Praise for
Journey

"Remarkable . . . Superb literature." —*The Pittsburgh Press*

"James Michener has amassed a peerless reputation as the heralded dean of the historical tome. . . . *Journey* is a book that envelops the reader in an atmosphere of hazardous escapades."
—*Richmond Times-Dispatch*

"Michener paints a vivid picture of the greed, deception, wild-eyed and irrational behavior of those stampeding to instant wealth. . . . The pictures and sounds of the Canadian wilderness at its most beautiful and its most terrifying will put the reader in awe of the majesty of nature. The poetry included in the book will give the reader an appreciation for British verse in a setting packed with the imminence of death." —*The Grand Rapids Press*

"*Journey* is an intimate look at the lives of five misplaced adventurers. . . . A fine addition to both the Michener library and to the lore on the Klondike gold rush." —*The Indianapolis News*

"An outstanding tale by a brilliant storyteller."
—*Wichita Falls Times Record-News*

"Epic in its portrayal of men facing adversity and their reactions, for good or evil, to their predicament. This slim volume stands strongly on its own." —*King Features Syndicate*

"Michener's fine novel is at least the equal of anything that Jack London wrote about the frozen North." —*Copley News Service*

"Unforgettable . . . Michener is back on the scene with another of his choice historical novels. . . . An adventure into the brutally cold gold rush country but also a journey into the souls of men . . . Solid, thorough, authoritative . . . Michener scores again." —*Macon Beacon*

BY JAMES A. MICHENER

Tales of the South Pacific
The Fires of Spring
Return to Paradise
The Voice of Asia
The Bridges at Toko-Ri
Sayonara
The Floating World
The Bridge at Andau
Hawaii
Report of the County Chairman
Caravans
The Source
Iberia
Presidential Lottery
The Quality of Life
Kent State: What Happened and Why
The Drifters
A Michener Miscellany: 1950–1970
Centennial
Sports in America
Chesapeake
The Covenant
Space
Poland
Texas
Legacy
Alaska
Journey
Caribbean
The Eagle and the Raven
Pilgrimage
The Novel
James A. Michener's Writer's Handbook
Mexico
Creatures of the Kingdom
Recessional
Miracle in Seville
This Noble Land: My Vision for America
The World Is My Home

WITH A. GROVE DAY
Rascals in Paradise

WITH JOHN KINGS
Six Days in Havana

JOURNEY

Mrs. Garner, 1897

JOURNEY

A NOVEL

JAMES A.
MICHENER

THE DIAL PRESS

NEW YORK

2015 Dial Press Trade Paperback Edition

Published in the United States by The Dial Press, an imprint of
Random House, a division of Penguin Random House LLC, New York.

THE DIAL PRESS and the HOUSE colophon are
registered trademarks of Penguin Random House LLC.

Originally published in hardcover in the United States
by Random House, an imprint and division
of Penguin Random House LLC, in 1989.

ISBN 978-0-8129-8675-4
eBook ISBN 978-0-8041-5154-2

www.dialpress.com

Book design by Carole Lowenstein

INTRODUCTION

Steve Berry

I grew up in the 1960s, a time when the extent of reading material for kids was, to say the least, limited. R. L. Stine, J. K. Rowling, Suzanne Collins, and so many others had yet to come along. In fact, what we now know as the young adult genre had yet to be invented. Back then, at least for me, it was Hardy Boys and Nancy Drew. A limited selection, but what gems those tales were—each loaded with action, adventure, secrets, and conspiracies. Wondrous stories to fuel young imaginations. I devoured them.

Then one day when I was sixteen years old, a friend handed me a dog-eared paperback copy of *Hawaii* by James Michener. Its thousand pages immediately intimidated me, as did the small print. I'd never seen so much information packed into one book. The opening sentence alone contained thirty-six words—monstrous in comparison to the prose of Franklin W. Dixon.

But what a sentence: *Millions upon millions of years ago, when the continents were already formed and the principal features of the earth had been decided, there existed, then as now, one aspect of the world that dwarfed all others.*

I kept reading.

What unfolded was a saga spanning many centuries that described how a tiny group of islands in the Pacific Ocean were formed by nature and then settled by man. The epic involved Polynesians, Chinese, Japanese, Europeans, and Americans. Its massive chapters, hundreds of pages long, featured one expansive episode after another—each intertwined—forming a chronicle that defined both the land and its culture. I read it cover to cover. Then I found more books by this guy Michener and read every one. Eventually, I started collecting them, and now, more than forty years later, I own a first edition of each, save one—*Tales of the South Pacific*. That book is hard to find. Only a few thousand were printed and, if by some miracle one of those 1947 first editions can be found, the price is through the roof. I keep every one of my Michener books prominently displayed, wrapped in plastic. I see them every day. They are a source of pride and comfort. Today, I write modern-day thrillers in which history plays a central role. Without question, the seed for that technique was planted the day I discovered *Hawaii*.

James Michener led an incredible life. Born in 1907, he was orphaned but was soon adopted by a woman named Mabel Michener, who was already raising two other children. Some of his biographers have hypothesized that he was actually Mabel's natural son, the adoption story used to protect both of their reputations. No one knows the truth, and as an adult Michener refused to comment on the subject.

By the time he turned ten, the family had moved to Bucks County, Pennsylvania. They were poor, barely able to put food on the table. His classmates, and even a teacher or two, tormented Michener about the secondhand clothes and toeless sneakers he wore every day. Later in life he recounted that taunting with a sly smile and a twinkle in his eye. He would say that those early years instilled in him an appreciation for life that he never forgot. They taught him about living simply and not attaching too much value to material things. And though he eventually earned hundreds of millions of dollars from writing, he always feared ending up poor.

Before he'd even reached twenty years of age, Michener had traveled across the country in boxcars, by thumbing rides, or simply by walking. He worked in carnival shows and other odd jobs, and he visited all but three states. Of that time, he wrote in his 1991 autobiography, *The World Is My Home*, "Those were years of wonder and enchantment. Some of the best years I would know. I kept meeting American citizens of all levels who took me into their cars, their confidence and often their homes." He would also say that those wandering years spurred inside him an insatiable curiosity about people, cultures, and faraway lands.

In 1925 he entered Swarthmore College, a prestigious Quaker institution, on a four-year scholarship, graduating with highest honors. He attended graduate school in Scotland, then returned home and taught at a school in Bucks County. He eventually ended up in New York City, editing textbooks at Macmillan Publishing.

World War II changed everything. At age forty Michener enlisted in the navy, where he discovered the enchanting South Pacific. He earned the rank of lieutenant commander and was made a naval historian, assigned to investigate cultural problems on the various islands. A near-fatal crash landing in French New Caledonia altered the course of his life. He wrote in his autobiography, "As the stars came out and I could see the low mountains I had escaped, I swore: 'I'm going to live the rest of my life as if I were a great man.' And despite the terrible braggadocio of those words, I understood precisely what I meant."

That brush with death also made him realize what every soldier was experiencing during the war, and that one day, when the danger had passed, people might want to recall those things. So each night he began writing down observations, recording comments, describing people and places. Fifty years later, in 1991, he said:

> Sitting there in the darkness, illuminated only by the flickering lamplight, I visualized the aviation scenes in which I had participated, the landing beaches I'd seen, the remote outposts, the exquisite islands with bending palms, and especially the valiant people I'd known: the French planters, the Australian coast watchers, the Navy nurses, the Tonkinese laborers, the ordinary sailors and soldiers who were doing the work, and the primitive natives to whose jungle fastnesses I had traveled.

All of that became *Tales of the South Pacific.*

The story of how that first manuscript made it to print is typical Michener—an unexpected combination of skill, determination, and luck. Using a pseudonym, he submitted the work to Macmillan, the publisher he'd worked for before enlisting. He omitted his name because he knew the company had a strict policy against publishing anything by an employee. Once the war was over he definitely intended to return to work there, but at the time of the submission he was technically a naval officer and not an employee. So the company bought the book, which was published in 1947. One year later *Tales of the South Pacific* won the Pulitzer Prize for fiction.

Michener changed publishers in 1949, moving to Random House, where he stayed for the rest of his life. More books followed—*The Fires of Spring, Return to Paradise, The Bridges at Toko-Ri,* and *Sayonara.* Also in 1949 he moved to Honolulu and soon began work on his most ambitious project to date. Four years of research and three years of writing were needed to produce *Hawaii.* Its epic scope, length, and breadth proved to be the stamp of Michener's trademark style, one he would master over the next forty years. Legend has it that he finished *Hawaii* on March 18, 1959, the day Congress voted to accept the islands as the fiftieth state.

In 1962 Michener ran for Congress as a liberal Democrat but lost. Then, in 1968, he worked as secretary of the Pennsylvania Constitutional Convention. Outer space was a lifelong interest, and he served on NASA's advisory council, an experience that led to his novel *Space*.

Honors were something Michener shied away from, but in 1977 Gerald Ford bestowed upon him the Presidential Medal of Freedom, the nation's highest civilian award. Eventually, he wrote nearly fifty books, including five on Japanese art. His work has been translated into multiple languages, and there are more than 75 million copies of his books in print. These latest editions, being rereleased with new covers, will only add to that already staggering inventory.

A myth associated with Michener speaks of his cadre of researchers, used to gather the enormous amount of historical detail included in each of his epics. The reality was quite different. Most of the work was accomplished with the help of only three secretaries. He was a disciplined writer, establishing a routine early in his career and maintaining it his entire life. An early riser, he would go straight to work, where he wrote using a manual typewriter. He then had a light breakfast, maybe a meeting or two, and went back to work until around one P.M. Evenings were a time to be by himself. In the final year of his life, at age ninety, he still kept to his daily routine, except he spent three days a week at a renal treatment center, undergoing kidney dialysis.

The treatment proved painful in a multitude of ways, perhaps the most difficult being that it prevented him from straying far from home. The man who'd visited nearly every country could no longer travel. He told an interviewer at the time, "I sit in the TV room and see shows on the big ships I used to travel or areas that I used to wander, and a tear comes to my eye. It's not easy."

And that explains his death—he simply decided there would be no more dialysis. Instead, he welcomed the end.

Michener died on October 16, 1997.

I recall the day vividly. A segment on the evening news reported that he was gone. A sadness came over me, as if I'd lost a close friend—which, in a sense, I had.

In preparation for writing this introduction, I reviewed many articles written just after Michener passed. Most came from folks who'd had some personal contact with him through the years—an experience that had clearly stuck in their memory. All of them recounted what happened as if they had been in the presence of a king or head of state. It seemed a privilege to have spent just a little time with James Michener.

And that legacy lives on.

Though he was known to be fanatically frugal, he gave away more than $100 million. Recipients of his generosity included libraries, museums, and universities. He donated $30 million to the University of Texas for the establishment of a creative writing program. Several million more went to the creation of the James A. Michener Art Museum in Pennsylvania. One wing of that building was named for his third wife, Mari Sabusawa Michener, who died before him, in 1994.

He never really liked talking about himself, and he could frustrate interviewers. "Famous is a word I never use," he would say. "I'm well known. I've written thirty or forty books. I've done a great deal. I let it go at that." He was extremely generous with his autograph, so much so that he once noted, "The most valuable books are those that aren't signed."

Of my own collection, only one bears his signature.

To the frequently asked question, "Which book are you most proud of?" he would just smile and say, "The one I'm working on next."

By no means was he perfect. He could be a difficult man to know. He wasn't the type to start conversations with strangers, and he detested small talk. He had few close friends, and those who counted themselves in that number knew to tread lightly. He could be abrupt, even rude, and quite aloof. After his death we learned that he utilized collaborators on some of the big books, a fact he refused to acknowledge in life. He was married three times and at one point maintained a mistress. He was a multimillionaire, yet he would constantly fret about not having enough money to pay his bills. And though he was an orphan himself and a co-founder of an adoption agency, in the 1950s he gave up his claim to an adopted child when he divorced his second wife.

All of which shows that he was human.

But still, what a remarkable man.

Michener possessed an incomparable ability to simultaneously enthrall, entertain, and inform. Nobody else could write a two-hundred-word sentence with such grace and style. And he chose his subjects with great care: the South Pacific (*Tales of the South Pacific, Return to Paradise*), Judaism (*The Source*), South Africa (*The Covenant*), the West Indies (*Caribbean*), the American West (*Centennial*), the Chesapeake Bay (*Chesapeake*), *Texas, Alaska,* Spain (*Iberia*), *Mexico, Poland,* the Far East.

Like millions of other readers, I loved them all.

I never met James Michener. I would have loved to tell him how he sparked the imagination of a sixteen-year-old boy, which led first to a lifelong love of reading, then to a career as a writer. When, in 1990, I decided to write my first novel, it was Michener who influenced me most. By the end of that decade, though, changes had firmly begun to take hold. Today you won't encounter many two-hundred-word sentences or millennia-long sagas involving hundreds of characters. Instead, in the twenty-first century, story, prose, and purpose are expected to be tight. In the Internet age—with video games, twenty-four-hour news, streaming movies, you name it—there is just little time for thousand-page epics. Toward the end of his life Michener gave an interview in which he doubted he would have ever been published if he'd first started in that environment.

Thank goodness he came along when he did.

Now his stories can live forever.

CONTENTS

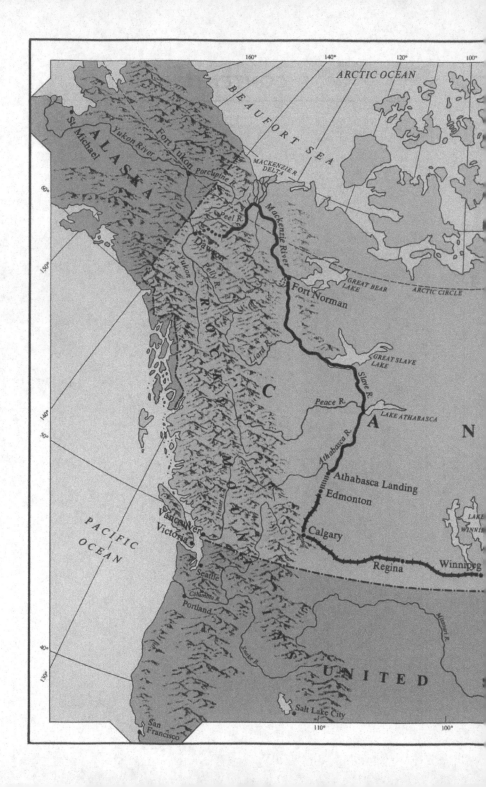

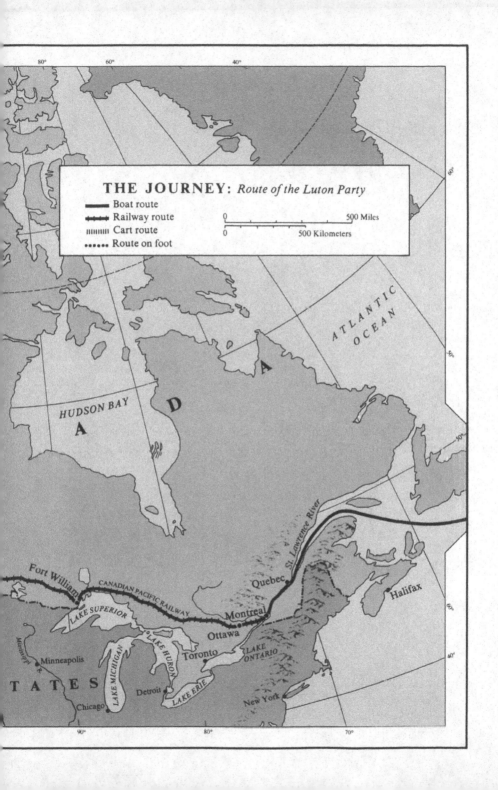

THE JOURNEY: *Route of the Luton Party*

Boat route
Railway route
Cart route
Route on foot

0   500 Miles
0   500 Kilometers

ATLANTIC OCEAN

HUDSON BAY

A   D   A

Fort William

CANADIAN PACIFIC RAILWAY

LAKE SUPERIOR

St. Lawrence River

Quebec

Halifax

Montreal

Ottawa

Mississippi R.

Minneapolis

LAKE MICHIGAN

LAKE HURON

Toronto

LAKE ONTARIO

T A T E S

Detroit

LAKE ERIE

Chicago

New York

ONE

HOPE

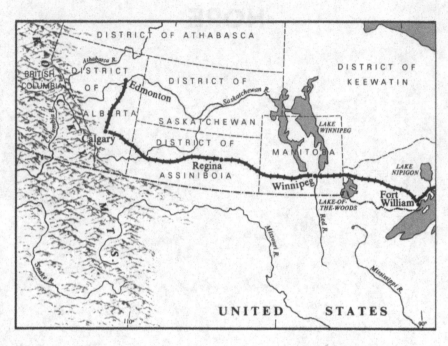

DISTRICT OF ATHABASCA

BRITISH
COLUMBIA

DISTRICT
OF
ALBERTA

Athabasca R.

Edmonton

Calgary

DISTRICT OF
SASKATCHEWAN

Saskatchewan R.

DISTRICT OF
ASSINIBOIA

Regina

DISTRICT OF
KEEWATIN

LAKE
WINNIPEG

MANITOBA

LAKE
NIPIGON

Winnipeg

LAKE-OF-
THE-WOODS

Fort
William

Columbia

R O C K Y

M T S.

Snake R.

Red R.

Missouri R.

Mississippi R.

UNITED   STATES

50°

110°   90°

WESTWARD HO: *by boat and rail*

—— Boat route

◆◆◆◆ Railway route

0   300 Miles

0   300 Kilometers

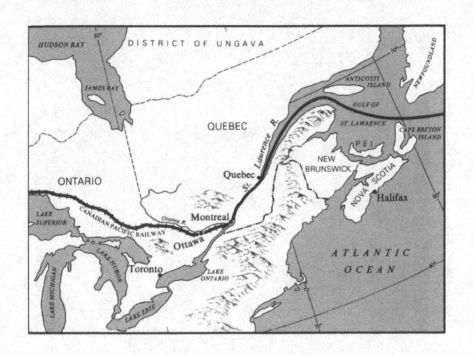

WHEN ON 17 JULY 1897 THE STEAMSHIP *PORTLAND* DOCKED AT Seattle, bringing belated news and hard evidence that an enormously rich strike of gold had been made the summer before along the Klondike River on the extreme western border of Canada, the world was startled by a felicitous sentence scribbled in haste by an excited reporter who visited the ship. Instead of saying that the miners had reached Seattle with "a huge amount of gold" or "a treasure-trove of gold," he wrote words that became immortal: "At 3 o'clock this morning the Steamer *Portland* from St. Michael for Seattle, passed up the Sound with more than a ton of solid gold aboard."

Those sensational words, "a ton of gold," flashed around the world, evoking wild enthusiasm wherever they appeared. Across the United States and Canada, men who had suffered sore deprivation during the great financial panic of 1893 cried: "Gold to be had for the picking! Fortunes for everyone!" and off they scrambled, with no knowledge at all of mining or metallurgy, and very little sense of how to protect themselves on a frontier. Shifty manipulators, who realized that they would have little chance of finding gold in riverbeds, nevertheless knew that with the proper card game or attractive young woman to lure those who did find nuggets, they might win fortunes by mining the miners. Proper businessmen also smelled opportunities; actors out of work visualized theaters with dancing girls, and a few born explorers of untested regions, like Lord Evelyn Luton and his military cousin Harry Carpenter of London, made immediate preparations to rush to the gold fields for the sheer adventure.

But if the news of the strike could have such electric effect upon so many, why had it taken almost a full year to travel the relatively short distance from the Klondike to Seattle, less than thirteen hundred miles as an eagle would fly? The explanation must be carefully noted, for it explains the tragic events that were about to destroy so many lives.

The Klondike was a pitiful little stream, too small to admit a boat of any serious size and hidden away in one of the most remote areas of the world. It emptied into the great Yukon River, which rose in the high mountains of the northern coastal range and roamed through Canada and Alaska for more than nineteen hundred desolate and uninhabited miles. So if the big river was available, why had not the miners who found the gold taken boats down the Yukon to bring the news to civilization? Unfortunately, the mighty river was frozen almost solid from early in October through to the first weeks in June. The men who had discovered the bonanza and would profit from it had made their strike so late in the summer of 1896 that they could not get down the Yukon until early summer of the next year. For nearly eleven months they had lived with their great wealth and their explosive secret, but now the genie was out of the bottle and chaos was about to ensue.

There were two other awesome facts about the discovery on the Klondike: although the gold fields, and they were unbelievably rich and extensive, lay entirely in Canada, there was no practical way to get from the principal settlements of western Canada to the region; the only feasible route was through Alaska, but anyone who tried that found himself facing one of the most fearsome physical challenges in the world, the dreaded Chilkoot Pass, at places almost straight up and passing through snowfields and mountain defiles. And if he did negotiate Chilkoot or the neighboring and equally formidable White Pass, which many failed to do, he then had to build himself a small boat from felled timber, to negotiate a series of deadly rapids and gorges and make a long, dangerous sail *down* the Yukon to approach the gold fields from the south. "In from the south, out to the north" was the rule at Dawson City, the Canadian settlement that sprang up near the spot where the little Klondike emptied into the wide Yukon.

It was this land—of frozen rivers, tempestuous gorges, impossible ascents through snow and ice, long sweeps of river through a thousand miles of wilderness—that in the late summer of 1897 attracted adventurers from all parts of the world, and not one of them, when he left Australia, or Indiana, or Ottawa or London, anticipated the hardships he would have to undergo before he reached Golconda.

In London, a few days after the news from Seattle appeared in national newspapers, a rich uncle and his impecunious nephew, members of the English noble family of Bradcombe, read of the "ton of gold" with considerable excitement. The older man, Lord Evelyn Luton, was the younger son of the redoubtable Marquess of Deal, eighth of that line whose Bradcombe ancestors had helped Queen Elizabeth establish a Protestant foothold in Catholic Ireland. Luton was thirty-one, imperially tall and slim, aloof, soft-spoken, unmarried and a man with a sometimes insufferable patrician manner. He despised familiarity, especially from underlings, and whenever a stranger presumed to approach him uninvited he tended to draw back, lift his nose as if he smelled an unpleasant odor undetected by others, and stare at the intruder. A friend at Oxford had termed this "Evelyn's silent-sneer," and when a listener had pointed out that all sneers are silent, the first student had replied: "Look to your dictionary. Anyway, when Evelyn hits you with his silent one, it speaks volumes."

Another friend had argued: "His critics may be right when they call him insufferable, but we suffer him because he's so . . . well . . . correct," and the first man had agreed: "He is always right, you know." But even this concession did not satisfy the first man: "Thing I like about him, when he embarks on any project, he's loyal to all who accompany him."

As a result of interminable practice when a boy he had, with only meager athletic skills to begin with, converted himself into one of England's finest cricketers. When not playing for his county team or representing England against Australia, he was an avid explorer, having penetrated to the upper reaches of the Congo, much of the Amazon, and, of course, the Nile to a point well beyond the great temples at Karnak.

Actually, there was a solid reason for his wanting to leap into the middle of what threatened to become a gold rush, since so many wished to join, but he scarcely admitted this to himself and certainly not to strangers. Having already probed both Africa and South America on daring expeditions, he fancied traveling next to the arctic and later to remote corners of Asia with the purpose ultimately of writing a travel book, perhaps to be called *An Englishman in the Far Corners,* in which he would exhibit, as he explained to himself, "how an ordinary fellow with a bit of determination could follow in the footsteps of the great explorers." He patterned himself after notable prototypes who had carried the British flag into the most dangerous parts of the world: Sir Richard Burton, who had written about primitive India and Africa, and Charles Doughty with his incredible *Travels in Arabia Deserta.*

Of all the intrepid explorations that had fired the imagination of an entire generation of Englishmen it was the expeditions to the high arctic in search of the fabled Northwest Passage that had most excited Luton. While up at Oxford he had read as many accounts as he could procure of the brave men who had led these northern explorations: Sir John Ross; Sir William Edward Parry, who had attempted to reach the North Pole; Sir Robert McClure, the first to discover the passage through the arctic waters. But none of these men's deeds had affected Luton as much as that of the noblest and most tragic explorer of them all: Sir John Franklin, who had perished with his gallant team in 1847 in his bold effort to discover the elusive passage.

Knowing intimately the travails of such Englishmen, Luton felt himself adequately prepared to face whatever challenges a mere gold rush might present. He would be venturing near the lands these men had discovered, perhaps even treading in the path of Sir John Franklin himself, who had once sailed the Mackenzie River in an early commission to map the coastline of the Arctic Ocean.

Luton had no doubt that he could succeed on his far lesser mission. On several occasions he had demonstrated that he was fearless by performing acts of some valor, but when asked about this he rejected that word: "Fearless? Who told you that? Did they also tell you I was so terrified I wet me britches?" To him the fragmentary word that reached London about the extensive dangers accompanying the gold rush presented an inviting challenge, but he would never have admitted that, for he had cloaked his former adventures as a seeking after scholarship, a thirst for knowledge, and this time he was already explaining to himself and others: "What I'd like, you know, is to give me nephew a spot of help." He pronounced the word *nev-ue*.

This nephew, Philip Henslow, aged nineteen, was the son of Luton's older sister, and since this made him a grandson of the Marquess of Deal, who was extremely wealthy, it might be supposed that young Philip did not want for money. But that was not the case. His mother, who as the daughter of a marquess enjoyed the title of Lady Phyllis, had displayed both temper and deplorable judgment in ignoring her father's strictures and eloping with a young chap named Henslow, whom the marquess refused to accept, for he was brash, liberal and Catholic. Growled the old nobleman: "Henslow's the shifty type Queen Elizabeth would have hanged, because he was plotting to remove her from the throne in favor of Mary the Scot."

Both Lady Phyllis and her son Philip had been in effect disinherited by the intractable marquess, and since the amiable Henslow had precious little money, the family was more or less strapped. Of course, when the marquess finally died, if he ever did, Lord Luton would be in a position to siphon off some of the Deal fortune to his sister and her son Philip, but while the old man lived, funds were needed.

For these contrasting reasons, love of adventure on Luton's part and need on his nephew's, the former dispatched his footman to Oxford to detach Philip from studies he was conducting during vacation and fetch him to His Lordship's club in Mayfair. "Really, Philip," Luton explained to his nephew as they dined that July night in his club, "it's a matter of patriotism."

"Why should one route to the gold fields be more patriotic than another?"

"Have you no sense of geography? Can't you visualize Canada?"

"I care little about Canada," the younger man confessed, "and very little about South Africa or India either." He was not teasing, this handsome nineteen-year-old from Eton, about to go up to Oxford, with his modest flair for the classics.

"Canada lies north of the United States, as I'm quite sure you know," Luton said, "and that's the infuriating part."

"I do not understand."

With bread rolls and tumblers, His Lordship laid out North America, with a teacup representing Alaska well off to the left: "This cascade of American gold we keep hearing about, it's all from Canada, you know. Not a farthing in the American part." And he used a small silver teaspoon to represent the Yukon as it wound its way across the Alaskan border into northwestern Canada. "Here's where the gold is, totally on our side."

"What's deplorable about that?" Philip asked, using one of the big words to which he was addicted.

"To reach the gold, which is all Canadian, you must thread your way through this deplorable Alaska . . ." He caught Philip smiling, and the young man said: "You've picked up one of my words again."

"Did I? Which one this time?"

"Deplorable."

"But damn me, it *is* deplorable to think that we're forced to pass through American territory to reach what's ours to begin with."

For Luton, like most men of his upbringing, considered all those areas on his globe which were shaded red to be British. He cared little for political matters and was oblivious of the self-government accorded Canada in 1867 when he had barely taken his first steps across the nursery. India, South Africa, Canada: they were all part of the unparalleled British Empire, unlike the American states which had unwisely and rudely rebelled against England's civilizing rule.

Philip did not need his uncle's attitude explained, and so he simply asked: "Is there no other way?"

"That's what we're here to find out, and we start our investigations tomorrow. We've got to put some funds in your exchequer."

Of course, Luton could easily have stayed home and sent his nephew to look after his own money matters, but that was not his style. He too had attended Eton, with no great distinction other than on the cricket field, and had later jollied his way through Oxford with a minimal degree. In both schools he had done a bit of boxing "to keep meself fit," as he phrased it, and a modest amount of chasing after young women prominent in the theater. He was known to his friends as an advocate of the telling gesture, as when he appeared dressed in full military regalia, but of the era of William of Orange, to hear the public speech of a general who had won minor honors in the Afghan war. A handshake from Luton was better than a contract attested by a notary, and his friends supposed that he would soon offer such a handshake to one of the various young women of good family whom he escorted to balls and to Ascot. Before he took this extremely grave step, for the Bradcombes did not divorce, he was now eager to lead a small group of like-minded Englishmen to adventure in the gold fields.

"I'll approach Harry tomorrow," he now told his nephew. "If we go, and I think we shall, I'd want him along."

"I, too," Philip said with unfeigned enthusiasm, for Harry Carpenter was one of those Englishmen who seemed to do everything easily. Thirty-seven and a graduate of a lesser school than Eton but a good one, he had received his degree from Cambridge with commendable honors but without much intense study. He had played rugby both for the university and his country and had served with his regiment on India's northwest frontier. He knew nothing of mining, nothing of Canada, but everything about living arduously on whatever frontier he found himself. He had climbed in the Himalayas while on leave from his regiment, but had stayed well away from the highest peaks: "I don't like cold weather and I'm afraid of high places." It was unlikely that he was afraid of much except his wife—one of the minor Bradcombes and a most determined woman—for he had more than proved his valor by tramping alone on a feckless scouting penetration from Peshawar on the Indian border, through the Khyber Pass and south into the markets of Kandahar to collect intelligence for a later strike against Afghanistan. He was a formidable man, secretive, self-disciplined and always eager to tackle the next assignment. He was aware that in civilian life he had performed only indifferently and that his place was with troops, but as he approached his forties with a slim or no chance of ever becoming a colonel—he simply hadn't the private funds to support himself in a position as head of a regiment—he had decided that he was too old to be knocking about as a mere minor officer in some frontier unit in the foothills of the Himalayas, so his cousin Luton knew that for Harry, a chance to try his luck on the gold fields would prove a godsend.

Next day, when Luton tentatively suggested a foray into the Klondike, Harry, with his customary diffidence, affected to know nothing about the gold there: "Is that the place they've been making a fuss over in the papers? Revolution or something?"

"Gold, Harry."

"Oh, yes. That Yukon bit."

"I was thinking of taking a look. Care to join me?"

"Love to, old chap. Anything to get away from London for a while. But I say, Eskimos and all that. Will we be eating blubber?"

"We'll be a thousand miles from the Eskimos, if I calculate correctly." Luton closed the conversation with an invitation: "I say,

Harry, I'm joining Phyllis's boy at the club tonight for dinner. Care to join us, to talk seriously about this?"

"I've found it dangerous to talk seriously about anything, but if you do go to the Klondike, consider me part of your team."

That night Lord Luton and Philip seated themselves in the foyer of the club so as to keep an eye on the entrance, and it was Philip who spotted Carpenter first: "There he comes!" and into the vestibule, where patrons deposited their cloaks to the care of an elderly attendant, stepped a man of medium height, sturdily built and with a rather large military mustache that projected about half an inch past the flare of each nostril. It was neither a garish mustache nor a flamboyant one; it was the rugged symbol of a rugged man, and opponents on many playing fields had grown to respect it.

"I say, it's good to see you, Philip. How's the pater and all that?" Carpenter was one of Luton's rare friends who always asked about Henslow the Catholic interloper, and when he did, it was with honest affection, for he had always liked Philip's father.

"He told me to say hello," Philip replied. "Said he wished he could join us."

"In this Klondike business? He'd better stay home and mind the shop."

"No, he meant for dinner tonight."

After a congenial meal, at which they discussed only county cricket, they wandered into the smoking room, where Harry said: "I've brought something you both must read, that is, if we're going to pursue this gold foolishness," and he passed along a worthy book published in London in 1868. It was by the English explorer Frederick Whymper, *Travel and Adventure in the Territory of Alaska,* and it recounted in delightful style his fifteen-month trip to that region in 1866.

But after Luton had given the book only a cursory glance he shoved it back: "Harry, the man was never in Canadian territory. Our plan must be to move only through Canada."

Before he could elaborate on the patriotic impulses that such a statement inspired, a white-haired club attendant came to suggest that since four members playing whist had protested the racket being made by Carpenter's rumbling voice, would the gentlemen please move to another room. Both Luton and Carpenter bowed politely to the servant, then to the whist players, and retired.

"Now, what we would do, assuming that I joined you," Harry said as if there had been no rejection of his book, "is hie ourselves to San

Francisco by one of the railroads they say they have, then catch a ship to Petropavlovsk in Siberia and take some Russian steamer across the Bering Sea to the mouth of the Yukon, and up we go to this place called Dawson City, wherever it is. It's certainly not on this map."

Lord Luton managed an icy laugh: "Harry, Whymper made his trip more than thirty years ago. If we wanted to go that route, we could take a train right out to this place called Seattle and then find us a big, comfortable oceangoing steamer straight to Alaska."

"Oh."

"But the whole purpose of our trip would be to make it exclusively on Empire terrain. Land in Montreal, go by train across Canada to a place whose name escapes me, go up one of the Canadian rivers, perhaps the Mackenzie, cross the Rockies, and drift easily down to the gold fields. Simple."

"Can it be done?"

"Join me in the morning. We'll visit the Canadian offices. They must have the information."

And as the summer evening passed, with fine cigars and ancient cognac, Philip listened intently while Luton and Carpenter reviewed the reasons why entering the Klondike by an all-Empire route was not only an act of patriotism but also a most appropriate act for a son of the Marquess of Deal: "Have you ever read, Harry, how my grandfather, the seventh marquess, was so badly treated by the Americans in that Oregon nonsense years ago? The braggarts changed the jingle 'Fifty-four-forty or Fight,' and my grandfather, who was in charge of negotiations for the English, said in this very club: 'Very well, if the scoundrels want a fight, let's give it them,' and he was prepared to lead volunteers into Canada, from which base he was ready to invade New York and Washington."

"What did the Americans do to humiliate him?"

"That's the proper word, *humiliate.* In the middle of the proceedings, with war inevitable, they called the whole thing off, surrendered their silly claim to what would have been half of Canada, and made my grandfather look rather foolish. Of course he was rather foolish, as you know, but he didn't like to be exposed."

"What happened?" Philip asked, and Luton said: "Nothing. It's sometimes advantageous when nothing happens." But then he tightened his lips and added: "It did leave our family with an abiding distaste for what our relatives called their 'ungrateful American colony.' Even today the Bradcombes try to avoid Americans."

However, he could not help laughing at himself as he revealed one of the trivial reasons why he was personally impatient with Americans: "Anytime I meet one of them I have to explain my name. To them Evelyn can be only a girl's name, three syllables, rather 1840, you know. I have to tell them that in civilized lands it's an honored man's name, two syllables, first one to rhyme with *peeve* or *leave*. I have sometimes thought that I would punch the next American who asks me about it."

In the morning Harry Carpenter stopped by to pick up young Philip Henslow after paying his respects to the boy's father. They proceeded to the club where Lord Luton was staying and then drove to the London offices of the Canadian government, where a commercial attaché awaited them. Taking them to his cluttered office, he sat them before a large wall map containing names with which he was familiar and they were not.

"Of course, we've known for years about scattered gold in these regions up here, but this Klondike thing is rather special, isn't it?" When Luton nodded, the attaché said disparagingly: "Since these lurid American newspaper stories, we've been so deluged with inquiries that Ottawa has had to cable us two pages of reliable information, which I'll pass along later. But for gentlemen of your standing, I must say our government would be most honored to receive you . . . well, I should think you ought to see a special cable which arrived only yesterday."

"We would profit from any information," Luton said, whereupon the attaché almost fell over himself to be gracious: "Could I have Miss Waterson fetch you some tea? Good."

With a pointer he reviewed what he called the "rather simple problem of getting from London to Edmonton."

"And why Edmonton?" Carpenter asked, and Luton interrupted: "That's the name I was trying to remember!"

"Your commodious Canadian steamer will disembark you at Montreal, a port equal in every way to New York, where the fast trains of the Canadian Pacific will carry you to Ottawa, Fort William and Winnipeg. Miss Waterson is from Winnipeg, and she can assure you it's a splendid stopover for a short rest before heading into the gold country."

Miss Waterson did so assure them.

"And now we come to the exciting part of our trip, the journey through the vast lands of the Northwest Territories. Winnipeg across our District of Saskatchewan . . ."

"What glorious names!" Philip Henslow cried, and the attaché nodded: "They are indeed. Indian, too. And then west to Calgary, from which a spur runs north to Edmonton, the end of the railway and the beginning of your great adventure."

"Where's Dawson City?" Luton asked, and the Canadian said: "Well, sir, it's not on the maps yet. It sprang up last year, overnight as it were."

"But where is it?"

The attaché explained: "I have a recent letter from Ottawa which sketches the new developments, and it places Dawson right about here," and he entered a dot on the map, siting it about a hundred and fifty miles nearer Edmonton than reality would justify.

"So you see, gentlemen, when you leave the train in Edmonton you're practically in the gold fields."

"What gear should we take?" Carpenter asked, for when frontiers were involved he had a practical mind.

"Oh, sir! Only your traveling kit. One bag, two bags. Because everything you could possibly need in the gold fields can be purchased in Edmonton, and at prices considerably less than those being charged in the United States, where, if the truth be known, they're apt to prey upon the traveler." Luton said, as if making his goodbyes: "I can believe that," but the young man had one more important caution: "Milord, you really must get one fact burned into your mind, because a great deal depends upon your understanding of it. Here in England it's July, glorious time of the summer, boating and croquet. But in northern Canada it's almost the beginning of winter. If you're going, go soon and go fast, because our northern winters can be terribly deep and tediously long."

Luton nodded, but Carpenter felt that anyone with a respect for geography and good sense would know what the young man had just said; he was impatient to get down to business: "What was the cabled information you spoke of?" and the attaché produced two extremely reassuring typed documents. The first had been issued by undesignated officials within the Edmonton Board of Trade, and it promised the traveler from Europe that the only sensible way for him or her to reach the gold fields was through Edmonton:

It is more direct, less tiring and cheaper. You have seen pictures of the dreaded Chilkoot Pass, which only the bravest and strongest can negotiate. Avoid it if you can. The ocean route to St. Michael is tedious and expensive, and when you get there you still have to move upstream along practically the entire length of the Yukon River.

Come to Edmonton. Use the all-Canadian route. And find yourself at the gateway to the gold you seek. From Edmonton you will have the choice of four easy routes which will be outlined to you by local experts, who will also provide you with guidebooks and maps. Come to Edmonton and make yourself a millionaire.

Both Luton and Carpenter dismissed this as an understandable effort by the merchants of a provincial city to lure business their way, but they were quite impressed by the cable which had arrived the day previous, for it summarized the reasoned views of two experienced travelers who had made the journey from Edmonton to Dawson and who assured prospective adventurers that the trip was not only practical but in certain respects pleasant. The first expert was a man named Ludwig Halverson, who told how one could come to Edmonton, head over an easy trail to the Peace River, cross a low divide, pick up the Liard River, move quickly to the Pelly, and drift comfortably down to a confluence with the Yukon, from which the gold fields would be only a few more miles, all downstream:

> This route will prove both the easiest and quickest to the target. Any well-trained man with a good packhorse and a light canoe should be able to cover the pleasant distances in less than seven weeks, and the vigorous experience of sleeping in the open and breathing the world's freshest air will prepare him for the easy work of panning for gold.

Halverson provided the prospector with various useful hints. One must not buy inferior equipment but wait till one reached Edmonton, where men long trained in frontier living would know what was best for travel in the north. Scurvy, which used to be a problem, was easily prevented by a proper diet, which local grocers would be happy to provide. When one found a rich placer deposit, one should have the gold assayed as promptly as possible and reduced to bricks for easier carriage. In fact, Halverson used the word *easy* so often that it became a kind of refrain, but the substance of his article was that by leaving from Edmonton and choosing one of the easy river routes to Dawson, the prospector would reach the fields much sooner than those who went by the American routes. He would thus be in a position to stake the best claims.

Harry Carpenter, well versed in the difficulties of travel in harsh places, knew intuitively that the trip might require somewhat more than seven weeks, but since he did not trace out the distance on the map, he visualized a trip not of twelve hundred miles but of something like four hundred. He said frankly that he, for one, would be more interested in the other major route, the one that was downstream most of the way, the one that focused on one of the great scarce-explored rivers of the world, the Mackenzie. It was a perplexing waterway, because it bore many different names—Finlay, Peace, Slave—a result of the fact that at different dates it had been discovered piecemeal and always from the warm south, but always it was the same great river, two thousand, six hundred miles in length from its birth in high mountains near Alaska to its entry into the arctic seas. It was a river to inspire the imagination of men, and Carpenter wanted to test it.

An explorer who had traveled it in both directions, Etienne Desbordays, explained in the second half of his report how efficient and awe-inspiring and, yes, even delightful the trip down the Mackenzie could be:

> Wild animals in great profusion feed along the riverbanks as your boat or canoe glides past. Tall mountains grace the distance, and every turn in the river provides some new excitement, for you are traveling through some of the wildest and most beautiful land in North America.

> Swiftly, silently the vast river carries you to your destination, and after a thousand miles of this effortless travel you approach the Beaufort Sea, an arm of the Arctic Ocean, but you are not headed there. Choosing any one of a dozen convenient rivers which feed into the Mackenzie from the west, you head west along the pleasant waterways, cross a low divide, and find yourself in the headwaters of the Klondike River itself, down which you drift, pausing to prospect at likely sites as you go.

Desbordays concluded that there could not be a more pleasant or effective way to reach the gold fields than to follow the Mackenzie.

"And one of the glories of this route is that it is entirely Canadian. You pay no United States duties on your necessities when you come this way. You are on Canadian terrain all the way." As with the other route, there were a few facts of which he must have been aware but which in the service of salesmanship he chose to disregard.

The Canadian office in London was so pleased with the specific data provided by this long cable that steps had already been taken to publish it as an instructive pamphlet with maps and quotations from earlier correspondence, for as the attaché reminded Lord Luton: "You must remember, we've known about gold in Canada for the past six years. It's just that this latest strike has gotten a little out of hand."

"Who are these Halverson and Desbordays?" Carpenter asked the attaché, who in turn asked Miss Waterson if she knew of them. When she replied: "I'm from Winnipeg. That's more than six hundred miles from Edmonton," the Englishmen caught some sense of the vast distances involved. Young Philip, good at math as well as classics, studied the wall map for some moments, then said: "You know, Uncle Evelyn, Edmonton to Dawson is a long way, a very long way," but the impact of his discovery was blunted by the attaché, who said enthusiastically: "Evelyn. That's a fine English name we rarely hear in Canada," and the conversation turned to other matters.

It was decided that Lord Luton's team would be comprised of himself, his cousin Harry Carpenter, his nephew Philip Henslow and an adventurous friend of Philip's, an Oxford man of twenty-two named Trevor Blythe whose frail build and sensitive manner belied his courage and tenacity. These four would form an admirable team; two older men of mature judgment and great force supported by two younger gentlemen who had done well in school and who promised to do just as well in life. All four were resourceful, educated, and representative of the best that their exalted class could produce. On the night that they met together at Luton's club for the first time, Luton had said with reserved pleasure: "I say, if any four in this city stand a chance to fight their way to the gold fields, it would be us." He saw his team as the next group of highly disciplined Englishmen to follow in the steps of the great explorers, who had all had backgrounds like theirs: a distant boarding school at age seven, knocked pillar to post by older boys at Eton or Harrow, rollicking through their university days at Oxford or Cambridge, serving in the army or navy when required, and on to a gallant life. The four were terribly able but also terribly deceptive; when you saw them move out as a group they might be headed insouciantly either for an afternoon's punting on the Thames or to a nine-month probe of the headwaters of the Amazon.

That night Lord Luton started the next installment of the journal he had kept on all his explorations against the day when he might want to write of his adventures:

> I doubt I could have put together a more trustworthy four-some: two grizzled veterans like Harry and me, and two stalwart young fellows just beginning to show their mettle, Philip and his friend Blythe. We understand the responsibilities of being Englishmen and I trust we shall conduct ourselves according to the highest traditions of that calling.

But it was clear both to Luton and Carpenter that a fifth man was needed, someone to do the heavy manual work, and it was fortunate that one of the country places pertaining to the Marquess of Deal was located in Northern Ireland, where Lord Luton had spent many of his summers. During his visits to the area where his father had lived before he inherited the marquisate, and where the old man had developed his distrust of Catholics, Evelyn had come to know rather well a fellow two years younger than himself who displayed a spirit and an ability that anyone would have respected. Timothy Fogarty was the son of poor farmers whose land had been absorbed generations ago when Queen Elizabeth moved Scottish crofters and English lords across the Irish Sea "to civilize," as she said, "the people of that unfortunate island."

An early Marquess of Deal had been one of her agents in this effort at altering the character of a land, and he had been a holy terror, rooting out priests and establishing in their stead reliable Protestant ministers. Subsequent members of the Bradcombe family had been more conciliatory, but all had one propensity: they lived in Ireland as long as they bore the subsidiary title Lord Luton, but once they inherited the marquisate, they moved promptly to one of their several senior estates in England and rarely saw Ireland again.

The present Lord Luton, who stood no chance of inheriting the marquisate, was not at all like that; he liked Ireland, its gentle ways and lyrical manner; in particular he liked what he had seen of Fogarty. From the brash young lad's first days on the Luton properties he had displayed such an innate understanding of animals and fish that Evelyn had quickly designated him an apprentice to the elderly Irish gamekeeper who minded the wildlife on the estates. He proved exceptionally qualified to be a ghillie, the Scottish term that Luton used for his field helpers, and in addition, he was well-mannered and could sing like the paid choristers in a London church. He was big of chest, but not overly tall, and when he applied himself to a task he could do prodigious amounts of work. He had only a sparse education, which he fortified with common sense, and if a group of traveling Englishmen with money wanted a factotum, they could find no one better suited to this task than Tim Fogarty. Married to a responsible lass named Jenny, he was nevertheless always eager for a new challenge, and since he had the native intelligence to attack it in a new way, he was almost ideal for the job Lord Luton had in mind. However, he did have one weakness about which the noble lord did not know: Tim Fogarty, though in training to become a traditional Irish gamekeeper, was one of the canniest poachers in Ireland. No trout stream was safe from his attentions, and even those he was hired to protect fell prey to his nighttime explorations, for he was a master of the shaded light, the well-cast line. He did not consider his poaching criminal in any respect, for as he confided to his priest: "A man cannot love horses and roses and prize hogs unless he also loves fish . . . and I do love them."

Lord Luton could not command his ghillie to accompany him to Canada—the days of peonage were over—but he could make the trip so enticing that the Irishman had to accept. When Fogarty crossed the Irish Sea and presented himself in London, he listened only a few moments to the proposal before he said enthusiastically: "I'll go," and asked forthwith for permission to return to Belfast for his kit. Luton took out his wallet and said: "Not necessary. Take this, but buy only the necessities this afternoon. The rest we'll get in Edmonton." Fogarty demurred: "It's not only me kit. It's me wife. Jenny would be . . ."

Lord Luton stiffened and a foreboding scowl darkened his face: "Buy it here, not in Ireland. Each moment of summer is precious," and Fogarty, accepting the proffered money, nodded.

Next day, when the Luton party entrained for Liverpool, Fogarty was aboard, because English gentlemen and Irishmen could act almost precipitately when they had to. Since both Luton and Carpenter wanted to reach the gold fields promptly, they booked passage on the first ship bound for Canada.

They embarked on 25 July 1897, and were agreeably surprised to find themselves on one of the most elegant ships to ply the North Atlantic: the *Parisian,* pride of Canada's Allan Royal Mail Line. Long and sleek, she boasted four towering masts from which hung a forest of yardarms and a blizzard of white sails. But the power of this vessel was indicated by two big, blunt smokestacks amidships, for the *Parisian* was powered by both sail and steam, which made her a mistress of the seas. The gentlemen's cabins were spacious and comfortable and the saloon well appointed with oak and ash floors, its walls and slender pillars decorated in leather. Chairs of walnut burnished to a soft glow offered a welcome seat after a bracing walk on the promenade deck.

The captain, at whose table they were seated that evening, commended them on their discernment in choosing his ship. The *Parisian,* he explained, had been cleverly designed with saloon amidships which dampened the pitch of the steamer in high seas and made dining on board as tranquil as on shore. The captain continued his proud description with details of the innovative bilge keels that kept her steady in the water and explanations of how he used both her steam and sail power to best advantage, but Luton, tiring of his boasts, distracted him with a question: "Why the name *Parisian* if she's a Canadian ship?" and the captain replied: "It's a mark of the respect, sir, that we Canadians hold for France." Luton bristled at this reminder of what his family considered Canada's blemished past under French rule, and quickly changed the subject: "How long d'you think before we see Montreal? The twelve days we were promised?" and the captain said: "Aye, twelve days, if the weather doesn't blow."

During their calm crossing one of the basic rules of the trip evolved, and in a somewhat unpleasant way. Trevor Blythe, whose family kept a staff of seven, began summoning Fogarty, who slept on a lower deck, and giving him orders as if the Irishman were his assigned manservant. This had to be done conspicuously, because the four gentlemen in Luton's party occupied first-class quarters, while Fogarty shared a cramped cabin with two other men in steerage. So when Blythe felt he needed Fogarty's services he had to take obvious steps to summon him.

Fogarty did not complain; he knew he was a kind of servant, but Lord Luton was distressed by Blythe's action, and after this infraction of the tacit rules of such an expedition occurred for the third time, Luton and Carpenter asked the two younger men to join them in a secluded corner of the ship's luxurious saloon.

"This isn't pleasant and it isn't crucial, so let's not make an affair of it," Luton said after a deferential cough. "But I think we must understand certain rules. Nothing in writing, no saluting or the raising of voices." He coughed again and was obviously uneasy: "Harry and I've been through this often, and I'm sure you young fellows will catch on immediately."

When Henslow and Blythe looked at each other in bewilderment, Luton snapped: "Dammit, you make it difficult to say, but Fogarty is the expedition's servant, not at the beck and call of individuals."

Now Blythe realized that he was the subject of the meeting, and before either Luton or Carpenter could speak further, he apologized profusely: "I say, I am most fearfully sorry. It was thoughtlessness, Evelyn, sheer thoughtlessness."

Luton, relieved to see that the young man was taking the admonition properly, sighed, thrust out his hand and clasped Trevor's: "Thanks. I knew you'd understand. Harry, lay out the rules."

"Quite simple. It's as Evelyn said. Fogarty is at the service of the party as a whole, never of an individual. I think an example will clarify it nicely. When we're in camp and require wood for the stove, it will be Fogarty's job to see that we get the wood, but each of us in proper turn will help him do it. And should he suggest that Evelyn chop down that tree over there, I would expect Evelyn to hop to it smartly and chop the thing down."

"Highly sensible," said Blythe without a sign of rancor.

"Now, if young Philip here needs his socks washed because he's worn them too long on the trail, he need not call for Fogarty. He jolly well washes them himself."

"Understood?" Luton asked, and when the young men nodded, he added: "Good. But Fogarty has agreed to cut our hair during our long trip, and for that, each of us must pay him in cash. Understood?"

Not once on their long journey together would anyone call the Irishman anything but Fogarty, which was understandable, since none knew his first name or showed any interest in learning it, but that night in his notes Lord Luton did praise the ghillie:

There are few people in this world more pleasant to deal with than a well-trained Irishman who knows his place, and our ghillie Fogarty is one of the best. I spotted him young and have had him work with our finest hands. In due course, fifteen, sixteen years, he'll be my gamekeeper, and I doubt I'll ever have a better.

Harry and I have had to lay down the rules to our two young men. How could they know the niceties if we didn't tell them? And I am proud to say they snapped to and saluted like proper soldiers. That's the way to launch an expedition properly, and tonight I appreciate more than ever the stalwart abilities of Carpenter. I'd not like to go ahead without him.

The latter part of the twelve-day crossing to Montreal established patterns which would prevail during the months ahead. Philip spent long hours in the ship's library, which overlooked the saloon, reading and then almost memorizing parts of Whymper's account of his journeys in Alaska, and whenever the Yukon River was mentioned he took special notice. In time he knew that waterway as intimately as one could from maps and a book, but his uncle almost ridiculed this effort: "The part of the Yukon you're reading about is entirely in American territory, and we're not going that way." Nevertheless, the young man continued his preoccupation with the river.

After some days of browsing the ship's limited collection of books, Trevor Blythe concentrated his attention on one of the small volumes he had borrowed from his mother, Palgrave's well-regarded *Golden Treasury,* the 1861 anthology of what was considered at that time the essence of English lyrical poetry. Trevor had, of course, made himself familiar with most of the poems, but since he aspired to adding perhaps a lyric or two of his own to the grand assembly, he wished to know the works intimately. On this excursion, through prolonged study of the more gracious poems, he hoped to learn the secrets of effective prosody.

During his two years at Oxford, Blythe had attracted favorable attention for his youthful poems and some university critics had gone so far as to say that he had the authentic English voice. He did not think so; his reverence for the songs of Sidney, Herrick and Waller was so profound that he doubted he could ever add to their flawless statements, but he did want to understand the sorcery whereby they had achieved their miracles. So as the ship sliced through the North Atlantic swells he would sometimes cry with the joy of late discovery: "Philip! Did you ever catch the felicity, there's no other word for it, of Waller's cry? I must've read it a dozen times but never before . . ." And as the ship plowed westward he would read those lines which had for centuries tugged at the hearts of young men:

> Go, lovely Rose!
> Tell her, that wastes her time and me,
>   That now she knows,
> When I resemble her to thee,
> How sweet and fair she seems to be.

Lord Luton and Harry Carpenter were engaged in more practical matters; endlessly they reviewed the technical aspects of the trip, and each agreed that to purchase even a handkerchief prior to reaching Edmonton would be unwise, for as Luton said: "Stands to reason, don't it, that those chaps on the frontier will be better informed about arctic conditions than anyone in places like Montreal or Winnipeg." They gave much attention to modes of locomotion, and here Luton was determined: "I'd say, get to the Athabasca River as soon as possible, no matter the overland portage, and buy a boat there, or even build one, and start floating downstream. Cross the Great Slave and . . ."

Always Harry broke in at this point: "Let's look at this again, Evelyn. Can we, in common sense, hope to get across the Rocky Mountains, wherever we encounter them, this autumn? I mean, before the rivers freeze?" While Luton restudied this, Carpenter would add: "I'm eager too, you know."

But when pressed, Harry would state firmly: "Evelyn, it's nearly August. From what I've been reading—Whymper says the same—these rivers start to freeze in late September, maybe earlier in the far north."

"Then you see no chance for this year?"

Carpenter was the kind of steady, careful man who disliked arbitrary statements; too often he had seen men of great resolve contest the odds and make their own rules, so he avoided giving a direct negative: "As we go down the Mackenzie we might hear of some river we don't know about coming in from the west, hooking up with the

Yukon. If we could find that river, we'd be drifting down the Yukon right into Dawson."

"You've ruled out overland?"

Now Harry had to be firm: "Evelyn, old friend, I've been looking at the maps. It's a far distance from Edmonton to Dawson overland. More than a thousand miles, I calculate. Could you and I haul our tons of gear on sleds for that distance in the time available this year?" Lowering his voice, to indicate the gravity of the decisions he must share, he whispered: "I doubt it."

Drawing upon his experiences with rough travel in Asia and Africa, he knew it would be advantageous if members of the party memorized the terrain between Edmonton and the gold fields, and to that end he conducted study lessons on a table in a corner of the ship's card room. Here he spread the team's various maps, and after he had summoned Fogarty from below, the five men pored over sketchy and often inaccurate maps depicting the recollections of former travelers. As Harry compared the maps he noticed one compelling fact: regardless of which route the gold-seekers elected, it would be impossible for them to leave Edmonton and reach the Klondike without at some point climbing and crossing the Rockies. Whatever map he focused upon, it contained that ominous black line coming down from the northwest and running diagonally to the southeast. Even on flat paper, those mountains were a brooding, repellent barrier.

Once when he drew Blythe's attention to the forbidding line, he noticed that the young poet studied with unusual interest the way it twisted about as if protecting the gold fields from intruders, and later Harry saw the young fellow scratching in his notebook. Always interested in what men younger than himself were engaged in, he asked politely: "I say, Trevor, could I have a peek?" and almost shyly the young man shoved the little book forward with the brief comment: "Toying with words. Idea for a poem, maybe," and Harry read:

In gathering darkness we pursue
A Grail of Gold protected by jealous elves
Who keep it rimmed by jagged mountains . . .

"Fine conceit you have there, Trevor," Harry said approvingly. "A proper poet could make something of it . . . polishing . . . simplifying . . . don't you know?" After he had returned the book he said to the others: "I hope the rest of us realize the aptness of what

Trevor's written. He's got it just about right, you know. We find no gold till we penetrate those mountains.

"As I consult my maps, and they have a few good ones on this ship, I grow most dubious about these two reports we saw in London." He laid before them his copy of the glowing statement by Ludwig Halverson regarding the ease with which one could travel overland from Edmonton to Dawson City and the later one by Etienne Desbordays describing the floating comfort of a trip down the Mackenzie River. "This one"—and he indicated the overland trail—"seems absolutely impossible, regardless of what Halverson says he did. And this one"—pushing aside the Desbordays with contempt—"has not a word of information that I would consider solid."

"Where's that leave us, Harry?" Luton asked, and Carpenter said: "In a fix. But not one we can't work our way out of. After all, we know that people are getting to the gold fields. The outflow of gold proves that, and so shall we."

In cautious, statesmanlike terms Lord Luton stated what their strategy must be: "Immediately upon docking in Canada we shall rush by train across the continent to Edmonton, and there make the most penetrating inquiries as to the truth of the two routes. Only when we have more detailed and reliable facts in hand shall we decide our next step, but I assure you of this. We shall get to the gold fields." And the other three supported this resolve, with Philip adding: "If Yankees can get there in their fashion, we can certainly do the same in ours."

None of the team had ever been in Canada, nor had they read much about it. Lord Luton said he knew all that was needed: "When the Americans broke away back there, Canadians had sense enough to stand firm." By that he meant that they had remained in the Empire, and he could not for the life of him understand why the Americans had not.

"England has everything a man wants—good government, a king we love or a queen we love even more. Wealth . . . order . . . membership in the best group of nations in the world. It will take the Yankees generations to catch up with what they already had, but tossed away."

He was therefore disposed to like Canada, and when the *Parisian* started picking its way through the clusters of big islands guarding the entrance to the St. Lawrence River, and then entered the spacious river itself, he said approvingly: "What a splendid way to enter a country!" He felt even more encouraged when the ship passed by the tall cliffs at Quebec City which were surmounted by the gracious Château Frontenac, a new hotel whose reputation had already reached the ears of London society.

"Marvelous beginning," he said, but when they docked at Montreal his ardor diminished, for he saw that he was now in the middle of a society that was completely French, and this he did not approve: "I could've got to real France by crossing the Channel and saved a bundle. I was on a ship of the right name for that." His day in the city was not a happy one, for he felt as if he had been cut off from England and thrust into an alien setting he had not anticipated: "Might as well be Albania."

Trevor Blythe, listening with amusement to Luton's barrage of acerbic comment, thought: He's a young man with an old man's ideas, but since he himself was a guest on the trip, he deemed it best not to speak.

The Englishmen received their first indications of the gold mania that had hit Canada when they hurried to the railway booking office to pick up their tickets: "Oh, Your Lordship! You were so wise to cable ahead for reservations. If you hadn't, I don't know what we could have done. Hundreds every day clamoring to go west. You'd have found every seat sold till well into next week."

"Even first class?"

"Especially first class. Gold-seekers are happy to pay a premium. They're convinced that in six weeks they'll be millionaires."

Safely aboard the handsome new Canadian train that had recently begun to run uninterruptedly from the Atlantic seacoast to the Pacific, the four Englishmen again received the kind of joyous surprise that made travel a pleasure, for a train of eleven cars, five of them luxurious, was waiting to speed travelers along the first short leg of the journey—Montreal to Ottawa—in maximum comfort. The four Englishmen, of course, were traveling first class, Luton and Carpenter in one delightful bedroom saloon, Trevor and Philip in another, while Fogarty had fairly comfortable sitting space in one of the less expensive cars.

The saloons were handsomely appointed in heavy dark-red upholstery and spacious let-down beds, but it was the long dining car that gained accolades. The compact galley, big enough for two cooks, was forward to protect the car from intrusions by riders in the lesser seats, but the remainder of the car clear to the rear door consisted of tables handsomely draped in thick linen containing along the edges revealed to the public the carefully embroidered initials C.P.R. Tables on one side of the carpeted aisle seated two, the chairs facing, but somewhat larger tables on the other side were for four, and when Henslow first entered the car his immediate impression was of endless white decorated with sparkling glassware and gleaming silver. "A car for gentlemen," Luton said as he surveyed the place and waited for the head attendant to show him to a table for four.

It was a gala meal intended to display the riches of Canada: seafood from the east coast, rich beef from the prairies, fruits and vegetables from Ontario and desserts from French patisseries in Montreal, all served by two professionally gracious white headwaiters assisted by blacks trained to show professional smiles.

"This is a grand introduction to Canada," Luton said. "I hope it's an omen."

But as he observed the other diners on this first night of his trip across the continent, he saw so much that perplexed him, so many different styles of dress and speech, that he became bewildered. What troubled him most was the breeziness of the people on the train, their informality, their lack, as he expressed it, "of any clear-cut social structure." He soon learned that he could not easily determine from what level of society a man came: "They all speak the same, bottom to top, no differentiation at all, except for those who've obviously had their education in England." Men pushed and shoved and paid little deference to those of obviously superior status, and when at Fort William several American travelers boarded the train, even what few proprieties the Canadians did observe seemed to fly out the window.

"At times," he told the two young men, "you'd hardly know it was a British colony, everything so jumbled."

Philip said he was pretty sure Canada wasn't a colony any longer: "Didn't they have a dominion office in London and all that? And their own prime minister?"

"If it makes them feel good, such concessions do little harm. But when an Englishman travels in India, for example, everything is so clear. There you are, white skin and all, dress easily recognized, officers in spanking new uniforms, women of all ages carrying on the best traditions of the home country. Sharing the place are the Indians. You can't miss them. Mind you, some of them can buy and sell the average Englishman, Oxford and all that, and they've learned to fit into the finest clubs. But Indians are Indians, and no one ever forgets it, isn't that right, Harry?"

Carpenter grunted agreement, then said that when he served in the Punjab on the Afghan frontier there were no finer troops than Probyn's Horse: "Mostly Indians, and I never fought with better."

"But of course they had English officers?"

"Yes. But I'll tell you this, Evelyn, if push should come to shove in Europe, and it might, I would expect a Canadian battalion to give a good account of itself, very good indeed." He was struck by the fact that the average Canadian man they were seeing seemed an inch or two taller than men of similar status would have been in England: "They're stout chaps, Evelyn, a new type of Empire man," but Luton thought the Canadian women dowdy and lacking in refinement.

"Travel by these trains isn't cheap, I can tell you that," Luton said, "so we've got to suppose we're seeing the best of the crop. Not too impressive, I'm afraid."

He feared that Canada had probably been corrupted by its proximity to the United States, and whenever he spoke of that massive republic lying just to the south he expressed ambivalent feelings: "Man would be an ass not to recognize the accomplishments of those energetic people. Remarkable, really. Fine cities and all that, but you must remember we got them off to a flying start during the hundred and fifty years we guided them. But I'm sure their effect on Canada has been destructive."

Carpenter, laughing at his friend's reluctance to accept Canada for what it was, said: "Evelyn! On this train you're enjoying a luxury not surpassed anywhere in Europe. Relax. Enjoy it," and Luton raised his glass: "To Canada, such as it is!"

Tim Fogarty was having a less opulent trip, for he was riding in what the new railway called a Colonial Car, an ingenious affair containing many little alcoves consisting of facing double seats, with between them enough space for the wooden table which when needed could be dropped from its resting place upright against the wall and returned there when the picnic-style meal was finished. But what pleased the Irishman most were the arrangements for sleeping, for he had soon tired of the endless vistas of lakes and trees his window afforded of the land north of the Great Lakes.

At night the space between the seats was filled in with a structure that also came down from the wall, thus forming, with the facing seats, a fine, level bed, upon which two passengers could sleep in relative comfort, especially if they had been forewarned to bring blankets of some kind. And that wasn't all. If four people occupied an alcove, the sleeping accommodations for two more were arranged for by an invention which simply delighted Fogarty and which he occupied even during daylight hours.

From a spot high up on the walls came strong link chains which supported the outer edges of bedlike platforms. These were thus suspended, as it were, from the ceiling and passengers could climb onto them with the aid of a little ladder. There, high above the others, they could stretch out, adjust their blankets if they had any, and sleep their way across the continent. What made these upper ledges especially homelike was the fact that in the rear of the car stood a well-designed wood-burning stove on which the travelers could cook such food as they had either brought with them or purchased at one of the many station halts. This meant that there was throughout the car, especially near the ceiling, a constant odor of the normal family kitchen.

The only drawback that Fogarty could detect was that the seats were upholstered in the hardest, shiniest, most unforgiving mock leather, only slightly more resilient than a board, and after even one day's travel, this unrelenting hardness began to tell.

The trip from Montreal to Edmonton traversed an awesome distance broken into four distinct segments: Montreal to Fort William at the head of Lake Superior, 995 miles in 32 hours; Fort William to Winnipeg, capital of western Canada, 427 miles in 14 hours; Winnipeg to the interesting frontier town of Calgary, 840 miles in 30 hours; and Calgary due north to Edmonton, 192 miles in 11 hours. The trip would thus cover 2,454 miles in 87 hours, without allowance for time in the station, time for refueling and taking on water. Since passengers were eager to avail themselves of hotel or inn accommodations at the terminal points of each segment, the journey took at least six days. This was fortunate, because it enabled Canada to introduce itself by conditioning stages; to have thrown the Englishmen direct from French Montreal to frontier Edmonton would have been too disorienting. To break the journey at little Fort William was advantageous, and the Englishmen noted that in a sense the gold rush began here, for this was the beginning of the western reach of the national railroad, and to it had come prospectors from all parts of Canada and especially from the little feeder railroads that came into Canada from the United States. Here also the big ships that plied the Great Lakes terminated their long runs; the traveler could, if he had the time and money, deviate from the normal rail route which traversed northern Ontario, go instead to Toronto and onward to Windsor on the Detroit River, board a luxurious steamer and spend several delightful days transiting Lakes Huron and Superior, disembarking at Fort William to resume the rail trip west to the Pacific.

In the summer of 1897 a constant horde of gold-seekers boarded the trains at Fort William for Winnipeg and Calgary, and the Luton party, seeing such men close up for the first time, judged them to be an ungainly lot, single men mostly, although some came in groups of three or four from some small town in places like Ohio or Michigan, with an occasional man and wife, the woman always big and strong and capable. A surprising number of the Americans who joined the caravan had been in the United States only briefly; they were Germans and Scandinavians, with now and then an Irishman and very rarely an adventurous Frenchman. They were men on the move, most of them in their late twenties or early thirties, sometimes a few in their grizzled forties and fifties. With their rough clothes, pasteboard suitcases and blunt language they were not an appetizing lot.

Some hours before the Englishmen arrived in Winnipeg, where they rested overnight, their train finally emerged from what had seemed to them an endless landscape of dark trees, still lakes and rock, brightened only by the flash of a silver birch tree and an occasional waterfall. Even Blythe, enamored at first with the wildness of this vast forest, had tired of it during the second day. Now the forest had stopped and the prairie stretched unbroken to the far horizon, and they began to comprehend fully both the immensity of Canada and its radical difference from any other part of the British Empire. "It really is a continent," Trevor said as he pored over maps, "and we're barely halfway across," but Luton dampened this uncritical enthusiasm by asking: "Does a thousand miles of empty prairie with no history, no culture, equal a hundred miles in an historical corner like Germany, Holland and Belgium?" He could express little interest in the vital sprawling new capital of Manitoba, and was unimpressed by the new electric streetcars which rumbled through the city, to the evident pride of its citizens.

West of Winnipeg, when the train halted at towns with names like Moose Jaw, Swift Current and Medicine Hat, the Englishmen saw that the passengers who now boarded the cars bore almost no similarity to types they had known in England and little to those in eastern Canada. Here no one spoke French, and English seemed no more commonly spoken than the foreign tongues of Baltic nations. There were no men's suits from fashionable London shops. These were men who plowed the prairie, tended cattle, and ran small country stores, and their women looked as competent as their husbands. A surprising number of women were traveling alone or in pairs.

Adding to the jumble of nationalities already on the train were the large numbers of gold-seekers who had come north from the western United States, big uncouth men with squarish faces indicating Slavic origins, or with light-blond hair indicating northern Europeans. Now every car in the train was crowded with would-be miners, many carrying with them all their family goods; the white-and-gold dining car was filled with dialects not heard before, and Fogarty's Colonial Car was so jammed that he had to share his bed aloft with a Swede who said he came from Montana.

The other Englishmen in his party were amused by the effect of this flood of newcomers on Lord Luton: "My word, they're a vigorous lot! No wonder they wanted to steal Oregon from us and half of Canada. Wonder the old marquess was able to hold them off, because these chaps could fight if they had to." Studying the Americans aloofly, he thought: They're either brash and forward, with no sense of proper social distinctions, or they're brutish clods recently arrived from some minor European country, little better than the peasants you'd find in any French village. And it irritated him to think that these latter Americans in their rough country clothes were presuming to occupy first-class accommodations, the only ones they were able to obtain on the crowded trains. You'd not find them doing this in England, he thought, and he was increasingly pleased that he had engineered it so that his team could avoid America completely, knowing he'd not feel at ease spending an extended period among such people.

The two young Englishmen, forced to accept what seats were available in the crowded dining car, struck up an easy conversation with their tablemates. "I say," Trevor asked, "where do these people come from?" and one of the men pointed to one pair of diners after another: "They're German, I happen to know them. That group I would judge to be from a Russian religious group who found refuge near here. The next? They could be anything," and he leaned out from the table to ask: "Where would you be from?" but as soon as the man began to speak, Trevor cried: "Scandinavian, aren't you?" and the man said: "Norwegian."

When Luton's party disembarked from the main line of the Canadian Pacific in Calgary in order to catch the train to Edmonton, everything changed, for nearly a thousand gold-seekers from all parts of the United States had crowded in to augment the hordes who had streamed in from eastern Canada. When the smaller train started due north to Edmonton, every seat was taken, so three cars normally used for cattle transfers were attached, and more than a hundred people rode the hundred and ninety-two miles to Edmonton standing up, and happy to be doing so.

Lord Luton, surveying this crush of humanity, said: "It's been like the meander of a major river over a long course. Smaller streams keep feeding into it from distant points, until the thing becomes a flood." He had scarcely uttered these words when someone heard Fogarty address him as "Milord." Word flashed through the mob that a real British lord was traveling north. Soon gawking Americans were pushing in to see how a British nobleman looked and more experienced Canadians watched approvingly from a distance.

Seeking refuge, Luton fled to his private saloon, but at dinner several strangers stopped by his table to pay their respects and wish him well. He was so distressed by this that he drew back, took refuge in his silent-sneer, and prayed that the trip would end quickly. Eleven hours later he heard cheering coming from the three cattle cars and looked out to see Edmonton, which had exploded from less than five hundred people last year to more than two thousand in the period since those fatal words were shouted in Seattle: "Ship's in with more than a ton of solid gold!"

Luton's first impression of Edmonton was of a city of tents, for the gold-seekers had thrown up thousands of temporary canvas dwellings along the flats of the North Saskatchewan River. Shops of every description had mysteriously appeared, most with some bold sign assuring the newcomer that inside these doors he would find all he needed for his forthcoming journey to the Klondike. The burghers of Edmonton reveled in its sudden notoriety, while hawkers pestered strangers on its impromptu streets, seeking to guide them to this shop or that. One man dressed like a carpenter, with overalls and bib containing six pockets for nails, harangued the travelers, and handed out leaflets warning them not to go north without the necessary hardware. He said that a minimal kit could be purchased at his brother's store for $43, which provided basics such as shovel, pick, whipsaw, hammer, rope, ax, drawknife, chisel, bucket and gold pan. However, he recommended what he called "the complete kit, listed here in detail, more than a hundred and ten necessities, only $125." This contained such useful items as a brace and bit, a block and tackle, a magnifying glass and a Dutch oven.

Philip accepted one of the leaflets, and when he returned to the hotel he recommended to his uncle that they buy the $125 assortment, but Luton said: "Harry's doing the buying, and he's much more practiced in outfitting expeditions than your carpenter friend."

While the four gentlemen attended to such matters as hardware, Fogarty moved quietly among the Americans and the Edmonton shopkeepers, and as he talked with clerks he began to uncover disquieting news. When he asked who the expert was who had prepared that pamphlet his team had acquired from the Canadian office in London, one sharp-minded fellow working in an outfitting shop asked: "What expert?" and Fogarty said: "I think his name was Halverson." The clerk sniggered: "Oh, him," and when Fogarty named the expert on the Mackenzie River, Desbordays, the clerk laughed outright: "They're the same man. Peter Randolph. He works at the newspaper."

"Has he ever been to Dawson?"

"He hasn't been as far north as the Athabasca River."

"What did he do, ask a lot of questions?"

"About what?"

"You know, talk with the other men who had been there."

"Nobody from here has been anywhere. I mean, down the Mackenzie River a short ways, maybe. On fishing trips, yes."

"But to the gold fields?"

"Nobody. At least not yet. There's talk that a government expedition might set out next year. But not now, with winter heading in."

Fogarty, loath to accept such disheartening information, quietly left the outfitter and strolled from one shop to another, asking not proprietors but minor clerks about the trails to the Klondike, and consistently he heard that Peter Randolph had never been out of Edmonton and that no one at present in the town had made the trek to Dawson, for as several pointed out: "Dawson wasn't even there till all this started."

"But could they have been to the Klondike?"

"There was no such place till last year when those Americans gave it that name."

As Fogarty walked down the dusty back streets of Edmonton, trying to digest his disturbing discoveries, he saw that he must do two things: try to speak with this man Peter Randolph who had written the spurious documents and then inform Lord Luton of his findings. At the office of the town's newspaper he asked for Randolph, and was told: "He doesn't work here anymore." When Fogarty asked: "What's he doing?" he was told: "He's taken a job giving advice to prospectors at a store that opened last week."

It took Fogarty a while to find which of the many new businesses had hired this imaginative man, and when he did he presented himself as a solitary would-be prospector. "Yes indeed!" salesman Randolph said enthusiastically. "You can get to the fields before the ice freezes everything. We'll provide you with the best clothing and equipment possible, food supplies too, and with one horse, which you supply, you can make it."

After Fogarty talked with him for some time, he began to suspect that not one word of what the man said was true. The whole Edmonton operation could be a gigantic fraud engineered by a few rapacious businessmen and a group of inattentive town fathers. It looked as if no one, when these pleasant days of summer were still long, stopped to reason that in sending lone travelers north into the teeth of the oncoming winter, a sentence of death was being pronounced, and that in dispatching even carefully prepared teams like Lord Luton's, disaster was being invited.

With this partial but frightening information, Fogarty returned to the hotel and told Luton: "If you'll excuse me saying so, Milord, we better get the others." When they assembled he said: "I think we're in a trap. The two men who wrote those reports you mention so much, they're one man, a fellow who's never been out of Edmonton, not even as far as the Peace River. I've been told by many men in town that there's no way people starting now can get to the gold fields before winter."

"Fogarty," Luton said, with just a show of irritation, "are you certain of all this, or is it just a batch of village rumors?" and when Fogarty protested that he had checked the veracity of his informants as carefully as possible, Lord Luton cut him short and snapped at Carpenter: "Harry, go out there and find out what's happening."

While Lord Luton was looking the other way, Fogarty slipped up to Carpenter and whispered: "His name's Peter Randolph. You'll find him tending shop in that place with the stuffed bear in the window"; and Harry went in search.

He found Randolph eagerly selling equipment to strangers who had no conception of the dangers they would be facing, and he was repelled by the young man's brazen lies. For nearly half an hour he hung about the edges of the crowd that was eagerly buying Randolph's gear, listening to the deceptions and correcting them to himself: "Dawson's just to the north, three, four hundred easy miles." Must be twelve hundred of hellish difficulty. "Seven pleasant weeks before the snow falls should get you there." More like seven months, with snow most of the way.

What really terrified him was the information quietly passed him by an Edmonton man who said he was ashamed at what was happening: "You look a proper sort. England? I thought so. Believe not a word that one says. He's never been north of this town. Only one man in history has completed the journey from here to Dawson, trained scout familiar with our climate. Powerful chap, top condition, had the help of Indians, too."

"How long did it take him?"

"A year and two months. Arrived nearly dead."

"Then it's criminal to send these unsuspecting people along such a trail."

"It's worse. It's murder."

Rushing back to where Luton waited, Harry said bitterly: "Everything Fogarty said is true, Evelyn, except that he discovered only half. Even to attempt an overland trip from here to Dawson would be suicide. And Fogarty was also correct about Randolph. His forged reports are founded on nothing, not a single trip to anywhere, just dreams and willful delusions. Evelyn, this deception is so shocking, I do believe we must warn those gullible fools out there not to attempt such folly." He was so statesmanlike, never raising his voice and thinking only of others, that Luton was persuaded that an alarm must be sounded. Before this could be done a wild noise of cheering and whistling flooded their quarters, and all turned out to watch not a tragedy, nor a comedy either, but merely the latest in line of the Edmonton insanities.

A farmer named Fothergill from Kansas, who had made not a fortune but a competence raising corn and feeding it to his hogs, had arrived some days earlier on the train, bringing with him some two dozen large pieces of cargo that he had assembled into what he called "the Miracle Machine," which would carry him to the Klondike. Basically, it was an agricultural tractor, heavily modified for the gold rush, and on the flat fields of Kansas it might have been a sensation, for it consisted of a sturdy iron-strapped boiler which, when heated by wood chopped along the way, would activate four giant wheels.

"You'll notice," Fothergill told the admiring crowd, "that the wheels are pretty big across. That's to help them roll over obstacles. You'd be surprised how that helps." But then he showed them the secret of his success: "Maybe you didn't notice at first, but look at those spikes fitted into the wheels, and these three dozen extras in the box back here in case one breaks."

"What do they do?" a suspicious Canadian asked, and Fothergill explained: "They dig into the soil. Give the contraption a footing and send it forward as neat as you please." As he spoke, his eyes shining with expectation of the gold he was going to find, it became obvious to the Englishmen that he had pictured the trail from Edmonton to Dawson as an American prairie, flat and easily negotiated but with a necessary tree here or there, for when one Edmonton man asked: "How you goin' to get it through forests?" the American replied: "We may have to avoid a tree or two, go around maybe."

And now the time had come to start his drive of more than a thousand miles, with no map, only a few spare parts and just one ax to cut the needed wood. Lord Luton, watching this tremendous folly, whispered to his nephew: "Someone ought to halt this madness."

As the fire below the boiler began to flame, the already heated water started to produce steam, and with a violent creaking of parts the huge machine, capable of carrying twenty men, inched forward, felt its power, and struck out for the modified Edmonton prairie, moving quite splendidly forward with Fothergill in the driver's seat waving to the cheering watchers. But when, one hundred yards later, the huge spiked wheels encountered a stretch of flat earth where rains had accumulated, the contraption did not proceed onward; instead, the wheels dug themselves ever more deeply into the swampy soil, the big spikes cutting powerfully down and not ahead, so that soon the entire body of the vehicle was sinking into the mire, with all forward progress halted.

Before the confused farmer could halt the supply of power to the four huge wheels, they had dug themselves into a muddy grave from which six mules would not have been able to dislodge them. Dismayed, Fothergill climbed down from his perch, looked at the laughing crowd, and asked: "How am I ever going to get this to Dawson?" By chance, he directed this question to Lord Luton, who drew back as if the man and his stupidity were distasteful, and said: "Yes, how indeed?"

Back in quarters, Luton resumed the point that Carpenter had been making when the launching of the miracle machine had interrupted: "We must alert these fools to the perils they face if they attempt such nonsense . . . or even attempt to leave on foot . . . or with horses."

For an entire day the four moved among the gold-crazy hordes, warning them that the Halverson and Desbordays documents were fraudulent, but they found themselves powerless to dissuade the starry-eyed travelers. They met two men and a woman who had bought a pony that was expected to carry their entire pack to Dawson. "Please, please! Don't try it!" Carpenter urged, but even as he spoke the trio set off for a journey that would take them at least a year, if the pony lived, but since Harry was certain it would die before the week was out, he supposed its three owners would also perish.

When he encountered a fine-looking woman in her late thirties who proposed making the entire overland trip on foot, by herself, with a small packet of dried fruits, he lost all patience, and scolded her: "Madam, you will be close to death at the end of the first week, and surely dead by the second." When she explained, tearfully, that she must have the gold because she had two children in Iowa to support, he made a move which astonished both her and him: He took her in his arms, pushed his heavy mustaches against her face, and kissed her soundly on the cheek: "Madam, you're a handsome woman. And a wonderful mother, I'm sure. But for God's sake, go back to Iowa. Now!" And before she could protest, he had given her fifteen Canadian dollars and taken her by the arm to the depot from which she could start her journey home.

Philip Henslow was having an experience that was somewhat similar, but one which would have a surprisingly different outcome. He was strolling idly, asking questions of any strangers who looked as if they might be informed concerning the various routes to Dawson, when he came up behind a woman, probably a good deal older than himself, he thought, who was conspicuous for her outstanding mode of dress. It looked like a modified military uniform made from some sturdy, tightly woven dark cloth: ample skirt but not long, soldier-type jacket but puffy at the shoulders, visored kepilike cap worn at a jaunty angle, heavy, durable shoes and, even though the weather was warm, stout gloves.

He was so taken by this unusual garb that he did something he would never have dared back in England, but the free and almost wild spirit of Edmonton that summer emboldened him. Hurrying ahead to pass her, he turned to ask politely: "Ma'am, are you headed north?"

When she looked up to see him, he almost gasped at the total charm of her appearance. She was, as he had guessed, in either her late twenties or earliest thirties, but she had the lithe figure of a teen. Her face was not beautiful in an ordinary sense of flawless complexion, prominent cheekbones and perfectly harmonized features; it was more like that of an eighteenth-century Italian statue of some distinguished matron: gracious, appealing, yet carved from timeless marble and somehow as hard.

She seemed in that first enchanted glance to come from some foreign country, neither Canada nor America and certainly not England, for her hair, which showed handsomely beneath the odd tilt of her kepi, was so light a straw color that it could almost have been called beaten silver. But her salient characteristic was a slow-forming smile which seemed to deliver contradictory messages: "Come closer so we can talk," but also "Stand back so I can calculate who you are."

From that first brief question of Philip's she had made the same deduction as he: this one is a foreigner; and in a voice remarkably low and soft she asked in an accent he could not identify: "From where do you come?"

"London."

"Heading for the gold fields, yes?"

"Like everyone else."

She said: "You look like a boy. Too young to be making such a trip," but when she saw him wince she quickly added, like a mother wanting to reassure a child: "Maybe you have more courage when you're young."

"Have you heard any reports about the overland route to Dawson?"

When she heard these words she actually sucked in her breath and drew back: "You're not thinking of trying that route, are you?" and when he replied: "That's why our team is out asking questions," she actually grabbed his right hand with her two gloved hands and said with a voice of deep concern: "Oh, young man! Don't let them drag you along that path!"

She was so agitated that when Philip asked: "Did something terrible happen to you?" she did an unexpected thing. Turning away from him, she raised her right arm and signaled a group of three men clustered some distance away. Catching the wave of her gloved hand, they hurried to her.

"He do something to you?" one of the men, chunky, swarthy-looking fellows in their thirties, asked menacingly, and she held them back with a disarming laugh: "No, no! A nice young man from London. He's asking about going north." She introduced the three men: "Steno Kozlok, my husband; his brother Marcus; my brother Stanislaus. All farmers from North Dakota, and that includes me."

"Why did you call us?" Steno asked, and from his heavy accent and dark, squarish face Philip deduced that he and the two other men must be immigrants from one of the Slavic countries or perhaps from Russia. The three looked as if they had been hewn foursquare out of some Middle European oak tree, and Philip thought: I'm certainly glad that I didn't offend her, because if these three came at me . . .

"My name is Irina Kozlok," she said in softly accented words that seemed to sing.

"Where are you people from? I mean, before North Dakota?"

"Ah," she laughed, "you'd never guess." And she said that her husband Steno and his brother Marcus had come from a distant corner of the Austrian Empire. "His proper name, Kozlowkowicz, but when we marry I find that no one can spell it or say it, so I made him change it to Kozlok. Now everybody can spell my name."

"But you . . . and your brother?" Philip asked, and she replied almost teasingly: "You would never guess," and he said: "Well, you do have light hair. His is even lighter. Swedes?" Again she laughed: "Everyone says that. No, we come from a place you never heard of. Estonia."

"Ah! But I have heard of it," he cried like a child who has solved a puzzle. "It's part of Russia."

Her smile vanished. "It's Estonia, a part of nothing else. Just Estonia." Then, afraid that she had seemed harsh, she said brightly:

"Men, I want you to tell this nice young Englishman who's thinking about risking the land route what it would be like."

As soon as she said this, her three companions stepped close to Philip, all speaking at once, and from the jumble of their words, he knew he was receiving just the kind of information Lord Luton sought: "Murderous . . . they should shoot the son-of-a-bitch sent us that way . . . no marked trail . . . you wouldn't believe how many dead horses rotting in the sun . . . and you got to ford a dozen streams . . . snow comes, everyone on that trail freeze to death."

The young woman stemmed the flood of complaints: "They're telling only half."

"You people actually tried the trail?"

"We did," Steno said, and his brother added: "But we smart enough to turn back." Irina broke in: "If your team even thinks about going that way, stop them now."

"If we'd'a tried to push on," Steno said, "we'd'a been snowed in, proper, all winter."

"And without heavy clothes or food," his wife added.

"What now?" Philip asked. "Back to North Dakota?"

"Hell no!" the three men said almost together. "We came for gold. We gonna get it."

"How?"

"Only sensible way. Right down the Mackenzie, haul our boat over the Divide, and into Dawson."

At this firm point, Irina grasped Philip's hands again and stared deep into his eyes as she said softly: "I'm so glad you stopped me . . . asked me those questions. Please, please, listen to them. Don't take that route. If you do, you'll die."

This was said with such gravity that Philip was momentarily struck silent. Then he said, with a slight bow to each of his informants: "I hope you reach the gold fields, you kind and helpful people from North Dakota," and Irina spoke for all when she replied: "We intend to." Then in a gesture of the brotherhood that linked all gold-seekers that summer in Edmonton, she astonished him by gripping his hand tightly, smiling at him briefly, and repeating in a voice as cold as steel exposed in winter: "Do not go the overland route. You're much too young to die," whereupon she reached up and kissed him.

Half expecting her husband to come flying at him, Philip instead heard Steno saying: "Listen to her, young fellow. We do," and the four trailed off to start their journey to the Mackenzie. As they

disappeared in the lingering twilight, Philip, still dazed by that farewell kiss, thought: Wouldn't it be wonderful to have a wife like that,
so daring, so quick to laugh, so generous toward other people? I
wonder if all women in America are like that?

When Lord Luton's four investigators reassembled to report their
findings, he listened firm-lipped to their distressing news and inter-
rogated each: "Did you reach the conclusion by yourself?" and each
told him of the shocking facts that had become so apparent under
questioning. Satisfied that they had been honest in their seeking and
in their decision that any version of overland travel was insane, he
rose abruptly, nodded, and stalked from the room: "I've got to hear
this for myself," and into the warm night air he disappeared.

Tall, thin, carefully dressed, with his aquiline nose slightly lifted
as if he wished to avoid the smell of the rabble, he poked his way
about, remaining aloof from the gold-seekers who had been unable
to find quarters and were sleeping on the ground, their belongings
piled about them. With brief and restrained questioning he satisfied
himself that in all this rabble, no one knew anything, and a profound
sadness overtook him: They're fools who have been deluded by fools,
and they're doomed. When he came upon two men from a small
Canadian village who were going to attempt the overland route on
bicycles, dragging behind them little wheeled carts holding their gear,
he stopped to ask them: "What will you use for greatcoats when the
blizzards hit?" and they replied smartly: "Oh, we'll be in Dawson by
then." He did not try to enlighten them, but his depression increased.

Still moving slowly among them like a recording angel, wise, just
and impartial, he muttered again and again: "Doomed! That trio
won't survive even into November," and he formed a sound resolve
that *his* expedition was not going to plunge blindfolded into such
folly: We are men of sound sense, dammit, and we'll not comport
ourselves like idiots.

Just then he saw an older man who seemed to be moving with
some purpose, as if he had serious business to attend, even though it
was now close to eleven at night, and Luton accosted him: "My good
fellow, can you help me bring some reason into this madness?"

"Madness it is," the man replied in a heavy Scottish brogue as he
surveyed the people sleeping on the ground. "What is it you seek?"

"Answers, answers. How can I and my party get from here to the
gold fields and escape the certain devastation that faces these blun-
dering idiots?"

"You've come to the right man," the Scot said. "I work for the Hudson's Bay Company and I'm the only one around here who's made the trip, and because I could rely upon my company's various caches of supplies, I traveled extremely light. Almost no gear. And I had Dogrib Indians to help part of the way."

"How was it?"

"Wretched. It's a crime to send untested men north at this time of year. Many will die."

"What would you advise?"

"You look strong and sensible. What of the others in your party?"

"Young, able."

"If I were you, I'd stay here in Edmonton till next June when the ice melts. Then sail down the Mackenzie, a majestic river if ever I saw one, and stay with it almost till it empties into the Arctic Ocean. But stay out of the delta! It's a wilderness of interwoven streams and small islands. As the delta begins, you'll find the Peel River entering via the left bank of the Mackenzie. Paddle up it ten or fifteen miles, and you'll come to the Rat River, feeding in from the west. Go clear to its headwaters, portage over the mountains, not easy but it can be done. There you'll find the Bell. Drift down it, easy paddling, and in due course you'll hit the Porcupine, a grand river. Turn right. Keep going downstream, and with no trouble, little paddling, you'll reach Fort Yukon. And, as the French say, '*Voilà!*' you're on the Yukon River where you catch an upriver steamboat which carries you direct to Dawson."

This good man was so eager to correct the errors perpetrated by other Canadians that with his forefinger he drew in sand a map of the many twists and turns he recommended: "It'll be demanding, but relatively easy doing it this way. Portages, yes, and some paddling upstream, but not excessive."

When Luton looked down at the map he scowled: "We shouldn't care to use the Yukon steamers. We've decided to do it on our own. The challenge and all." Then he pointed to the mark that represented Fort Yukon: "And under no circumstances would I consider entering the gold field through American territory."

The Hudson's Bay man contemplated this rejection, checked his temper, and said quietly: "Sir, you interpose conditions that make no sense in this part of the north. I would accept a push from a crippled old woman if it would enable me to complete a difficult journey." He bowed stiffly and disappeared into the starry night.

As Luton started back toward his hotel he was diverted by a light in the distance. He moved toward it, hearing a rumble of low voices as if many men were conversing, neither in anger nor in jubilation. When he drew closer he saw a large group of Indians, men and women together, engaged in a midsummer ritual dance, their heads tilted back as if imploring the moon to appear, their feet occupied in a formless shuffle, their arms limp at their sides as if semidetached from their bodies. It was neither an exultant dance, nor one of leaping and shouting, but the number of participants, their steady shuffling movement and their low whispering song was almost narcotic, both to themselves and to those watching.

For many minutes Luton remained in the shadows, unperceived by the dancers but participating in their quiet dance through the swaying of his own body. Even as he followed the rhythm he thought: Savages! I've seen them in Africa. And along the Amazon. Same the world over. Halting his swaying, he brought his right thumbnail to his teeth and gnawed at it as he contemplated the hypnotic scene: How many generations before these savages evolve a decent civilization?

His reflections were broken by a man who sidled up from the rear, speaking in broken French: "Blackfeet. Most powerful Indians on frontier. Don't let dancing fool you. Start a fight, two hundred knives at your throat."

As a cultured Englishman, Luton, of course, spoke French with only a slight accent, and although he resented the Frenchmen of Montreal, he welcomed this man in the wilderness, where, he thought, it was proper for him to be: "Why are they in Edmonton? The Indians, I mean?"

"They've been coming here for centuries, they claim. You built Fort Edmonton on their dancing ground, they claim."

"Are you a Blackfoot?"

"Métis. Long time ago, maybe grandfather Blackfoot, father Scotch, they claim."

"Your name?"

"Simon MacGregor."

"Scotsman." The two watchers fell silent as they watched the monotonous drag-foot dancing of the Blackfoot braves, then Luton asked: "Does anything happen in the dance? Should I wait, perhaps?"

"Just same thing, maybe five hours," the Métis said in English.

When Luton whistled at this surprising information, two Indian men heard him, stepped out of the shadows, and almost diffidently asked in broken French: "You like dance? You want to join?" and when he failed to state strongly that he had no desire for such meaningless posturing, they interpreted this as agreement. Politely, almost gravely, they took positions beside him, edging him not toward the shuffling dancers but to a flat area close to where he had been standing, and there they led him in steps which imitated those of the group.

Since the men were dressed in full Blackfoot regalia—decorated deerskin jackets, tight trousers with brightly colored leather tied below the knee, streaks of red and blue down their cheeks—and since Luton's magisterial bearing showed to advantage between the two braves, they formed a handsome trio. The light from a central fire cast deep romantic shadows across their aquiline faces, prompting the Métis to break into soft applause: *"Très bien! Les danseurs magnifiques!"*

Luton, astonished at what he had let himself into, attempted a few additional movements, but when the men actually laid hands on him, trying to guide him into other proper steps, he pushed them away and fled the scene. Startled, the Indians stared at his departing figure, interpreted his rejection as one more evidence of white man's ill will, shrugged, and moved off. Luton, once more alone, again could think only of other savage dancers he had seen, and his unease regarding the Indians of Canada increased. If he did not relish his imaginary view of the United States, he felt a similar dislike for Canada's Indian lands, and with confused reactions to what he had witnessed under the stars he returned to his hotel.

Although it was late when he reached his quarters, he routed out his three companions and dispatched Philip to fetch Fogarty. When all were present he directed Harry to unfold his big map, and proceeded in low, masterful accents to line out a chain of decisions, and as an augury of the good luck he trusted would attend them, the short, crisp directives he issued were exactly right: "Under no circumstances will we attempt the overland route and I wish never again to hear a word about it. That leaves us with two alternatives, and I will ask Harry to present them, for on this you have the right to influence the decision. I can survive with either choice."

Clearing his throat in the deferential manner he affected, Carpenter said: "Men, you've heard what Evelyn says. The choice is up to us. We can remain here in this bleak outpost village that strives to become a town for seven long months waiting for the Mackenzie to thaw—no libraries, no theater, no music, no decent food—or we leave for the Mackenzie tomorrow, get us a boat, sail her down as far as we can get before it freezes over, and when it is about to freeze, head her into some protected cove and see if we are men enough to brave an arctic winter north of the Circle, hibernating like bears. Let me hear which you prefer? Edmonton for seven months?" The groans, except from Fogarty, were so loud they were almost palpable. "Sail north to the Arctic Circle and test our courage?" Cheers, to which Lord Luton added: "How I would have deplored it if you had voted otherwise."

Then, asking Harry to move aside, he resumed command of his expedition: "Gentlemen, you have chosen a difficult way, but the only way. It can succeed only if we discipline ourselves rigorously. When we are iced up, we scout the land for what timber we can find, drift-wood perhaps, and build a kind of hybrid tent-cabin. Total usable space, about like that corner over there. We shall all have tasks. And if we do not have respect one for the other, we shall fail."

After the four listeners had applauded quietly, he gave final orders: "Up at six tomorrow to make your last purchases to sustain us for a year, in case trouble strikes, and each man to provide two good books."

As the men began to bask in the euphoria of a well-made decision, Carpenter, long trained in subduing alien terrain, felt obliged to bring the team back to reality. Relying upon the map to fortify his points, he reminded everyone of the terrible contradiction of the Mackenzie River: "This river, which will hold us prisoner, runs parallel far to the east of the Yukon River, which we want to be on. If we stay on the Mackenzie long enough, we end up in the Arctic Ocean and no good done. We'd be nowhere. So our problem is: At what point heading north do we escape the tyranny of the Mackenzie and head west, to seek the benevolence of the Yukon?"

"I've asked about that, Harry," Luton said evenly, "and the map is clear. On our way we will pass a score of rivers coming in from the gold-field territory. All we have to do is go up one of them till we encounter a river heading down the other way, and it will carry us right to the Yukon and the gold fields."

Harry was not finished, for after dipping his finger in a glass of red wine—"It's not fit to drink," he apologized—he drew a bold line from farthest north in Canada, right on the Beaufort Sea, down into the first shadow of the United States. When he was done he stepped back so that all could see: "The Rocky Mountains. High here, low there, very high here, but always present, never to be avoided, not by men or rivers or eagles." Looking intently at each of the other men, he said almost ominously: "No matter where we go, or how, if we want to reach those gold fields, at some point we must climb with all our gear and maybe even our boats, and cross the Rocky Mountains. There is no avoidance, unless we want to turn back and go in the way the others go, through Alaska."

Lord Luton, standing very erect, his arms folded behind his back, assumed a posture of command and said softly: "We shall sail north on the Mackenzie, find the likeliest river heading west, and the lowest stand of the mountains, and cross over to our target." That said, he folded the map and advised his men: "Thanks to your common sense, yours too, Fogarty, we have avoided the deadly errors of the land route. May God direct our proper choices on the river."

In the morning the five men fanned out through the shops of Edmonton, picking up last-minute requirements, including a shovel, two axes and extra ascorbic acid. Two of their purchases would prove significant. Harry Carpenter, having been on safari and trek, sought a store that sold books, where he purchased three volumes, whose covers he promptly tore off, to the dismay of the clerk: *Great Expectations,* the poems of John Milton and a Bible.

Philip Henslow went to the store with the bear in the window, and there the imaginative Peter Randolph was clerking. The author of the pamphlet for stampedes convinced him he must acquire a special pair of boots for the north.

They were rubber, heavy enough to keep out the cold, Randolph said, and tall enough to reach well above the knee. They were highly polished and created a pleasing seventeenth-century impression when worn with trousers tucked in, but when Carpenter saw them he grew angry: "Who sold you such boots?" Philip would not reply, and Harry became stern: "Son, rubber boots like that are for farmers who work in muck. What you need are stout, heavy leather boots like mine, with high lacing."

"I like mine," Philip said, whereupon Harry took another tack: "They do look stout. But one doesn't wear rubber boots on a journey like this."

"They're waterproof. The man said so. And we'll be in water a lot, the way we plan to go."

Carpenter referred the problem to Luton, who chided his nephew:

"If you want to drag around boots that heavy, so be it. But never say we failed to warn you."

In the middle of August 1897, when from all over the world adventurers were heading toward the Klondike, Lord Luton, his three friends and the Irishman Fogarty rode north in two rented Red River carts to intercept the Athabasca River, some ninety miles away. Down this river they would sail in the boat they would order built when they reached the waterway, and because of careful planning by Luton and Carpenter, they would have a fighting chance of reaching the gold fields next June, if they selected wisely among the various rivers leading in from the west.

At about the time they set forth, three men from Australia departed by the overland route, as did a dentist from Salt Lake City and three of his companions. A Frenchman, a Norwegian, two Germans and some fifty men and women from various parts of the United States, as well as many Canadians and two other parties of Englishmen, departed shortly thereafter. None of these adventurers using the land route came anywhere near the Klondike.

One man who left Edmonton in that euphoric summer did so on a farm wagon with huge wheels, pulled by two pairs of goats that he proposed to feed on the browse they would encounter on the way. His effort would end the second week when there was no browse. Another man intended to be hauled along by dogs, and another left Edmonton with only a knapsack and a supply of specially prepared nuts and fruits which he claimed would sustain him till he reached the gold fields in early September. Seventy like them who either had left or were about to leave would perish en route, sad proof that this was a time of general insanity.

Lord Luton had estimated that if his party could cover the relatively easy ninety miles to the Athabasca River, they would find themselves well launched on the great Mackenzie River system. So, anxious to waste not even one day of summer, and never parsimonious, Luton was willing to hire draymen to haul them to Athabasca Landing, but only if it could be done speedily, for he was determined to be among the first to sail north. "We really must," he told the draymen, "put ourselves well down the Mackenzie before it freezes."

"It's ninety-four miles overland, Guv'nor, and at twenty miles a day . . . you can figure for yourself . . . more than four days."

"Make it three and a half, there's an extra quid for each of you."

"In dollars?"

"Five Canadian," and it was a deal.

In this way they found themselves among the hordes speeding out of Edmonton, and it seemed strange to be so attentive to the freezing of rivers, for this was still summer and they traveled these first miles in their lightest hunting dress. As they passed through lonely settlements the inhabitants, accustomed only to hunting parties, called: "Are you after moose or gold?" and Philip always cried back: "Gold!"

On the layover during the third night, Harry Carpenter unfolded the modern map of the Mackenzie he had purchased in Edmonton, and with the ruler he had contributed to the expedition made careful calculations of what lay ahead for them once they entered upon the Mackenzie system at Athabasca. Since he insisted that all members of the team understand the task they were about to attack, he recited mileages carefully: "If we can buy a boat of some kind tomorrow, August eighteenth, start sailing immediately and keep our minds to it, we'll have sixty-four days till the start of normal freeze-up of the Mackenzie. From here to Fort Norman, a probable target, is only eight hundred and sixteen miles as the crow flies, but . . . ."

Philip completed the sentence: "We ain't crows."

Harry nodded in his direction and said: "The winding way we'll have to go looks to be just over twelve hundred miles," and Philip whistled.

"But wait. If you divide twelve hundred miles by sixty-four days, you get an average distance to be covered of under nineteen miles, and that's possible."

Now Luton took over: "We have three enormous advantages in our favor. We're going downstream all the way on a steady and sometimes swift current which would carry us quite a distance each day, even if we did nothing to help. And most of the way we'll sail with a wind behind us. Most important of all, once we get into our boat, and under sail, we could move north twenty-four hours a day, every day till the freeze."

"On those terms we could get to China," Philip said, and his uncle continued: "Another advantage in our favor is that we don't have to reach Fort Norman, or any other arbitrary point, for with the careful planning Harry started in London and completed in Edmonton, we can halt wherever we please, erect our cabin, and face the winter with impunity."

"Then why hurry so?" Philip asked, and his uncle had the answer that motivated all the gold-seekers leaving Edmonton in those late days of summer: "Because we want to be far down the river next spring, when the ice melts and we're free to travel again. Gentlemen, the excitement of this trip starts tomorrow, but also the hard work. This will be your last night in a comfortable bed properly made in a very long time. Make the most of it."

At Athabasca Landing—a collection of several permanent frame houses and an equal number of storage barns belonging to the trade companies—they came upon scores of white tents, indicating that other prospectors had come here for purposes similar to theirs. Luton, offended by the disarray, turned to Carpenter and Fogarty: "We know nothing about boats suitable for the Mackenzie. Circulate among these people and determine which would be better, to have a new boat built for us or to buy one already built." The two had made only a few inquiries when they found that everyone they asked was directing them to a shack occupied by four hard-working German brothers, the Schnabels, who were whipping out most of the boats going down the Mackenzie that summer.

"We can build you a sturdy boat for two . . ."

"We're five, bound for Dawson," Carpenter said.

"Just as easy for us."

"Have you any already built?"

"Them two," and Luton's men saw tied to trees along the shore two radically different craft, one a fine big boat about thirty-seven feet long, ample in width and with a small cabinlike shack aft big enough to sleep two. The other was a small, compact craft not half as large as the first.

"Are they both for sale?" Carpenter asked, and one of the Germans said: "In a manner of speaking."

"What do you mean?" and the German explained: "The big one has been ordered by a group of men from Saskatoon who want to trade up and down the Mackenzie. The small one has been built to the specifications mailed us by a dentist from Detroit."

"Then they're both sold."

"Not really. We're ahead of schedule, so if you want them, you get them. We can replace them before the owners get here."

"We'll take the big one," and all the Schnabels who heard this decision broke into laughter, and one of them said: "Just a minute.

Two different boats, two different purposes. Like I explained, the big one is for navigating the Mackenzie . . ."

"That's what we'll be doing."

Schnabel ignored him. "Only the small one is for going down the Mackenzie and then getting across the Rockies to the gold fields."

"What's the difference?" Carpenter asked, and when Schnabel replied with only one word: "Portage," Harry slapped his leg and uttered a self-deriding laugh: "How stupid of me. Of course it would be impossible to lug that huge thing anywhere."

Now he and Fogarty turned their whole attention to the smaller boat, and Harry asked the Germans: "Give us honest advice. Would we be better off if we waited till you built us one exactly suited to our purposes? Five of us?"

"It would be better by this much," and when one of the builders indicated with a thumb and forefinger a difference so small it was hardly detectable, Harry said: "I'm sure we'll want this one intended for the dentist, but I must consult with Lord Luton . . ."

"A real lord?"

"Yes, and a fine gentleman," and he sent Fogarty running to fetch Evelyn. When Luton arrived the four Germans clustered about him, and one said: "We don't get many real lords up this way," and another said: "We don't ever get any," then quickly they reviewed for him the crucial difference between buying a big heavy boat intended for permanent duty up and down the Mackenzie and a small, sturdy boat for getting to the gold fields. Before they were finished Luton broke in: "We'll take the small one," but then he repeated the question Carpenter had asked: "Would we gain anything if we waited for you to build us exactly what we wanted?" The oldest of the Germans stepped forward: "I know what's in your mind, sir. You think we may be trying to sell this one because we have it already on our hands." He chuckled: "Look at that crowd. More coming in every day. We can get shed of everything we have by nightfall."

"And this one will do us?"

"It will," and the deal was made.

But the Germans were honest workmen and they wanted Luton to be satisfied with his purchase, so they sprang about adding small grace notes to an already fine job—an extra inch of coaming all around, double reinforcement for the housing into which the mast would be stepped when the wind made the use of two small sails practical—and when all was done and Luton and his party were summoned to view it, one Schnabel appeared with a brush and a bucket of paint: "Now, what's her name to be?" Lord Luton looked about with his two hands raised palms up as if seeking counsel, so Trevor Blythe offered a felicitous suggestion: "It must be properly English. Perhaps *Sweet Afton,* in hopes the Mackenzie will flow gently."

When everyone applauded, Luton was inspired to invite onlookers in the area to a christening spread of wine, cheese, cigars and such sweetmeats as could be purchased at the Landing. Cracking a bottle of wine against the prow of the little craft, he intoned: "This may not be champagne, but I christen this ship *Sweet Afton,* and may God protect all who sail in her."

It was the kind of boat the Schnabels had found adapted to the Mackenzie system: flat-bottomed for negotiating rocky rapids, relatively light in weight for the brutal task of portaging, and high-straked to repel waves that often swept the bigger lakes. Well aft, the Schnabels had erected a small, low shack intended primarily for the stowing of gear but also big enough to sleep two, not in comfort. To port of the shack ran a wooden bench providing a position from which the steersman could operate a long sweep to swing the boat from side to side while avoiding rocks in the rapids or the floating logs which menaced ordinary stretches of the river.

The *Afton* was a craft which summarized much Mackenzie lore, and when the Schnabels turned her over to her new owners, she was about the best that could have been devised for tackling the great, wild river.

As they prepared to embark, Luton was perplexed to find that in addition to the bright-red name of his boat, the Schnabel with the paintbrush had added, at the halfway mark, a thin red line running vertically right across and around the boat, inside and out: "What's that for?" and the painter explained: "To guide you when you're sawing."

"And why would I be sawing?" and the man called to his brother: "Tell him."

"Oh, sir, even though you will be sailing down the Mackenzie, your main job will always be to get over the mountains and into the Yukon . . ."

"I've heard that before," Luton said, half smiling at Carpenter.

"So you must choose one of the rivers that come into the Mackenzie from the west."

"I'm aware of that, too."

"They're all serviceable. Liard is quite usable. Gravel can be excellent. But whichever you choose . . ."

"I was advised last night by a Hudson's Bay official to avoid those early rivers and head straight for the delta, and then take . . ." Here he produced from his pocket a notebook in which he had written down the complicated tangle of rivers in the extreme north: "Peel to the Rat, portage to the Bell, and on to the Porcupine."

"The wise ones, old-timers, seem to choose that route. But when you do get safely into the Rat you face situations which force you to saw your boat in half. The little rivers are too winding for the full-length boat to get around the corners. You just cannot manage it, but half a boat twists and turns nicely. And before long, especially with the Rat, the water grows so shallow that you can no longer sail or pole. Then you attach hauling ropes, leave your boat, walk along the bank, and pull her upstream."

Luton interrupted: "But what do we do if there is no bank to walk on?"

"Then you catch your breath, step down into the cold mountain water, and hike right up the middle of the Rat, hauling your boat behind you. And at that moment you'll thank us for telling you to saw it in half."

Another brother said: "And of course, when you reach the end of the Rat, you must haul your boat on land over the mountain pass, portage we call it, to the headwaters of the Bell. You do this by hand— strength of your arms and back—and when you're draggin' her up that last half-mile ascent, you'll be damned glad you sawed her."

Departure was somewhat disrupted by the arrival on horseback from Edmonton of the Detroit dentist, who, when he saw his boat sailing down the Athabasca River, galloped along the bank, shouting: "Pirates! That's my boat!" but he was mollified by Harry Carpenter, who called back: "They'll build you a better!"

The sail down the three hundred and fifty miles of the Athabasca established a pattern for the entire trip, with Lord Luton, passionately eager to reach some spot far down the Mackenzie before the winter freeze imprisoned the boat, driving his men relentlessly. At the various portages around rapids, where the laden boat had to be hauled over uneven ground, he employed waiting Indians to help, but he himself pulled from the lead position, setting a pace that his four followers sometimes found difficult to match. However, if the distance overland was extensive, it was Fogarty's dogged strength which kept the *Afton* crawling forward.

But the regimen that enabled them to cover extraordinary distances, once sailing again, had been established that first night out of Athabasca Landing when Luton refused to pull into shore: "Starlit night. Good omen. Keep sailing." And they did, with him at the tiller, and thereafter, except when storm prevented, the *Sweet Afton* forged ahead day and night, piling up remarkable distances. During one spell, an unusually swift current combined with a stiff breeze to push the *Afton* along at a steady four miles an hour for a day's run of ninety-six miles. "We're flying!" Philip cried. But of course, there were those other days at the portages when they were lucky to cover one mile.

The other regimen he established was that on these night expeditions either he or Carpenter must be in charge, with one of the younger men or Fogarty in assistance. By a process of natural selection his partner became Trevor Blythe, and in the dark passages of the night they discussed those things which interested Luton: courage, deportment, sportsmanship, cricket, the responsibility of Englishmen to hold the world together, provided they received occasional help from Germany or Russia. He had little respect for France and practically none for the United States, which as he explained to Blythe, "Lacks every virtue we've been discussing."

During daylight runs the travelers learned a great deal about this part of Canada, because what they saw was an endlessly repeated landscape with almost no redeeming features: formless hills, vast expanses of graceless forest, bogs with stagnant water. "Not one of my favorite trout streams," Luton said as the dismal landscape continued, not for miles but days, without showing signs of improvement. But when they reached the Slave River on the second of September they faced not boredom but real problems, for this short stream contained many rapids, some difficult to navigate, others so impassable as to require exhausting portages. And as each of the wasted days grew markedly shorter, the men had sobering proof that winter was crowding in. However, they were about to encounter a problem of such magnitude that these comparatively petty annoyances were promptly forgotten.

The Great Slave Lake, which those unfamiliar with northern Canada had never heard mentioned, was immense, larger than either of two renowned Great Lakes—Erie and Ontario—and when the *Sweet Afton* blithely swung into it, the passengers had in mind a pleasant day's sail, or perhaps two, because the map showed that they would be skirting no more than the southern edge. "We won't see the lake, really," Luton told his men, "and that's a pity because it does look a bit of something, doesn't it?"

They spent six anxious days on the vast lake, covering one hundred and twenty miles, hugging the shore and cringing as sudden gales out of the northwest whipped up waves that should have been expected only in midocean. Navigation became so perilous that only Luton or Carpenter was allowed to steer, but with sails furled they frequently had to seek safety in coves or behind some headland.

Luton was in charge one afternoon when he heard Carpenter shout from his position forward: "Evelyn! My God!" and down upon them crashed a monstrous wave which engulfed everything and required frantic bailing. The *Afton* pitched and rolled through a nasty six minutes with everyone grabbing for whatever he could reach, but Luton refused to panic, and soon had the little craft righted.

But they had been so beat about that all agreed they should find some projection of land behind which to shelter, and as night approached they spotted a cove protected by spindly trees, and when they neared the shore they saw that another craft, less fortunate than theirs, had been swamped by the storm and thrown upon the rocks, a shattered wreck.

"No one can be alive," Luton said as he surveyed the mournful scene, but when they drew closer they saw one lone figure standing beside the wreckage, signaling frantically, and as the prow of the *Afton* beached itself, Philip uttered a joyous cry: "It's the girl from Dakota!" and he leaped ashore to rush toward her as she stood shivering in her drenched uniform. Distraught, she did not recognize him, but realizing that he had come to save her, she threw herself into his arms.

When Lord Luton gently took her away, she told in sobs and whimpers of the disaster that had overtaken their craft: "Two long days ago . . . fearful storm . . . worse than today . . . Steno guided well but we didn't know . . . When the boat started to break up their first shout was 'Save Irina' and they threw me ashore . . . none of them made it . . ." Her voice trailed off, and despite the fact that Luton was trying to hold her, she slipped through his arms and onto the beach, all fortitude gone.

Harry took charge, washing her stained face with lake water while she was still unconscious, then drying her forehead with his sleeve. He directed the others to search the beach to see if any bodies or gear had washed ashore, but there were none. Even before she revived he had the others considering what garments of their own they could lend this castaway, and by the time he had gently slapped her back into consciousness he had arranged for her rejuvenation. When she saw the gifts and realized that she was indeed saved, she broke into tears and asked: "How can I dress?" and she indicated the five men clustered about her, and Harry said in a fatherly voice: "I'm married. I have a daughter. I'll ask the others to go over there," and he helped her slip into dry clothing.

When she moved to the beach fire that Fogarty had started, she clasped with two pale hands the mug of tea Trevor Blythe prepared and told her pitiful story: "Little money, great hopes. Farming in Dakota poor, poor. *A ton of gold*. . . We saw it in the paper and went crazy . . ."

"And you ended up," Luton asked, interrupting, "on the beach alone for two nights?"

"Yes."

"And nothing . . . nothing washed ashore?"

"Terrible storm. Everything lost, you can see that."

"How did you get to Edmonton in the first place?" Harry asked, but she avoided the question: "At Athabasca those four nice Germans. We hadn't much money, but they let us have a boat. Not a big one. None of us had ever sailed a boat before, they gave us lessons, and they sold it to us for almost nothing." She hesitated. "One of the Germans begged me not to go. Said it would be too rough. Told me to go back home, and as we sailed away he crossed himself."

"What did you do when you first realized your plight?" Luton asked, always concerned with human response to disaster, and she said: "I cried, I prayed for Steno. I became aware that I had no dry clothes, no food . . . was completely alone."

"I mean, what did you do then?" and she replied with that solidity of character Philip had noticed that first night when he saw her steel-set eyes: "I told myself 'Don't panic. Either they'll find you or they won't.' And I jumped up and down trying to keep warm."

"Did you panic?"

"About dawn today. Night didn't scare me, but when I saw daylight and realized that no one knew where I was, I thought maybe I'd go crazy . . . nobody . . . nobody."

Lord Luton, as head of his expedition, was capable of making swift decisions, and without consulting the others, said: "We must move forward before the ice catches us. You can join us, but not stay with us. We'll try to intercept a trading boat heading south and send you to safety."

"What will I do?"

"In Edmonton, I'm sure they'll find a way to get you back to Dakota."

They were astounded by what she said next: "No! I came to find gold and I'll find it," and Luton was so appalled by such a statement at such a time that he confronted her fiercely: "We'll have none of that. You escaped death only because we came along. Next time it'll find you." When she lamented the loss of her dreams, Carpenter comforted her, but Luton put a stop: "Ma'am, you'll be on your way back on the first riverboat we intercept, and now I would be obliged if my nephew would utter a brief prayer of thanks for our salvation from the dreadful storm and your rescue from a certain death."

The storm-tossed gold-seekers bowed their heads as Philip whispered: "Dear God, like Peter whom You saved from that storm on the Sea of Galilee, we give thanks for Thy saving us on Great Slave." He hesitated: "And we give special thanks for saving Thy heroic daughter Irina who survived only because of Thy miracle. Guide us to the safety of the Mackenzie."

After the amens, Carpenter lifted the young woman into the *Sweet Afton,* which proceeded without further incident to the exit from the lake. As soon as they were upon the river again, the condition that Philip had alluded to in his prayer took effect: they felt safe and once more in proper hands.

Irina Kozlok remained with them for several troublesome days. Because Lord Luton was determined to forge ahead against the coming of winter, they traveled continuously, and this presented problems about tending to their needs with a woman aboard. Previously the men had adopted simple, sanitary systems, and now they were inhibited, but the ice was broken by Fogarty, who, after he could control himself no longer, finally blurted out: "Madam, will you please look the other way?" and with the quiet ease of a duchess she replied: "Gentlemen, I've been married. I have brothers. This is no problem," and then she added, flashing the first smile since the wreck of her boat: "And I'll expect the same courtesy from you."

Philip was mortified by this discussion, for like any young romantic he had to believe that it had been more than accident that Irina saved his life in Edmonton, for that is how he now thought of her caution against the overland route, while he had saved hers on the shore of the Great Slave. To himself he mumbled: "It was fate," and the more he saw of her courageous resolve, and the handsome appearance she made when her uniform was dried and she could wear it again, the more he was reminded of his reaction on that night of their first meeting in Edmonton: Wouldn't it be wonderful to have a wife like that . . . ? and by the end of the second day with her he found himself a confused mixture of pity, admiration and deep attraction. In his infatuation he interpreted her slightest gesture of politeness as reciprocation of his feelings.

The first of the other four team members to recognize that young Philip was falling in love with a woman much older than himself was Lord Luton, and like a true Bradcombe he stiffened, summoning all the traditions of his ancient and distinguished family. The Bradcombes had survived when many other families had crumbled, he reminded himself, because through the centuries they had consistently protected their young men from the snares of attractive French women, and English commoners, and pert Irish lassies and, in recent decades, from the daughters of aspiring American millionaire families. With unerring rectitude they had allowed marriages only with the safest young women from the best English families, and although Luton himself was not yet married, he felt certain that when the time came the elders of his family would identify some young woman of impeccable qualification. He never visualized himself as "falling in love," but only as "getting married" in the pattern established long ago by the cautious men of his family.

In this context Irina Kozlok was a threat, an uneducated girl . . . from where was it? He did not care to remember a name like North Dakota. And it was his inherited obligation to see that his nephew, a Bradcombe, did not become entangled with her to any degree more complicated than unlucky chance had already provided. The boy must be prevented from repeating the grave mistake his mother had made. Since Harry was also more or less a Bradcombe, being married to one, Luton enlisted him in his schemes: "Harry, we've got to get that woman off this boat. To protect young Philip."

"Highly sensible, Evelyn. You've spotted a real danger."

"How far is it to the next settlement . . . of any kind?"

"If I recall, Fort Norman. We might make it before the freeze."

"And if we don't?"

"Seems obvious. We'd be stuck with her through the winter."

"Oh my God!"

And that afternoon they had real cause for worry, because they heard Irina tell Philip: "Those are handsome boots, really, but with that polish they're more suited for an expensive fishing trip than for mucking about in the arctic."

"Do you think so?" he asked, all eagerness to please, and she said: "Indeed I do. What you need are heavy leather boots like mine," and when, some time later, he asked his uncle and Carpenter: "D'ya think that perhaps I ought to wear leather boots?" they could scarcely hide their irritation, for back in Edmonton they had lectured him on this very matter and he hadn't listened. Now this American girl was delivering the same caution but with a smile, and the ninny was beside himself.

Disgusted with his nephew, Luton whispered: "Damn me, Harry, we've got to do something," but what he did not know. During one conversation he told Carpenter: "When the others aren't looking, we could shove her overboard," but as the last word left his lips he felt his arm caught in a tight grip and heard Harry's voice coming at him with unprecedented force: "Evelyn! Even to think such a thing in jest is a mortal sin." Then, asserting his elder status for the first time on the journey, he said almost menacingly: "We'll have none of that, Evelyn. None, I warn you."

Shaken by the fury of Harry's words, Evelyn asked contritely: "But what shall we do?" and Carpenter replied: "God obviously sent us to save her, so she's our obligation until we can rid ourselves of the burden. Good Samaritan and all that."

But this did not ease Luton's feelings, which were intensified when he watched as Irina sat forward with Philip, kepi off and the wind blowing her silvery hair attractively about her face. Her little gestures in pushing it back were, Luton thought, so damned Slavic she could be a Russian princess, and then he found himself speculating on whether Estonians were Slavs; he decided they weren't.

He was not merely frustrated; as leader of an expedition and at present the captain of a ship, small though it was, he could not stop himself from reviewing scenes from British naval history in which disruptive forces had destroyed otherwise solid explorations, and in his distress he called Harry aft for a serious consultation: "Have you ever read the old accounts of how this chap Bligh, an untidy sort, lost his ship that had been commissioned to carry breadfruit from Tahiti to Jamaica?"

"Of course."

"What did him in? Native girls corrupting his sailors. And did you follow what happened when the mutineers fled to that tiny island somewhere?"

Harry hadn't, for that part of the old naval tragedy was not so well known, but Luton had: "Same thing. The English sailors handled things quite well, really, if you forgive them their mutiny, but they fell to squabbling over native girls, and I believe they killed one another. None survived."

The two veterans contemplated this for some moments, agreeing that to have any woman penned up with five men in a small cabin over a prolonged winter was running a risk that was formidable, and, said Luton, pointing forward to where Irina's silvery hair was once more tumbling about in the wind: "To have that particular one amongst us would be suicidal. I could see Philip and Trevor battling for her at first, and ultimately, believe me, you and I would be at it. And she would sit there all the while in the corner of the hut like some Circe, smiling and combing her hair and plotting to turn us into her swine." His fear of what Irina might very possibly do had generated a hatred so intense that he could not think rationally.

Nor did she help. Eager to prove to the men that she would not be a hindrance to their voyage, she kept discovering ways to be helpful and performed more than her share of the tasks: she prepared the meals once Harry laid out the rations that only he controlled; she cleaned up afterward; she was remarkably alert in moving out of the way if the men had duties in adjusting the sails; and regardless of what she did, she maintained her appearance of responsible gravity, broken now and then by that ravishing smile which seemed to fill her entire squarish face. In short, she made herself an ideal passenger.

For Lord Luton that was the problem, because he could see that her impeccable behavior was winning over not only youthful and impressionable Trevor Blythe, who read her poems from Palgrave, but also Harry Carpenter, a married man who should have known better. After carrying out her voluntary duties, she would move to the front of the boat, "where everyone has to look at her," Luton grumbled to himself, "and take off her kepi, allowing her beautiful hair to dance in the breeze." At such moments he saw her as one of the Sirens, perched not on the prow of his boat but on a jagged rock toward which she was luring his men to their destruction; he imagined she carried a lyre which she strummed as she worked her charms.

Even Fogarty proved susceptible, and one evening Luton caught him staring as she fixed her hair, his eyes glazed over. "Fogarty!" Luton cried snappishly. "Tend the sails!" The Irishman's response was most unfortunate: "She does remind me of me wife, Jenny." Luton, infuriated, wanted to cuff some sense into his ghillie, but controlled his temper, muttering: "Him too?"

Realizing that only he was impervious to her seductive plotting, he resumed his study of ways to dispose of her: I could maroon her at some promontory where the trading ships would have to see her; of course we'd leave food for her. But I doubt the men would permit this. Or when we make camp, we could build a little hut for her, off to one side. But I'm sure the others would sneak over there at night, after I was asleep. And then came that hideous image, of pushing her off the *Afton* on some dark night, and the others running about: "Where is she? What could have happened?" This hateful nightmare he tried to chase out of his mind, but he was powerless to exorcise it.

Reprieve came in the sudden appearance on the Mackenzie of a sizable river steamer hurrying back to civilization at the completion of her last trading trip of the brief summer season, and when Luton signaled frantically, her captain hove to while the men in the *Afton* explained how they happened to have a castaway woman aboard: "Bunch of Dakota farmers wrecked their craft at Great Slave. You're to take her back to Athabasca so she can go on down to Edmonton and on to her home." When the captain asked: "Who pays her fare?" Lord Luton with indecent haste leaped forward to cry "I do!" and he gave the captain not only the requested fare but also a bonus of five dollars. While this was happening, Carpenter quietly slipped Irina a handful of bills and a fatherly admonition: "Go back to Dakota, Irina. Give up your dreams of gold."

In gratitude she went to each of her saviors in turn and kissed him. When she reached Philip he blushed furiously, but the reaction was quite different when she came at last to Lord Luton. Stiffly, with his best silent-sneer, he drew back, refused to kiss her but did accept from a proper distance her warm handshake.

Ignoring this rejection, she transferred to the larger ship, and after reaching down for her tiny package of clothes the men had given her, she remained at the railing as the two craft separated there in the center of the great river, with never a tree or a hut visible. As Philip watched her slowly vanish upstream, his heart felt a heaviness it had not known before. He acknowledged to himself that she was much older than he, and that she was an American of uncertain lineage, but he also knew that she was a vibrant, heroic woman with a sense of humor and compassion, and he was aware that her naturalness had overwhelmed him. But his two older companions who were watching him closely, Evelyn and Harry, knew from their own experiences as young men that this sense of romantic tragedy would pass. It always did.

Luton and his party continued their journey on the Mackenzie without seeing one evidence of human habitation and scarcely a sign that others had ever passed this way. As they stared at the banks lined with increasingly dwarfed trees they agreed that this was indeed one of the ends of the earth.

When they finally turned northwest for the climactic run of nearly seven hundred miles to the delta, they had an opportunity to see the great river at its most powerful; at times it broadened out to two or three miles, until Philip and Trevor thought they were entering another lake, but then it would contract into a swift-moving channel. The vistas were endless and the loneliness almost terrifying, but the grandest part came during the night runs when occasionally the heavens would be charged with electricity as the enormous northern lights filled the sky with luminous patterns.

One night as Luton and Trevor Blythe tended the craft while the others slept in the little deckhouse, the display lasted for three breathless hours, at the end of which Trevor said: "I've headed a new page in my notebook *Borealis*. Wouldn't that be a wizard title for a small book of poems about the arctic?"

Now Luton's party became willful players in one of the most tantalizing and fatal games of geography. Always aware that the Mackenzie was running roughly parallel to their target river, the Yukon, which lay a constant three or four hundred miles to the west, they asked continually: "Where will it be most practical for us to leave the Mackenzie and leapfrog over to the Yukon, which we can then use to float down to Dawson or row up, depending upon where we make our interception?"

The variables in this game were many, for numerous inviting streams, some considerable rivers, joined the Mackenzie from the west, and if one paddled and portaged upstream to their headwaters, one would be close to some other stream which dropped down to the Yukon. But even the most inviting route posed two harsh requirements. It would be murderously hard to row upstream against the current, and when one did reach the headwater, one still had to portage a heavy boat and all gear over the Continental Divide, as Harry Carpenter had pointed out repeatedly and kept reminding them as they drifted north.

Now the travelers entered into a kind of hypnotic trance which rendered sensible decisions impossible, for even though they knew that winter was approaching, the days remained tantalizingly inviting, and often they sailed with no covering but their flimsy shirts. The sun continued visible and warm, and the mighty river itself almost lulled them to sleep, so purposefully did it seduce them northward, always bearing them closer to the Arctic Circle. It ran so steadily, its current was so smooth and rapid that it seemed to sing: "I'm not luring you away from the gold fields; I'm carrying you always closer to the goal." But the goal to which it was speeding them was the river's goal, the arctic, and not the men's.

Every man aboard the *Sweet Afton* was aware of two conditions. Winter was perilously close, requiring them to find a place to pitch camp and dig in for seven or eight months, and they were drifting along without the courage to make a hard decision as to how they were to survive the winter and then get across to the Yukon. They were men morally disarmed by the vastness of the north, the complexity of the decisions they must make, and the sweet seduction of the Mackenzie. "We must soon make up our minds," Lord Luton said several times at sunset, as if on the morrow he would force a decision, but when day broke, and the peaceful river rolled northward, it carried them along, and decision was postponed.

The apt simile for their curious behavior came, as might have been expected, from poet Trevor: "We go forth, like all significant voyagers, in quest of our Holy Grail, but we approach it by running away, as if we were afraid to challenge the rim of Dark Mountain behind which it hides in self-protection."

Toward twilight on a day in October, Luton was inspecting carefully a stream which debouched into the Mackenzie from the west, and after some minutes of close study he said: "I do believe it's got to be the Gravel." Everyone crowded the port side to see this ominous yet fortuitous river, for they knew that it was the last viable escape route to choose if they wished to avoid the difficult tangle of rivers at the delta, where the Mackenzie would finally break through to the Beaufort Sea.

If they elected to leave the Mackenzie here and row up the Gravel, they would encounter at its headwaters the easiest portage over the Rockies and a fine free-flowing river, the Stewart, to whisk them down to Dawson in the spring. Lord Luton, aware of the amiable possibilities, cried: "We'll anchor in her mouth tonight and decide in the morning whether to keep drifting down the Mackenzie," and his men steered the *Sweet Afton* hard to port and into the Gravel for an overnight stay and some tough decision-making in the morning.

But that harsh obligation could once more be postponed because as soon as it was light Harry Carpenter announced: "I think our spot for the winter has been chosen for us." And when the others looked, they saw that the edges of both the large river and small had begun to freeze. The ice did not yet reach out far from shore but frail fingers did enclose their boat, a stern warning that soon the entire system would be frozen.

"Well!" Luton said as he studied the situation. "This comes a mite sooner than I had intended. I was so eager to have us reach Fort Norman. It can't be more than eighty miles downstream."

"Milord," Harry said, and by using his friend's formal title he indicated the gravity of what he had to say, "you're right. It is only a few miles to Norman. But in Edmonton and Athabasca, too, they warned us that the Mackenzie can freeze like that," and he snapped his fingers. "If we were to be trapped in the middle of this powerful river, with blocks of ice crushing down upon us, we could vanish in the midst of some floe, with our boat reduced to kindling."

Luton required only a few moments to appreciate the inevitability of this judgment: "We'll build our cabin a hundred yards up the Gravel. To escape the ice." So, aided by long ropes carried ashore and tied to trees, the men warped the *Sweet Afton* out of the larger river and berthed her safely a short distance up the left bank of the Gravel.

Ironically, Luton had been forced to choose the Gravel, after all, but he was putting it to the wrong use, a haven for the winter rather than a highway westward toward the safety of the Yukon.

TWO

COURAGE

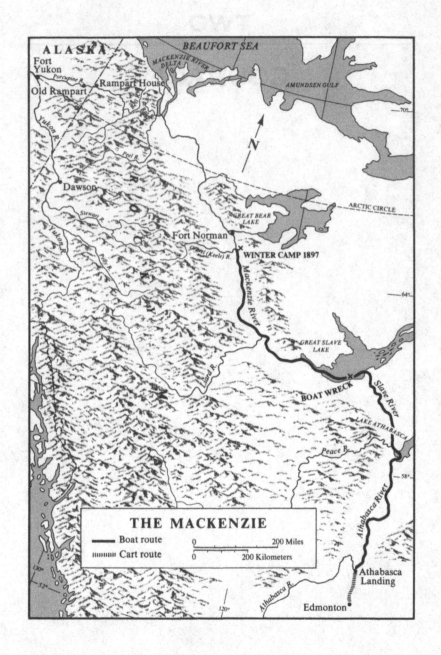

THE MACKENZIE

— Boat route

⊪⊪⊪ Cart route

0 ————————— 200 Miles

0 ————————— 200 Kilometers

THE REGIMEN LORD LUTON'S PARTY ADOPTED IN THEIR REFUGE on the left bank of the Gravel was evolved through committee discussion, for Evelyn did not act dictatorially except when a decision might mean the life or death of his enterprise. He was a shining example of the ancient English principle of *noblesse oblige,* always mindful that as a noble man, he had the moral obligation to act honorably and generously toward those about him. In reaching decisions which might affect Fogarty, Luton even allowed the Irishman to participate in the discussions. "We're civilized human beings," Luton was fond of saying, "and shall conduct ourselves accordingly."

His style of leadership was manifested immediately as the *Sweet Afton* was safely drawn onto the shore, for he sought advice from all members of his team regarding the location and size of their winter quarters: "You're to be living in them October to May, so share with me your best thoughts."

He began by stepping off what he considered an adequate living-and-sleeping area, and marking the proposed corners with small piles of rocks, and as soon as he had completed this, Philip, Trevor and Fogarty lay down within the indicated space to demonstrate where the beds would have to be. When Luton himself dropped to the ground, inviting Carpenter to do the same, it became apparent that his first estimate for the size of the living area was ridiculously small, and he began to adjust its confines outward, warning his men: "With each step I take, your work is doubled." After some silent calculations, Carpenter agreed: "You know, men, he's speaking the truth. Enlarging in any direction increases the work tremendously."

Harry eased the problem by an ingenious suggestion: "Let's pull the *Sweet Afton* up here to ground level, wedge her on her beam ends, and use her as one flank of our cabin," and Philip elaborated the proposal with one of his own: "Let's orient the *Afton* so she protects us from the north winds." Carpenter countered: "Sound idea, Philip. But on this spot the winds will come howling down the Gravel out of the west," and the boat was shifted to provide protection in that quarter.

So Luton transferred his piles of corner rocks to the new terrain: "Harry, that was a splendid idea. See how it obviates one entire wall. A lot of chopping saved by that device and we can use the cabin jutting in as our cupboard." But Trevor Blythe chipped in with one of the best suggestions: "Let's tie our largest canvas into this free end of the *Afton*. Lash it down securely and provide ourselves with a kind of protected storage area. Too cold for sleeping but valuable as a place to hold things." He smiled at Fogarty: "Say the frozen carcass of a moose you've shot." And this idea, too, was incorporated into the overall plan, with the canvas being erected immediately and tied securely to the *Afton*.

When Luton visualized his finished three-part winter dwelling he christened it "Our Hermaphrodite Igloo," and when the others protested that this part of the world had never known an igloo, he said: "In my storybooks there were nothing but igloos, and I've always wanted one," but Harry said more soberly: "You know, what we'll have here is pretty much what the Eskimos along the oceanfronts have always had. A big canoe lashed down on its side to protect a kind of dugout in the earth. An entrance area much like this tent." Surveying the site, he said: "We're in the grand tradition. And if thousands of Eskimos have survived the arctic winter in dwellings like this, so can we."

Then the philosophizing and the frivolity ended, for the laborious work of building a fairly large cabin had to be accelerated against the coming of blizzards, and each of the men went studiously about his assigned tasks. Philip and Trevor were given ropes and sent to search for usable timbers from the bleached driftwood that cluttered the banks of the Gravel. Like all arctic rivers that passed through an al-

most treeless terrain, its shores contained such an inexhaustible supply of wood that Trevor cried: "Where can it come from?" and
naturally they asked Carpenter.

"Simple. The banks here contain few trees. But up in the mountain, small forests."

"How does this tangle reach us?"

"Winter snow blankets the forest. Spring thaw erodes the banks,
and down come the trees. *Voilà,* the next flood brings them right to
our doorstep." Within a short distance east or west along only the left
bank they had at their disposal enough straight, fine wood to build a
cathedral; choosing only the best timber, they worked far into the
dusk hauling up to site level the wood that would be needed to face
their cabin.

Carpenter and Fogarty, meanwhile, had taken upon themselves
the most arduous task, that of felling and trimming the four stout
poles that would form the corners of the cabin. With the expedition's
two hefty axes they sought out larch or spruce, girdled the chosen
tree as close to ground level as practical, then took stances on opposite sides of the trunk and chopped away until the tree was felled.
Then, by common agreement, they took turns resting and hacking
off the lower branches and the unneeded crown of the tree, so that
the end result was a sturdy corner post. It was strenuous work but
necessary, for although driftwood of nearly proper size was available,
both men feared it might have been so weakened by floodwater and
bleaching and rough transit down the Gravel that it could not with-
stand winter blasts when wind pressures could be tremendous.

While the others were thus engaged in the demanding business of
assembling the wood for their cabin, Lord Luton was painstakingly
grubbing away with an improvised hoe-cum-scraper to provide a
level base as the floor, and when that was finished to his satisfaction,
he reached for the expedition's sole shovel, and began the fatiguing
task of digging four postholes for the corners. Almost immediately
he learned that this was not like digging in a Devon garden where the
loamy soil seemed almost to step aside to let the shovel pass. This was
brutal, demanding work, each inch of niggardly soil defended by
rocky deposits, and when he found that an hour of his best effort had
produced a hole only a few inches deep, he summoned the others.

"I'm not a shirker," he told them. "You know that. But this digging the postholes . . . really, I'm getting nowhere," and he showed
them his pitiful results.

This led to serious discussion, with Lord Luton and Trevor Blythe suggesting that a meager footing might be adequate if properly buttressed by stones above the ground, and Carpenter and Fogarty counseling from their greater experience: "A corner post not properly sunk is an invitation to disaster." Now a subtle change came in the structure of the Luton party, for without ostentation or any move which might denigrate his leader's position of authority, Tim Fogarty lifted the shovel from where Luton had dropped it, saying almost jocularly as he did so: "The fields of Ireland have far more rocks than those of England, Milord. Harry will need help chopping on that third post."

When time came to attack the fourth post, Carpenter said: "Fogarty, give Evelyn a hand on that last one," and just as quietly as the Irishman had behaved when taking over the back-breaking work of digging the postholes, Harry took away the shovel and asked: "Evelyn? Where did you have in mind for this one?" By these easy steps, Lord Luton was removed from command work but protected in his apparent leadership of the expedition as a whole.

It was Fogarty who suggested the solution to the chimney problem, for it was known in the arctic regions that to live in any cabin for seven or eight months without adequate ventilation for removal of smoke and noxious gases might not only damage eyesight but also result in death. Each winter in remote northern lands a handful of men, often two or three crowded in one small cabin, would perish in their sleep because there was no way for smoke to escape. Those who found their peaceful bodies in the spring would often say: "It's an easy way to die, but not necessary."

Carpenter and Fogarty knew it was obligatory to devise some arrangement which encouraged smoke and fumes to escape while preventing wind, rain and snow from entering. Since the team had not brought with them from Edmonton a stovepipe or anything that could be used as such, the men had to devise a reasonable substitute. Several ingenious ideas were suggested, including Trevor's that the stove should be located in one of the corners, with that section of the roof left open and a wall of some sort erected across the corner to keep the smoke out. This proposal was rejected by Carpenter on the grounds that the chimney would have to be so huge an opening that there would be no upward draw: "The wind would howl down it and suffocate us all with smoke."

Fogarty, at this point, found a collection of slablike rocks, rough on one side, smooth on the other, and he proposed constructing from them a stone chimney, wide at the bottom, narrow at the top, and when he put it together it was applauded by Carpenter, who pointed out: "Best feature is that the wooden wall will be faced by stone. Prevent fires, the kind that kill sleeping people in the north."

In this quiet way Carpenter and Fogarty assumed effective command of the expedition during the period of building the winter retreat. They decided how deep the difficult postholes must be, where the chimney should be located, how beds should be constructed, and how the tent area should be incorporated into the whole, but even between them an unspoken struggle for leadership evolved, although neither trespassed the other's prerogatives. When Harry decided that for maximum safety the cabin section must have an additional central post, Fogarty did not even comment, but when Harry himself started to seek out and cut down the added post, the Irishman quietly took command of the two axes and said: "Mr. Harry, time you learned the secrets." Off they marched to fell and trim the post, and when that job was completed, Fogarty also dug the fifth hole.

In this subtle manner each of the men acknowledged and performed his special function. Lord Luton decided the questions of policy, or anything requiring a resounding speech; Harry made the strategic decisions upon which the life and death of the expedition rested; Fogarty determined the practical ways to achieve ends with a minimum of oratory. And even the two young members differentiated their contributions, with Philip providing muscle and boundless energy when required, Trevor an ingratiating willingness to do the most menial jobs, such as washing dishes, gathering firewood, or taking waste to an improvised disposal dump. He also surprised the others at times with suggestions of the greatest practicality, as when he constructed and positioned three different sites from which the lanterns could be suspended, depending upon where their light was most needed for specific tasks.

When the log cabin was properly roofed, its sides erected and lashed securely to the corner posts, the two younger men rejoiced that the hard work was over, but Carpenter and Fogarty soon disabused them of that foolishness, for as Harry announced when the roof was in place: "Now the tedious work begins. All of us scour this land, miles in every direction, to find moss, and twigs and mud, especially the clayey type, for caulking every hole you see up there." And he pointed to the roof, where a hundred ill-matched joints provided entry for snow and rain and especially wind: "Caulk along the walls, too."

Philip turned to the *Sweet Afton* and said jocularly: "I'll caulk that wall," but he was one of the first down to the creek searching for mud, and far upstream he came upon one of those apparently random deposits of earth which had a modified clay consistency. He became the hauler of buckets of clay and river weeds to the other four as they strove to render their arctic home reasonably weatherproof.

After the talents of these energetic and willing men completed the building of their winter refuge, they had indeed what Lord Luton still called his Hermaphrodite Igloo, a weatherproofed cabin defended from blizzards by the resting *Sweet Afton,* enlarged by the unheated space of the strong tent, and warmed by the big woodpalisaded room from which the smoke escaped through Fogarty's chimney and to which proper light was delivered by what Trevor Blythe called "my peripatetic lanterns."

When the hard work was finished, mainly as a result of Carpenter and Fogarty's solid leadership, Lord Luton was not only free to resume command but was also subtly invited to do so, and he began enthusiastically by lining out sensible rules for the governance of daily conduct in what he called "Our Kingdom of Kindred Souls": "No one will lie abed all day unless he be ill and confined there. At least once each day every man will exercise. Harry, mark out a quarter-mile running oval and we'll give it a whirl. I calculate we're still well south of the Arctic Circle, so we'll have hazy light for such running, but even during the darkness we must protect our health."

Carpenter had several sensible suggestions: "We must change our socks at least twice a week and wash the worn ones in soap and hot water, else we'll develop a horrible fungus. It's not good to sleep in your clothes or to wear your underthings more than a week. The latrine is to be kept well back from the cabin, and I want to find no one just stepping outside the door and pissing."

But both Luton and Carpenter directed their major planning to the avoidance of scurvy. "I've seen it," Harry said. "Hideous disease. Comes from an improper diet. Most people like us have had no opportunity to experience scurvy, so we underestimate it. You ever see it, Evelyn?"

Luton said he had not but he'd heard enough to frighten him. So Harry continued: "I saw it during a long sea voyage. We should've known better, but the men began to fall sick. Teeth drop out. Legs become necrotic."

"What's that?" Trevor asked, and Carpenter explained: "They die before the rest of the body dies. You punch your finger into the leg, and when you take your finger away, the hole stays there."

"What must we do?" Philip asked, and Carpenter answered: "Canned fruit, pickled cabbage, the acid pills we bought in Edmonton. And we think that fresh meat provides just enough of what's lacking . . ."

"What is lacking?" Blythe asked, and Carpenter said: "Various theories. We'll know one day. So if anyone can shoot a deer, catch a fish or wing a duck, do so. Your life may depend on it."

The five men, as congenial a group as could have been assembled for such adventure, spent their first two weeks of isolation in routinizing their existence. Snow did not yet cover the ground, and since this stretch of the Mackenzie received only moderate precipitation, snow, even when it did come, would not be a major problem, for as Carpenter explained: "Arctic regions like this receive far less snow than places like Montreal and New York."

He laid out the running track, and he and Luton ran three laps morning and afternoon. The two younger men ran four laps in the late afternoon. Fogarty, who was often absent chasing game, ran on any day in which he had not walked extensively. And the health of all flourished. The latrine was dug, driftwood was collected from the riverbank and chopped to feed the effective little stove, and the men watched as the days swiftly shortened.

It was when the long nights started that the group showed itself to be exceptional, for under Luton's wise leadership the men organized themselves into a kind of college in which each member except Fogarty would assume responsibility for a given night, during which he would expound upon something he knew, no matter how obscure or how apparently lacking in general interest. On one of his nights, for example, Luton explained the ramifications of the Bradcombe family and its role in English history. He told of the marriages, the scandals, the murders, the services his forebears had provided the crown. Later he and Harry spent more than an hour recalling fascinating examples of how the rules of primogeniture had operated in their family to ensure the longevity of the line. "It's a thoughtful system," Evelyn said. "Eldest son inherits all—title . . . castles . . . land . . . lease to a good stretch of salmon river."

"Odd to hear you defending the system, Evelyn," young Henslow said, "seeing that you're younger brother to Nigel, and he inherits all."

"But that's what I mean, Philip. The law spells it out, item by item, so there can be no quarreling between Nigel and me."

"But aren't you envious? Just a wee bit?"

"I have my own title, an estate in Ireland, that's adequate. Envy? I doubt I've ever had a shred."

He then reviewed several fascinating accounts of how the principle of entailment had operated to protect important holdings in the Bradcombe family. "It's like this. My father cannot sell or give away either the castle at Wellfleet or the two old houses in Ireland. They're entailed. They must stay with the title."

"Interesting situation," Harry said. "Evelyn's father can't sell the Rembrandt or the Jan Steens, either. They're entailed." He laughed: "You ever hear about the public scandal when my grandfather tried to sell off the pictures entailed to our family? Wanted the money to support an English actress he'd met in New York. Came home on the ship with her. Fearful scandal. The women in our family weren't too worried about the actress but they raised hell about selling the Titian. Got the law to stop him."

When it came time for Carpenter to conduct his first evening session, he surprised the group by announcing that on his nights he would read aloud the entire novel *Great Expectations,* which a tutor had told him was one of the best-constructed of all the English novels, and in time the others looked forward to his sessions, especially when the real cold set in and the river fairly crackled from the ice it was moving about.

They had become involved because this novel was composed of masterful visual images: the dramatic appearance of the convict in the churchyard, Miss Havisham and her moldering wedding cake, Pip's boxing lesson, the wonderful scenes of London. "This is," said Harry, "a damned fine novel for a cabin near the Arctic Circle."

Trevor Blythe gave a series of four lectures elucidating the magic of Shelley, Keats, Byron and Wordsworth, and because both his tutor and his mother had loved poetry, he had as a result of their pressures memorized long passages of the poets' finer works, and he would sometimes sit with eyes closed, the light shining on his flaxen hair, and recite poems the others had known partially, and the cabin would be filled with the glorious music of the English language. Once on a very cold night when the land seemed to shudder from its weight of frost, with never a movement of air or breath of wind, he held a book open in his lap and without consulting it began reciting verses of Keats that he especially loved:

"St. Agnes' Eve—Ah, bitter chill it was!
The owl, for all his feathers, was a-cold;
The hare limp'd trembling through the frozen grass,
And silent was the flock in woolly fold. . . ."

He delivered the first forty lines from memory, then without breaking his rhythm he shifted to the book, but whenever he reached one of the sections he knew by heart, he closed his eyes again and filled the night air with those vast images that Keats had pressed upon his pages.

When Blythe reached the closing, with that marvelous line about the long carpets rising along the gusty floor, his listeners could see the lovers escaping and the drunken porter sprawled beside the gate. They could hear the door groaning and the warriors suffering nightmares. Such was the power of poetry that these long-dead words created living experiences, and the little cabin was alive with wonder.

On nights when Philip was responsible for the tutorial, as Lord Luton had dubbed these sessions, he could not compete in either wisdom or experience with his elders, and at first he was reluctant to try, but his uncle said firmly: "If you're one of us, you must be one of us," and Philip, with fear that he was making an ass of himself, reviewed the courses he had taken at Eton, and because he had been above average in geometry, he began to give the men a review of that precise and beautiful subject, until Luton stopped him: "It's fascinating, really, and we could profit from knowing what you know, but with your diagrams you're using all our paper."

By now Philip had gained confidence, so when he was deprived of geometry he turned to Greek mythology, and from that to the manner in which Charlemagne had established a great empire and then divided it among his sons. The older men listened attentively, happy to reacquaint themselves with subjects they too had studied more than a decade ago.

The hours of daylight, extremely brief at this latitude, were spent in vigorous outdoor activities—running, hunting, chopping—on those days when the temperature permitted, but when it skidded to fifty-below, all remained inside, edging ever closer to the fire to partake of the heat. Then the nights were twenty-four hours long, and orderly discussion under the flickering lights became treasured. The sessions had been under way for more than a month before Luton thought to include Fogarty as an instructor: "Fogarty, if we asked you to address this college on some subject about which you were an authority, what would it be?" The Irishman knit his brow, then bit his lip and looked almost appealingly at each member of his audience: "I could talk about horses, but you gentlemen already know most of what I'd say."

"Go ahead," Carpenter urged. "We can never know enough."

Fogarty, ignoring this encouragement, said: "But I doubt if you know much about poaching."

"You mean cooking eggs?" Philip asked, to which Fogarty said: "No, I mean real poaching." And forthwith he launched into a detailed account of how a master fish-and-game thief worked: "Mind you, I was good at picking off a rabbit now and then, and that's not an easy thing to do without making a noise, but me great love was to slip out on a moonless night and catch me a prize salmon."

"Salmon!" Carpenter echoed in astonishment. His forebears had shot men trying to poach salmon on the streams they commanded and had sentenced more than one to Australia for the crime.

"Aye, salmon, queen of the poacher's art." And as he talked proudly of his skill and patience he began to reveal just enough about the specific scenes of his triumphs that Lord Luton could not avoid identifying the Irish rivers Fogarty had plundered with the ones he himself owned, and it dawned upon him that this prideful Irishman had long been stealing salmon from the very streams he had been hired to protect.

Shaken by this unpleasant discovery, at one point Luton asked: "Aren't you speaking of the second pool below the stone bridge that General Netford built in 1803?"

"Aye. The very bridge. They said it had been put there to aid the army in case Napoleon crossed into Ireland."

Now Carpenter broke in: "That's the pool my uncle Jack wrote about in his book on the upper-central rivers of Ireland. He named it Mirror Pool because it reflected the sky so perfectly."

"The same." For nearly a century the sportsmen of England had written books about their favorite salmon streams, until every stretch of river in the British Isles that hosted the precious fish had been described and evaluated. Men like Harry Carpenter could sit in India or along the Nile and recall without error entire stretches of river and recount proudly how some distant relative had landed his prize salmon in 1873. Now Fogarty, round-faced and unaware of the agitation he was creating, was relating the poor man's version of the same chase: "I've never gone out within three days of a full moon, either before or after, and I used to advise young lads . . ."

"You taught poaching?" Trevor asked, and Fogarty said: "Not in the manner of a school, but if a young fellow of substantial character came to me with an earnest desire to make himself into a first-class poacher, I helped him learn the rules."

"What were the rules?" Lord Luton asked with an icy reserve which hid his seething disgust at the revelations he was hearing, and Fogarty gave such a detailed reply that the evening became one of the best of the seminars, for interested students were listening to an expert with an amazing breadth of knowledge.

"I stressed three basic rules, both in me own behavior and that of anyone I allowed to poach the streams I was controlling."

"You sold permissions?" Luton asked, to which Fogarty responded: "Heavens, no! That was me first rule. 'Never poach unless you need the fish and are going to eat it. Never sell it and don't give it to anyone but your own family.' To poach for money would be quite dishonorable, don't you agree?"

By such questioning, and by the controlled dignity of his approach to the stealing of salmon, Fogarty gradually brought his listeners into his confidence, and before long they were all participating in nightly forays and imaginary travels up and down the great fishing rivers of Britain. In particular, Harry Carpenter joined in the discussion, for he had fished most of the stretches and pools the Irishman was speaking of: "You mean, upstream of the one they call Princeps?"

"Aye, that's the one. With the willows on the far bank."

It was not until Fogarty had traversed a dozen streams that Trevor Blythe asked hesitantly: "But isn't this kind of poaching illegal?" and Fogarty replied with no embarrassment: "I consider it taxation in reverse."

"What do you mean?" Luton asked, and Fogarty explained with a self-incriminating frankness which astounded his employer: "The rich tax us poor people for almost anything we do, and a good poacher taxes the rich for a salmon or a rabbit now and then. It evens out, Milord."

Fogarty's beguiling revelations now lured even Evelyn into his net, for the noble lord began discussing poaching and rivers and the thrill of night fishing as if he too were participating in the challenging sport. At one point he asked: "What kind of fly would you use in well-rumpled water?" and Carpenter chimed in with his own expert knowledge.

But the younger members of the class were not content with Fogarty's answer on legality, and Philip persisted: "But it is illegal, isn't it?"

"Many things we do are illegal, or nearly so. Wasn't it illegal for Major Carpenter's grandfather to sell off the painting to please an actress?"

"But the courts stopped him."

"Aye, and the courts stop poachers, if they catch them."

"How do you feel about that?" Philip persisted, and Fogarty said: "I feel it's a great, fine game. A test. A challenge to all that's best in a man. His willingness to stand up for his rights."

"Rights?" Luton asked, and in the bitter cold Fogarty replied very carefully: "I suppose that rivers were created for all men . . . to enjoy the fish God put in them. Laws have changed this, and maybe that's all to the good, for thoughtful men like you and your father, Milord, you keep the rivers cleaned up and fresh for those who come after. But I believe that God sitting up there in judgment smiles when He watches one of His boys slip out at dusk to catch for his family one of the big fish that He has sent down, perhaps for that specific purpose."

"Isn't it risky?" Philip asked, and Fogarty pointed toward the much greater river that lay frozen outside: "Isn't it risky for you to be challenging this river at this time of year?"

As winter deepened, life in the tiny cabin produced unexpected problems. When the spirit thermometer purchased in Edmonton stood at minus-forty-three the two younger men did not relish running the oval, but Luton and Harry missed only when heavy snow was actually falling, which was rare. "A man must keep his mettle," Luton said, and once when the temperature dropped to minus-fifty and Carpenter was held indoors with a nasty cold, Luton ran four laps alone, and came in perspiring: "My word, that was bracing!"

The outdoor running did create one situation which could have become ugly had not Luton taken stern steps. Philip Henslow, still inordinately proud of his rubber boots despite Irina Kozlok's warning about their dubious utility in the arctic, tried doing his daily runs in them even though he knew that they provided almost no protection from the icy cold. In fact, their conductivity of cold was so immediate and complete that before he had run only a few steps in the bitter cold, his toes were colder than his nose, and that was perilous.

Out of pride in his choice of these boots and obstinacy in defending what he had done, he refused at first to acknowledge the resulting pain, but one evening when it became so intense that he winced when he took off his boots inside the cabin, his uncle heard the sudden intake of breath, looked down to see what had caused it, and guessed immediately that it was frostbite.

"Let me see those feet," he said quietly, kneeling to feel the gelid toes and confirm the lack of circulation. After he looked closely he cried: "Harry! Come see this dreadful mess!" and when Carpenter bent down he uttered a low whistle: "Another week of this and we'd have to cut off that left foot."

When the others gathered around to look, they saw a pitiful example of frostbite: the skin an ashen white, peeling between the toes, ankles that delivered no pulse or movement of blood. And despite the fact that the feet had now been exposed to the heat of the cabin for many minutes, they were still shockingly cold.

But no one panicked. Carpenter said, giving both feet one more inspection: "They can be saved. Without question, Philip, they can be brought back. I've seen it done."

Lord Luton issued a firm edict: "You will not wear those boots again this winter. You have heavy shoes and we have extra pairs of thin socks that you can wear inside." After turning away in disgust, he whipped about and said: "Harry, Trevor, you're to inspect his feet every night to be sure they improve. I have a very queasy stomach when it comes to cutting off a man's leg, especially a young man's, but I shall do it if it needs being done."

By placing Henslow's feet first in cold, then cool, and eventually in warm water, the cure was effected, and all might have gone well had not poor Philip uttered an unfortunate final comment on the messy affair: "Irina warned me about those boots."

This was more than Luton could tolerate. From a great height of moral indignation he glared down at his nephew and thundered: "*She* warned you? Damn me, *I* warned you. Harry warned you. And

I heard Fogarty warning you: 'Don't buy fancy rubber boots for the arctic!' But you wouldn't listen to us. You waited for *her* to warn you." By now he was shouting, but as he started to say: "Don't you . . ." he regained his self-control, and ashamed of himself, he dropped to his customary low-keyed voice: "Don't use her name again, Philip. It offends me."

As leader of the expedition, Luton felt that he must set an example by shaving daily, and he did, even though this entailed considerable effort and even discomfort. Fogarty, watching him struggle, said one morning: "Milord, I believe I could put a bit of edge on that razor." Luton replied: "You're not here as my manservant," but since he winced with pain when he said this, Fogarty insisted: "Apply more lather, Milord, and let me have that thing." So while Luton soaped, Fogarty honed and stropped. Thereafter he tended the razor three mornings a week, not as a servant but as a friend, and he nodded approvingly when Luton told the others: "Men can turn sour in situations like this. The proper regard for the niceties is essential for morale."

The men continued to honor the rule of urinating only at the latrine, and at the beginning they were careful to shave each day, but the tedium of doing so when temperatures were so low and space so crowded tempted first one and then another to forgo the daily shave, and once a beard started growing in earnest, all attempts to shave it off were surrendered. So by January everyone except Luton had a full beard, which was kept neatly trimmed by scissors applied in nightly sessions before one of the two camp mirrors; it was not uncommon to see a man tending his beard by the lantern while Carpenter read *Great Expectations,* which at the request of his companions he was reading for the second time.

As Lord Luton ran his laps or worked alone at some outdoor project or ruminated at night after Harry ended that day's stint of reading *Great Expectations,* he came to a conclusion which caused him pain: reviewing his pusillanimous behavior in not making a firm decision as to how his team was to bridge that awesome gap between the Mackenzie River to the east and the Yukon to the west, he saw clearly that he had been neglectful of duty in failing to direct his party up the Liard River, and one night he startled the others by rapping the table with his knuckles and crying: "Damn me, I should have grasped the nettle."

"What do you mean, Evelyn?" Harry asked, and Luton replied:

"On that long drift down the Mackenzie, I allowed myself to be mesmerized. My duty was to find our way over the Rockies to the Yukon and I failed the test."

"But, Evelyn, you still have three or four choices. The Gravel here. The ones at the beginning of the Delta. You're far from shamed, and you're even further from having let us down."

Luton would not be consoled, for he better than any of the others knew that he had been delinquent in allowing the days to slip by as the *Sweet Afton* drifted so easily down the great river: "I feel like a Greek warrior who, on the eve of battle, takes refuge in nepenthe and dreams away the day of confrontation . . . sweet sleep of forgetfulness."

In these days of self-flagellation it was curious that not once did he reflect on the fact that he was now by accident precisely where he ought to be when the rivers thawed in June: a quick push up the Gravel to where the boat could no longer make the bends, a swift sawing of the fine craft into halves, a brutally demanding but short portage over one of the best passes in the Rockies, an easy hookup with the Stewart River and into Dawson with no more trouble. Three or four times he had been reminded of this route, but the facts had simply not been allowed into his brain, for somewhere he had acquired a fixation that he must, as a matter of honor, sail to the end of the Mackenzie, then worm his way through whatever difficulties loomed while still remaining on Canadian soil. Ironically, the route up the Gravel would have satisfied most of those requirements admirably, but he failed to understand.

In his obstinacy he continued to berate himself until he was almost sick with self-recrimination, for failure lay heavily on a man like Luton. Once when he had captained a crucial cricket match against Sussex—at least he deemed it crucial—he had been forced to make one of those quick decisions which only cricket seems to produce: his team had a surprisingly comfortable lead, but to win the match outright he had to get Sussex out before time expired, so he made them follow-on, that is, bat out of turn in hopes that his bowlers could speedily dismiss them. But the Sussex rascals battled like demons, built up a big lead, declared before their last men were out, and made Luton's team take the field and try to catch up. An awful thing happened: Sussex bowlers became like mortars, hurling deadly bombs at Luton's men, so that instead of his having been clever in outsmarting Sussex, they outsmarted him and hurtingly. It was a disaster which he often recalled at night, "the arrogance of command," he called it, and its memory still stung.

He had the same regrets about having messed up the Mackenzie trip, and he refused to listen to Carpenter when his friend said truthfully: "Evelyn, it can all be salvaged. It's to be a grand trip, come the thaw."

Luton would not be consoled, and he felt so personally responsible for what he sensed as an impending disaster that he conceived a preposterous solution. "Gentlemen," he said one night before the prayers which he regularly led, "I've worked out the answer. It's so simple, really. It's less than fifty miles to the Hudson's Bay post at Fort Norman . . ."

"What's that got to do with us?" Carpenter asked, and Luton astonished him by replying: "They'll know the secrets about the river systems up ahead. Maps and the like. And with their help I can make the proper decisions about what to do when the thaw comes."

"Evelyn," Carpenter said with studied patience, "don't you realize that Fort Norman is downstream from us. Comes the thaw, we'll go right past there. Couldn't miss it if we wanted to. In thirty minutes ashore we can learn all they have to share."

Luton, refusing to consider this sensible solution, not only continued to make plans to travel the fifty miles to the outpost but startled his team by insisting that he would go alone. When they remonstrated against the foolhardiness of this, he cut them short and said with the calm authority he knew so well how to exercise: "This is my responsibility, mine alone, and I shall make my studies."

After one heated argument in which he said bluntly that he would be leaving next morning, Carpenter held private consultations with the two younger men: "Have you seen any indications of instability in Evelyn? I don't mean this trip. Before? At home?"

"None," Philip said firmly and Trevor had no comment, but when Harry continued: "What can ail the fellow?" Trevor said gently: "I think he castigates himself for not having made firm decisions on the river, especially since he was so ready to do so coming across the Atlantic . . . and in Edmonton." When no one spoke, the young poet added: "He may feel he owes us a debt . . . not us but the expedition." Feeling himself entangled in arcane matters, he ended lamely: "Such self-accusations can be quite pressing, you know."

• • •

On the morrow, Luton rose early, dressed in his warmest clothing, ate a hearty breakfast, then checked his rifle, his precious eiderdown sleeping bag, his supply of cartridges and his rations. When Harry took steps to follow with his own preparations for the foolhardy trip down the frozen Mackenzie, Evelyn said harshly: "I command you, Harry, to stay here and guard this encampment." Carpenter looked as if he were going to ignore the command, but Fogarty, to everyone's surprise, interceded: "He knows what he's doing, sir," and the noble lord, just turned thirty-two, struck out for the big river, made his way to its frozen center, and started the long snowshoe-and-ski push to Fort Norman.

Because he knew himself to be in excellent condition, he calculated that he could cover at least twenty-five miles a day and pretty surely reach the post at the close of the second day. He ate little and kept a sharp lookout for animals, not to shoot them but to record what wildlife was moving about at this time of year, but apart from a very few black and noisy ravens he saw little. Unaware of when day passed into night, he rested sporadically and on the second day kept traveling for nearly twenty hours down the breast of the great river, without incident: no fractures, no attacks by animals, just a normal caper down a vast river in thirty-degrees-below-zero weather and with sparse food. His spartan endurance put him into Fort Norman midway on the third day.

It had been for many years one of the farthest north of the Hudson's Bay posts, and traditionally was manned by three or four French-Canadian employees of the famous old Company, men who spoke both French and English plus two or three Indian dialects, and a half-French, half-Indian fur trader or two. These latter were never to be called half-castes or half-breeds, designations they considered offensive; they were Métis, and the Canadian North could not have survived without their knowing services. At different posts, depending upon the character of the white managers, the Métis were treated either as fellow explorers with valuable skills or as lowly servants deserving little consideration. At Fort Norman, the one Métis present fell, for good reason, into the first category. He was a forty-year-old trapper and fur trader, who was treated almost as an equal by the three French Canadians in charge.

He was the first to spot Lord Luton striding alone down the middle of the Mackenzie, and his warning cry astounded the others: "Man coming right down the river!" When the others ran to see, they expected to find someone near death, staggering up the long flight of wooden steps that led from their high ground down to the river's edge and begging for water and food. They were amazed when, upon sighting them, he waved his rifle spiritedly, left the river, and actually ran up the score of steps, crying as he came: "I say! How good to find you chaps right where the map said you'd be."

He did not stagger. He did not beg for food. Nor did he even accept the drink of water offered him: "I'm what you might say heading a small expedition. Five of us. Wintering in at the Gravel. All in super condition." Munching on a seabiscuit they provided, but not ravenously, he answered their questions. Yes, he had come down the river alone. Yes, the other three were Englishmen too. Yes, I did say there were five of us, the last's an Irishman. Why had he come to Fort Norman? To seek counsel regarding the most practical way to slip over to the Yukon and the gold fields at Dawson, but only after the thaw came, of course.

One of the Canadians would report later: "It was like he had dropped by his corner tobacconist's to pick up some Cuban cigars and the local gossip. Unconcerned. Unemotional. Damned good chap, that one, and we were nonplussed when he revealed under questioning that he was Lord Luton, younger son of the Marquess of Deal."

It was a remarkable six days that Luton spent at the post, interrogating the traders, comparing notes with the Métis guide by relating the trip he'd taken, and formulating the intricate plans that would determine the third portion of his expedition. He found the conversation with the Métis the most rewarding. The man's name was George Michael, and all pronounced his first name in the English fashion, his second as if it were the French equivalent, Michel, accenting the last syllable.

He told Luton that he had come north twelve years before from the District of Saskatchewan when some terrible battle with the English had driven his kind from their lands. Luton was stern in his questioning of Michael as to which Englishmen he had fought, and was greatly relieved when he understood that by "English" the man had merely meant Canadian troops. Michael said that Luton was the first nobleman he had ever met, and in awe of Evelyn's rank he called him "Duke." Then he spoke proudly of the noble blood in his own veins, the Indian blood, calling it the important half of his twin heritage. When the three white Canadians suggested that George

Michael hurry back to the Gravel to assure the Englishmen that Lord
Luton had arrived safely, he was delighted with the prospect of serving a duke and was disappointed when Luton said firmly: "No need.
They're all solid chaps. They'll know in proper time I made it. I'm
sure they expected me to."

Then, with the aid of his hosts, he launched his advanced inter-
rogations regarding the tangled rivers he would soon be attacking,
and after listening to them only briefly he said: "I think I've found
the four men in all Canada best qualified to advise me."

"First of all, Lord Luton . . ."

"Please call me Evelyn, since we're to be working at this for some
spell."

"You're not in a bad position where your camp is now, at the
confluence of the Gravel. You're aware, I'm sure, that when the thaw
comes, you can head up the Gravel and portage to the Stewart. Then
all's fair and a soft run home."

"I had rather fancied the route just beyond the Arctic Circle."

The men were not displeased by this rejection of their advice,
for his preference brought him into the territory they knew best, but
when they were alone one old-timer with the Company asked: "Do
you think he knows what he's doing?" and another said: "No Englishman ever does," but the third man cautioned: "This one may be different, he's a proper lord." The second pointed out: "Lords are worst
of all," but when the third man reminded them: "This one did walk
near fifty miles right down our river," they all agreed that he merited
consideration.

In preparation for their next meeting with Luton they drafted a
set of maps for him, marking with a heavy line the route that two of
them had used in getting from Fort Norman over the crest of the
Rockies and down into the important American trading station at
Fort Yukon, within easy striking distance of the gold fields. And the
men combined to drill into him, thrice over, the important decision
points.

"My lord, there'll be markers to help you leave the Mackenzie
and find your way into the Peel. That's crucial. Everything depends
on your getting out of this river and into the smaller system to the
west."

Another man broke in: "Crucial, yes, but the next turn is the one
that counts. Many miss it, to their woe. You'll find the Rat River on
your right, not big but the secret to success. Because it's there you saw

your boat in half, and the vital push begins. Up to the headwaters of the Rat, a short portage over the divide, and you're in the Bell. And then," the speaker's voice relaxed, "you're in a straight run home."

"To where?" Luton asked, and when the man said: "The Porcupine, which takes you straight into Fort Yukon, good water all the way."

"Oh, no," Luton said, drawing himself away from his ardent instructors. "I'd really not care to reach my goal through American territory."

This caused some consternation, two of the men judging such a restriction to be childish, the other two agreeing that it was sensible for a patriotic Englishman to want to keep his money and loyalty within the Empire, but it was George Michael alone who saw the solution to this impasse: "Duke, the Porcupine she is no problem. Turn right, you go into America. Turn left you stay in Canada, all way to Dawson."

Now the others became enthusiastic, applauding Michael's sensible statement: "And what's better, halfway to Dawson there's a kind of village, two, three cabins where trappers lay over in storms. Always food there." The men agreed with unanimous encouragement that their noble guest should follow that intricate but relatively easy Canadian route to the gold fields.

They were surprised, therefore, when Luton pushed aside their hand-drawn maps and turned to one large one published by the government: "I had rather thought we'd stay with the Peel. You can see its headwaters will bring us very close to Dawson."

This arrogant dismissal of their reasoned advice, and the proposal of a route completely contrary to what they had been advising, caused a hush, but then one of the Canadians inspected the map closely and said dryly: "What I see is that you'd be heading into one of the highest passes in this part of the Rockies," and another seasoned traveler warned: "That would be foolhardy, sir." Even George Michael agreed: "Duke, I travel on the Peel one time with the current helpin' me. Very swift. Hills each side river, they are close, close. To go your way, against current, those tight spots, they will cause you much trouble, you bet."

It was obvious that their arguments against staying with the Peel had not dissuaded him, and it was also clear that as a member of the nobility and leader of his expedition, he did not care to prolong the argument. The Fort Norman men saw that he had made up his mind and they knew that extreme hardship and perhaps tragedy would ensue, but that would be his problem, not theirs.

But when Luton was away working on his notes, one of the three French Canadians asked: "What makes Englishmen so stubborn . . . so blind to facts," and the oldest man, who had tangled with them many times in various parts of Canada, said: "Maybe that's what makes 'em Englishmen. They're born to do things their way," and the other one admitted grudgingly: "Maybe he's right. We know we can go Rat-Bell route. Maybe he'll find a better way startin' with the Peel," and the experienced man warned: "In a game, never bet against an Englishman," and the third one said: "But this isn't a game," and the oldest said: "For them it is. Else why would he walk down the Mackenzie in coldest winter? To prove he could do it. He'll go up the Peel just to prove we were wrong," and they burst into laughter.

Apart from those differences of opinion regarding routes, the six-day visit had been a respite, appreciated by everyone, and the Canadians were regretful when Luton said: "Tomorrow I must head back and get our team prepared for the thaw."

They asked if he had any conception of what happened to a frozen river when the ice broke up, and he replied: "I've heard it can be somewhat daunting."

"Unbelievable," they said, "and on this river, the worst of all." Taking him to their front porch atop the rise, they explained a peculiarity of the Mackenzie: "It runs from mountains in the south to very flat land in the north. When the sun starts back in March, it melts the headwater ice first and starts those waters flowing. Then it melts the high plateaus, setting free whole lakes of water, and every warming day it releases more and more water far to the south, while our part of the river up here in the north remains frozen tight. And what happens?" the men asked, looking to see if Luton had understood.

"Stands to reason, the waters flood in under the ice and dislodge it."

"Dislodge is not the word. It explodes the ice from below. It throws it about like leaves in a storm. Chunks bigger than you could ever imagine are thrown up as if they weighed no more than sheaves of straw. Believe me, sir, stand well back when the Mackenzie breaks its bonds. But it is a sight no man should miss."

Next morning when he proposed to start his fifty-mile journey back to the Gravel, he was surprised to find that the Hudson's Bay men were united in insisting that George Michael accompany him: "Common sense dictates it. As head of your expedition you dare not risk an accident."

"I made my way here. I can certainly . . ." When they refused to alter their plan, he asked: "But how's he to get back?" and the Métis said with a big smile: "No trouble. I will walk," and Luton thought: To give me comfort he'll walk near a hundred miles. With great reluctance he allowed George Michael to accompany him.

As the two men climbed down the wooden stairway to where the frozen river waited, the Canadians gave them three cheers and fired volleys in the air. Lord Luton turned and raised his hand in salute to them and their flag, a heroic outpost in this frozen wilderness.

It was providential that George Michael accompanied Luton back to the Gravel, for as soon as they arrived at the tent-cabin he cried: "Oh, Duke! You 'ave made terrible mistake!" In the dim light of day he ran about identifying scars on rocks and trees, and pointing in dismay toward the Gravel, the Mackenzie and the cabin.

Seeing his agitation and having had proof of George Michael's good sense, Luton stopped the man's running about and asked: "What is it, Michael?" and the Métis replied, with fear clouding his face: "You are in great danger, Duke. When thaw comes, ice here in Gravel and ice out there in Mackenzie, she will crash, sweep everything away." Then he kicked at the upturned *Sweet Afton* and with wild gestures indicated huge blocks of ice coming down the Gravel and battering the *Sweet Afton* and the cabin into small kindling: "Then what you do? No boat? No cabin? What in hell you goin' do?"

He would not delay even half a day, for the safety of this expedition led by a man he had grown to like and respect was of vital importance to him, and from long experience he knew that in these parts the preservation of the boat was paramount. Showing the men how to construct rollers from driftwood tree trunks, he marshaled all the ropes they could provide, used their shovel to smooth a pathway to higher ground, and with all hands pushing and hauling he tore the *Sweet Afton* away from her snug position as part of the cabin and dragged her to a spot well above where the crashing ice might be expected to reach.

Tireless, he then began the removal of the entire living area, even the latrine, to higher ground, and as he and Carpenter started to move the beds he stopped and said dramatically: "You stay down here, some night soon when you asleep, the ice she come and we don't see you never no more." Two nightfalls later the expedition was finally housed in a barely adequate substitute for the original cabin but one at a safer elevation. His task done, Michael sat heavily upon a rock, leaned back to allow the weak sun to reach his face, and said: "I very hungry. We eat?"

At the first resting period Lord Luton made a proposal that surprised the others: "Harry, take the shovel and scar out an exercise track for us up here next to our new cabin," and Philip protested: "The one down there's perfectly good. No trouble to run down for our daily spin."

"Ah!" Luton said with some force. "A great deal of trouble. Minus-forty and stiff breeze, which of us will want not only to run our circuits but also to run down that hill and back to do so? You, Philip, would be the first to demur. I can hear you arguing with me: 'But, Uncle Evelyn! It's bitter cold out there!' And the exercise you miss could well be the one that would doom you. Harry, mark it close to the shack." When it had been delineated, Evelyn was the first to utilize it, but George Michael, watching him run in the bitter cold, told the others: "He must be crazy. Nobody in Fort Norman run in the cold . . . summer neither," and Harry said quietly: "I'm sure they don't."

The Métis remained with the Englishmen a full week, during which he helped them complete the reconstruction of their living quarters and went hunting with Fogarty, whom he recognized as a kindred spirit. They were a pair of highly skilled hunters and brought a large moose to the far shore of the Mackenzie—Fogarty told the others: "He did it, not me"—and next morning after profuse thanks from Luton plus a gold sovereign he was gone, a lone figure striking out for the north, rifle slung across his back, right down the middle of the great river.

With George Michael gone and the camp, thanks to his assistance, at a safe elevation, life returned to its routine, with Lord Luton giving only the most fragmentary report on his extraordinary visit to Fort Norman: "We studied the maps and they copied several for us, so we're in firm shape," and he displayed them briefly. Carpenter quickly saw that Luton had apparently decided to follow the Peel into some rather high terrain, and he asked quietly: "Wouldn't picking our way through those smaller rivers and that lower pass be preferable? I was told in Edmonton . . ."

"Strangers can be told anything," Luton snapped as he took back his maps.

One morning, apropos of nothing that had been said before, he told the men: "At Fort Norman, I felt absolutely naked. Those huge men with their beards as big as bushes. Said they never shaved after the fifteenth of October—tradition, they assured me." Then, looking about the cabin, he pointed to Trevor Blythe, whose beard was so skimpy and faded-straw in color that it made a poor show: "I say, Trevor, want to borrow my razor and scrape that foolish thing off?" but the younger man parried the suggestion by admitting, with some embarrassment: "I simply abhor shaving. At home I allow Forbes to do it for me, and I wish he were here now."

But in some ways it was Blythe who accommodated most perfectly to the winter isolation, for he was attuned to the changes of nature and relished what he was witnessing: "Have you ever seen more heavenly pastel colors than those out there? I feared the night would be perpetual, but these midday hours are superb. Just enough light to bathe the world in beauty."

He attracted the admiration of everyone by an astonishing accomplishment. The men were surprised that even in the remotest and coldest parts of the arctic, ravens appeared, huge black creatures with an ugly cry. "What do they live on?" Blythe asked. "In this frozen waste what can they possibly find to eat?" In time, the ravens were eating scraps which he provided and shortly one of the more daring was coming close to his feet and snatching crumbs from the snow. To the other men, all ravens looked alike, but Trevor found in this one some identifying sign, and whenever the bird appeared, Trevor lured it always closer. Othello, he called it, and it seemed as if the raven recognized its name and responded to it.

One morning while Trevor was outside feeding Othello, the men in the cabin heard a soft cry: "I say, come here. But quiet." And when they opened the door slowly they saw the raven perched on Trevor's left arm eating crumbs which the young man offered with his right hand.

"Remarkable!" Luton cried, whereupon the bird flew off with a slight beating of its black wings, but on subsequent days it returned, and grew bolder, until finally it elected Blythe's left shoulder as an assured resting place. When the others saw this extraordinary spectacle of a young man swathed in arctic clothing, flaxen hair exposed, with a raven perched on his shoulder, all silhouetted against the blazing white of the snow, they tried to lure the bird, but Othello, sensing that Blythe was the one to trust, stayed with him.

The men had agreed back in Edmonton, when it became obvious that they must spend a winter in the far north, that they would keep a record of how extreme cold and prolonged night affected them, and they learned to their relief that any healthy man who did, as Luton insisted, "observe the niceties," survived rather well. "There is disruption," Luton conceded in his notes. "We eat less, seem to require more water, and have to guard against constipation. We also suffer minor eye irritation from incessant lantern light. But we can detect no negative mental effects, and as the worst part of winter approaches, we have no apprehensions."

Fogarty in the meantime was scouring the countryside for game, and sometimes the men would see him approaching the far side of the deeply frozen Mackenzie at the conclusion of some foray to the east, and they would watch his distant figure grow larger. They would study closely to see if he signaled for them to cross over and help him drag home a side of caribou, and if he did wave his arms in triumph, they would pile out, cross the river, and grab hold of whatever it was he had dragged behind him, and that night their cabin would be rich with the smell of roasting meat.

As January waned, Carpenter warned his companions: "February is the testing time. No part of the year colder than February." In 1898 it was especially bitter along the Mackenzie, with the spirit thermometer staying below forty for days at a time, but when the cold was most oppressive Carpenter would say: "When it breaks, we'll have summer in winter!" and he was right, for in late February the cold mysteriously abated and the men had a respite as lovely and as welcome as any they had ever known.

The thermometer rose to four-below, and since there was not even a whisper of wind, it was indeed like summer. Harry and Philip actually ran their laps with shirts off, chests bare, and experienced no discomfort. Othello made two turns of the snow-packed course on Blythe's shoulder, and Carpenter accompanied Fogarty on a long excursion to the other side of the Mackenzie, where they bagged a moose.

This reassuring respite heightened the spirits of the men, who restudied their maps and made plans for when the spring thaw would allow them to resume their journey to the gold fields. "What those bearded ones at Norman reminded me," Luton said, "is that when we have to saw our boat in half, it might well be at a spot where there's no timber to be had to shore up the open end. So what we must do on our way downriver, as soon as it's ice-free, is bring on board any logs that look as if they might be sawn into short planking."

"And where do you calculate the site for sawing the *Sweet Afton* apart might come?" Carpenter inquired, not in unduly curious fashion but merely to prepare his thinking, and Luton pointed almost automatically to a spot well up the Peel River. Carpenter was about to launch one final protest against taking a route which was sure to be perilous, but before he could voice his objections, Lord Luton anticipated them, swept up his maps, and disappeared before Harry could force the issue.

So the vital decision was never submitted to an honest criticism and evaluation. When Harry studied his own maps in secret they reinforced his apprehensions about the inherent dangers in trying to force a way up the Peel: The entire trip on the river is against a current which has to be swift. The rapids cannot be easy to portage if there's no path to walk on shore. And those damned high mountains at the end. Not promising, not promising at all.

Now when he did his daily turns on the new track, some fifty feet higher than the old, he calculated the odds on each of these impediments. At the end of one imaginary survey he ruefully cast the score: Impedimenta barring the way, nineteen; Lord Luton's party, nothing. And he could foresee no way to change those odds unless Evelyn entertained a revelation when he faced that lonely spot where the Rat River led to safety across the low divide: If he refuses to see or to listen, we're doomed.

He was certain of this, and yet he did not enforce his judgment upon his cousin. Luton was younger than he by six years and less experienced in the field by seven or eight major explorations. He was in no way superior to Harry in intellect or in his university performance. He was courageous, of that there could be no question, but he had never been tested under fire the way Harry had been. And although he had a stern moral fiber, what some would term character, it had not yet been required to assert itself in time of real crisis, the way Harry's character had been tested in India and Africa.

With the scales weighing those virtues that really mattered in

Carpenter's favor, why did he defer to his younger cousin? Because in the prolific and noble Bradcombe family it was the custom out of time to pay deference when facing difficult decisions to the man who held the marquisate of Deal, and remote though the possibility was, Harry knew that Evelyn might one day be that man. This rule had served the family well, and if an occasional marquess had been a ninny, most had not, and Carpenter could see that when Evelyn had a few more years under his belt, he would be eligible, if called upon, to be one of the best. This expedition to the gold fields of Canada could be the final testing ground that would make Lord Luton a whole man, one forged in fire, and Harry Carpenter would stand by him in the testing period, for in that regard, he, Harry, represented all the Bradcombes. Their leader was under scrutiny and they stood with him.

With the arrival of warmer weather in April the men assumed that the Mackenzie would begin to thaw, and it was Blythe, least experienced outdoorsman of the group, who pointed out: "Fellows! It's still ten degrees below freezing!" and Philip replied: "But it feels like summer."

It did, and the realization that the winter hibernation would soon be coming to an end spurred the men to start casting up their assessments of what their adventure in the arctic winter had meant. Lord Luton took it upon himself to make the summary statements in the official log, and he came close to the truth when he wrote:

> As I look back on this splendid adventure, I see that we were a team of five who respected nature and wished to test ourselves against the full force of an arctic winter. Harry Carpenter had wide experience in frontier situations in all climates. My nephew Philip Henslow was a keen sportsman and a reliable shot. His friend Trevor Blythe displayed an uncanny aptitude for domesticating wild ravens, something never before attempted to our knowledge, and even our trusted ghillie, Fogarty from Ireland, had an unmatched knowledge of the way of salmon. I had traveled to many distant areas, loved boxing and cricket and the dictum of Juvenal: *Mens sana in corpore sano.*

> At the beginning of our long hibernation we laid down sensible and healthful rules which all obeyed, and as a result we suffered not one serious illness or accident. Rigorous daily exercise seems a sure preventative for the idleness of an arctic

stay, and our experience is that it should be enforced out of doors even in the roughest weather. Among other benefits, it inhibits constipation.

But the remarkable fact about our stay is that all team members displayed unusual and unflagging courage. Never were spirits allowed to fall or pettiness to invade our daily regimen. When meat was needed, our members were willing to roam very far afield, even under the most daunting circumstances. Hard work was greeted almost as a friend, and we proved once more what honest Englishmen can accomplish in adversity, and even Fogarty caught the spirit, for his extended forays in search of provender were little less than heroic. Harry Carpenter was an older exemplar without parallel of such deportment and our two younger men were faultless, displaying great promise for future development.

In all modesty I make bold to claim we were a gallant bunch, and the arctic was powerless to defeat us in our quest.

When the others heard these lines read aloud, they protested that in the coda Lord Luton had not mentioned his own laudable behavior, and when he disclaimed the right to any special notice, Harry Carpenter took the journal and wrote, reciting the words aloud as he did:

"The other members of the Lord Luton party wish to record the fact that in all contingencies their leader was salutary in his own display of courage under difficult situations, none more so than when he went on foot fifty miles in each direction, alone and in the dead of winter with the thermometer at minus-forty and storms brewing, to find us data regarding our next target. In this feat, performed during days that allowed only two hours of daylight, he performed as none of the rest of us could have."

There were murmurs of assent when Carpenter laid down his pen, but as he himself looked at the final words of his encomium he realized that he had omitted the salient truth of Luton's journey: And he returned from his venture without having listened to a word of the advice given him.

• • •

In May came unmistakable signs of approaching thaw, but it was not until June that Fogarty set out for one last hunting trip on the opposite bank of the Mackenzie; he returned immediately up the Gravel, shouting: "Gentlemen! Come see the river!" When they did, they witnessed one of the most savage displays of nature, for the various tributaries lying far to the south where the sun returned early had long since thawed and sent their burden of melt-water and floating ice crashing northward. Now, as this icy flood reached areas still frozen, the whole river began to writhe and crack and heave. With astonishing reports, like the firing of a battery of cannon, thick ice off the mouth of the Gravel, locked there since October, broke asunder in wild confusion.

"Good God!" Luton shouted. "Look out there. That one's as big as a house," and when the men stared toward the middle of the Mackenzie they saw that he was wrong. It was bigger than three houses, a huge chunk of ice, and as it ground its way past the mouth of the Gravel, pulverizing the smaller floes which that small river had contributed, the men gained an appreciation of what an arctic river could do when it was shattered by the surges of spring.

Blythe and Henslow stood side by side, watching in awe as a gigantic iceberg came thundering down the river, holding embedded within its massive walls of ice a collection of intertwined evergreen trees that it had ripped from a hillside eight hundred miles distant. On it came, "a frozen forest," Trevor said as he tried to imagine the journey the trees had made. "That iceberg must hold a thousand bird's nests, and when they come flying back to find their homes the landlord will tell them: 'We've moved them to the shores of the Arctic Ocean. Start flying north.'"

For more than an hour the two young men watched little forests floating past, but then their attention was directed to Carpenter, who shouted: "Look what's coming to greet us over here!" and everyone turned to see what their relatively tiny Gravel could produce, for tumbling down it came a monstrous block of ice traveling at harmful speed. As it roared past, twisting and turning, it swept with awful crunching force right over the spot where the original cabin had been, and with such grinding power that it would have reduced both craft and cabin to pulp.

No one, watching the total erasure of their former homesite and means of escape from this wintry prison, could keep from thinking: My God! If we had remained in that spot! And all recalled George

Michael's rhetorical question: "What would you do if you lost your boat?" Carpenter summed up their reactions: "Thank God, Evelyn did go to Fort Norman and bring back that Métis. We escaped a terrible trap."

And then Philip shouted: "Look at that one!" and down this meager stream, the Gravel, came one more block of ice, as big as any on the Mackenzie, and it was rolling in such grotesque fashion that it struck and dug deeply into the right bank, opposite where the watchers stood, and gouged out a huge chunk of bank, leaving behind four trees with roots torn loose, so that their trunks and branches, lying parallel to the earth, reached far over the surface of the river but not quite in it.

Carpenter, who had seen this phenomenon in Africa, warned those about him: "Extremely dangerous, that. They call them sweepers."

"Why that?" Philip asked, and Harry said: "Because if you come down this river in an open boat—and what else would you have on a stream this size—you grow careless, and those low branches reach out and sweep you right off your boat, and the current is so swift you can't climb back. Take care with sweepers."

One night during the waiting period it came Trevor Blythe's turn to conduct the seminar, and since this was more or less the termination of their long confinement, he offered a surprising but unusually profitable exercise: "Under my goading, we've talked a lot about poetry, I'm afraid, and often we've referred to the inventive lines with which poems begin. Things like 'My true-love hath my heart and I have his' and 'Tell me where is Fancy bred.' Such lines are keys that unlock gracious memories, and they don't have to be all that fine as poetry. Their job is to set bells ringing.

"As we drifted down this great river, I was pestered by a ripping pair of lines:

> Ye Mariners of England
> That guard our native seas! . . .

Ever since we left the Athabasca Landing, I've been such a mariner," and after laughing at himself he cited a few more effective opening lines: " 'It is a beauteous evening, calm and free' " and " 'Oft in the stilly night.' "

But then he shifted sharply: "I've come to think that how a work of art ends is just as important as how it begins. A good opening

entices us, but a strong finish nails down the experience." Now he had
to consult Palgrave, for not even he was as familiar with the good
closings as with the lyrical openings. He deemed one of blind Milton's to be impeccable: " 'They also serve who only stand and wait.' "
But as a young man in love, a condition he had so far revealed to no
one, not even the young lady, he also favored: " 'I could not love thee,
Dear, so much, / Loved I not Honour more.' "

But he surprised his listeners by praising extensively the rough,
harsh ending of one of Shakespeare's loveliest songs: "It has one of
the perfect openings, of course: 'When icicles hang by the wall' and it
continues with splendid lines which evoke winter, such as 'And milk
comes frozen home in pail' and 'When roasted crabs hiss in the bowl.'
But after all the niceties of the banquet hall have been exhibited, he
closes with that remarkable line which only he could have written:
'While greasy Joan doth keel the pot' to remind us that somebody has
been toiling in the kitchen."

Trevor then came to his conclusion: "Point I've been wanting to
make, the real poet has the last line in mind when he writes his first,
and there's no better example of this than the ending to that special
poem of Waller's whose opening stanza I praised many months ago,
the one beginning 'Go, lovely Rose!' Do any of you remember how it
ends? Neither did I, and I'm not going to trust my memory now. It's
Palgrave, Number Eighty-nine, I believe."

While fumbling for the page, he said: "Remember how the first
three stanzas go. In the first the rose is commanded to go to his love.
In the second it's to inform her that young girls, like roses, are put on
earth to be admired. In the third the rose is to command her to come
forth and be admired. And now the wonderful last verse:

> Then die! that she
> The common fate of all things rare
> May read in thee:
> How small a part of time they share
> That are so wondrous sweet and fair!"

Silently the men contemplated the misery of death, then Lord Luton
spoke: "A noble ending to a grand winter," and as he looked at the two
young men he said loudly: "Do you realize how precious this winter
will have been when we look back upon it? Philip, Trevor! You'll tell
of this to people who will never have guessed that a majestic river like
this existed!" He smiled at Harry and added: "So shall we all."

Harry did not return the smile, for while the others prepared joyously to plunge into the swollen Mackenzie for a triumphant run downriver to its junction with the Peel, he could not erase from his mind a segment of map he had memorized. It showed that if one ascended the Gravel to its headwaters and made a relatively short portage across the divide, one found oneself at the headwaters of a considerable river, the Stewart, which did meander a bit but which finally deposited one right on the Yukon, less than fifty miles upstream from Dawson City and the gold fields. And it's downstream all the way, once you reach the Stewart, he told himself, and he became so convinced that Evelyn was doing exactly the wrong thing in turning his back on the Gravel that on the very morning of their breaking camp he launched one final appeal: "Evelyn, you have studied the maps more closely than any of us. Surely you can visualize what a sensible union the Gravel and the Stewart achieve?"

Luton refused to listen: "I have indeed studied the map . . . memorized it . . . and I visualize instead the Peel, which leads directly to our destination." And so the five men set forth.

THREE

DESOLATION

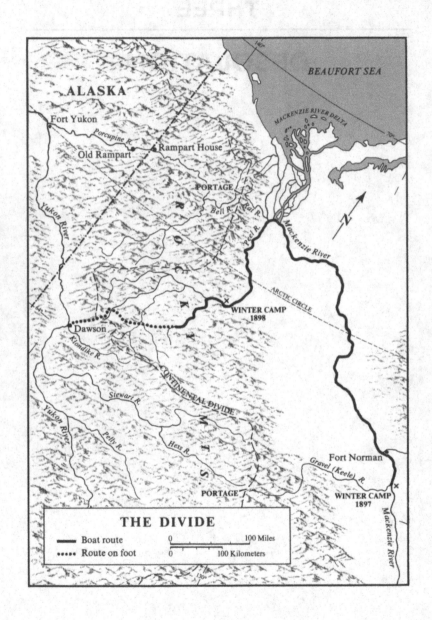

BEAUFORT SEA

ALASKA

Fort Yukon

Porcupine R.

Old Rampart   Rampart House

MACKENZIE RIVER DELTA

PORTAGE

Bell R.   *Rat R.*

Peel R.

Mackenzie River

Yukon River

ARCTIC CIRCLE

✕

WINTER CAMP
1898

Dawson

Klondike R.

CONTINENTAL DIVIDE

Stewart R.

Yukon River

Pelly R.

Hess R.

R O C K Y   M T S.

Fort Norman

Gravel (Keele) R.

PORTAGE

WINTER CAMP
1897

✕

Mackenzie River

THE DIVIDE

▬▬▬ Boat route

•••• Route on foot

| 0 | | 100 Miles |

| 0 | | 100 Kilometers |

O N 10 JUNE 1898, TEN MONTHS AFTER THEY DEPARTED FROM Edmonton, the Luton party was ready to resume its journey toward the Arctic Ocean, and their departure from the cabin which in its two locations had housed them for so long contained elements of sadness. Luton said the official farewells: "I doubt if any other five men could have occupied so small a space for so long without even a suggestion of friction. Gentlemen, I shall be forever indebted to you." And each of the men said goodbye to some particular aspect of this strange hibernation. Harry Carpenter took one last circuit of his running track, its surface muddy now but nonetheless still one of the agencies for the good health the men had enjoyed. Philip, clad once more in his treasured boots now that the freezing weather was over, sat by the dead fire and read a few pages of *Great Expectations;* he had acquired much useful information beside that fire. Luton saluted the cabin, and Fogarty gazed for some time at the surrounding hills he had come to know so intimately. Trevor Blythe had the most painful farewell, because although his raven was reluctant to move near the boat, it was obviously loath to leave the poet. It rode on Trevor's shoulder down to the water, but when the young man stepped aboard the craft, Othello flew off. In bewilderment it circled a few times, then cawed hoarsely as if bidding a dear friend farewell and flew inland to where its companions waited.

As the carefully reloaded *Afton* eased into the fast-moving waters of the Gravel, she seemed eager to complete her journey and fairly leaped forward to rejoin the Mackenzie. Carpenter had been nominated to get the voyage started properly and he was steering when the rushing waters of the Gravel veered suddenly to starboard, throwing the little boat right at the spot where the huge cake of ice just days before had gouged out the chunk of bank, leaving the dangerous sweepers.

Too late Harry saw that he was powerless to prevent the *Afton* from being driven under the branches of this fallen tree, but he did have time to shout a warning: "Down! All down!"

The men, remembering Harry's warning, obeyed, except for Philip Henslow, who was striving to save a rope that might be lost and remained standing aft as he reached for it. Before Blythe could shout his own warning, the sweeper caught Philip in the back and pitched him into the icy waters.

"Help!" shouted Blythe, leaping to that end of the boat, but now the mighty current of the Mackenzie took over, and by the time the others sprang into action, Philip was far out into the larger river. Even so, the agility with which Carpenter shot the *Afton* into the main current, plus the frenzied power when the others started paddling and rowing, would have enabled them to save Philip had it not been for those dreadful boots, rubber and heavy and reaching well above his knees; they filled immediately with water and made swimming impossible.

Had he been wearing short, loose footgear, which the knowing did, he could have kicked them off and saved himself, but impeded as he was, he could kick neither swiftly nor strongly and was unable to keep afloat until the boat overtook him. In the first terrible moment when he struck the water and felt his boots becoming dead weights, he tried with super-human valor to stay afloat. His lungs took in more oxygen. His heart beat faster. His arms produced unbelievable pulling power, and he battled to keep his head above the swirling waters of the Mackenzie.

But inexorably the boots, heavier than lead, pulled him down, and as he fought vainly to counteract their pull to death he uttered a wild and piercing scream: *"Help me!"* Each man on the boat heard it, and would hear it for many nights, and even months, but each was powerless. Trevor Blythe tried to leap into the water but was restrained by Harry Carpenter, who did not wish to lose two members of the team. However, he could not prevent Lord Luton from diving fully clad into the icy waters.

The gesture was fruitless. Luton did not come even close to his drowning nephew before the boy, with one terrible last scream, disappeared forever.

When the three men in the boat finally dragged Luton back aboard, they threw a blanket about him and sat beside him as the *Sweet Afton* floated swiftly down the broad crest of the river. "You did your best," Carpenter said, and Fogarty added: "No force could save him, Milord. You tried." But Blythe, standing at the rear of the boat, could only look through stinging eyes aft toward the dark waters that had taken his friend to their bosom. He remained there through that long, dreamlike spring twilight which seemed to last forever.

As the *Sweet Afton* continued down the Mackenzie the four survivors became painfully aware that each mile it carried them along took them farther from the Klondike. It was infuriating, yet inescapable, to be drifting down this great river and to be allowing it to divert them from their target, but that was the nature of the Mackenzie: one of the great rivers of the world, it led nowhere but its own end.

Harry spotted Trevor writing quietly, as he had done so often during the winter on the banks of the Gravel. Saying lightly "Examination time," he drew the book toward him, and what he saw was so pleasing that he did not stint his praise: "I say, Trevor, I do believe you've done it." Rapping for attention, he read aloud some dozen lines, which ended sardonically:

> *"Reluctant paladins we*
> *Who seek our Golden Grail by fleeing from it."*

Returning the book, Harry told the author: "See how much better it is when you compact your words and place among them images we can respond to?" and Trevor fell silent, for he was wishing that Philip had been alive to share this encouraging assessment of his first mature poem.

Shortly after dawn on the next day, Luton saw from his position in the bow the post at Fort Norman, and without alerting the others, he fired two salutes into the crisp morning air. The shots brought the Canadians to the head of their stairs, where they waited, but the Métis, George Michael, recognizing the boat and its occupants, leaped down the steps, shouting: "Duke! Duke! Throw a line." When he had it firmly under control, he drew the *Sweet Afton* to him as the Canadians hurried down to meet the Englishmen and renew their acquaintance with Luton, whom they remembered with respect.

When all were seated in the post's dining area, Luton opened the meeting with an acknowledgment: "Good friends, I want you to know that if your man Michael had not accompanied me home last time, all of us might now be dead." When the Canadians looked at one another in surprise, he explained: "He warned us to move our cabin and our boat to higher ground . . . against the day when so many ice floes would come roaring down that they would pile onto the land and crush all. He not only gave warning, he helped us move upland, and saved our lives."

As the Englishmen nodded toward their savior, the Métis looked carefully at each man and asked: "The other one, with the light hair? You leave him, maybe?"

Slowly and with visible pain Luton told the Hudson's Bay people the kind of tale with which they were familiar: "Drowned in the Mackenzie. A sweeper caught him in the middle of his back." There was silence—broken by Carpenter, who added: "Lord Luton dived into the icy water to save him. Hopeless. A dreadful loss."

The Canadians were so pleased to see Luton again that they wanted him to lay over two or three days, but they understood when he declined: "Our job is to get over the mountains and into the Yukon."

"We remember," said one of the men who had drawn him some maps of the delta area. "We certainly hope you've changed your mind about trying the Peel."

By the austerity of his look dismissing that ticklish subject, Luton let it be known that he would not welcome further discussion of routes, but he did express interest when the head of the post said: "We have few goods for sale this time of year. Our big supply ships don't reach here till July, but we can let you have a few things you might be able to use." While Luton disappeared with him to check what might be available, the other Canadians took Carpenter aside and advised him strenuously to argue some sense into Lord Luton, show him the folly of his plan to travel the Peel: "You will not be able to get through the rapids before the freeze sets in. It's as simple as that." But Carpenter silenced them: "It's his expedition and he's gone into difficult spots all over the world." One man replied with unmasked contempt: "Not at our degrees, he ain't. In Fahrenheit forty-five minus, in latitude sixty-six north."

The post people were able to provide Luton with six cans of meat, but nothing else, and as the Englishmen walked down to the *Afton* they assured the Canadians that they had sufficient stores to carry them into Dawson. The farewells were hearty, with Lord Luton at the last moment slipping a ten-dollar note into George Michael's palm: "For saving us with your help," but it was not till some time after cast-off that Trevor Blythe, wreathed in smiles, revealed his secret: "Look what George Michael slipped aboard when the Canadians weren't watching!" and he threw back a tarpaulin to reveal eight boxes of hunting ammunition.

Some days later, as they moved north of the Arctic Circle, Lord Luton for the first time lost his composure: "Damn it all! I wish we could leap over those mountains and land in Dawson," but this was not to be. At the conclusion of a river trip that had no parallel in the world, the Luton party approached the incredibly tangled delta where the Mackenzie fragmented into a score of separate rivers, each winding its way haphazardly toward the ocean. It was a jungle of swampland and muddy streams that not even the local Indians could thread, and Harry, who was at the wheel, shouted: "Everyone! Help me find the Peel or we drift out into the Arctic Ocean!"

All eyes scouted the left bank, but found no indication of where the Peel debouched into the Mackenzie; however, they were able to move slowly ahead, still looking, for at this time of year no night fell in this far latitude. As they crept along, Trevor Blythe, suddenly overcome by the thought of leaving the majestic Mackenzie, cried: "I cannot allow poor Philip to lie in the bosom of this icy river without a word of Christian farewell." For although each of the others had mourned privately for Philip, they had done so during the lonely night watches and at the rising sun of each new day. They agreed with Trevor and gathered with him at the rear of the *Afton*, where the young poet borrowed Carpenter's Book of Common Prayer, searching the pages for the service for the dead. When he found it, he passed the book along to Lord Luton, who read the noble words in stately cadence. A young man they had loved was gone and they eased his soul to rest. And when the prayers were ended, Trevor produced his copy of Palgrave, opened it to a place he had marked, and said softly:

"I should like to read a farewell to my dear friend." And he began in a clear voice: "John Milton lost a young friend, drowned in the Irish seas, and wrote 'Lycidas' to express his grief:

> Yet once more, O ye laurels, and once more
> Ye myrtles brown, with ivy never sere,
> I come to pluck your berries harsh and crude, . . ."

On through the majestic phrases he read, until it seemed as if some celestial organ were paying tribute to the dead young man, and it was improbable that Blythe realized how appropriate the final lines of this elegy were going to be when heard by Lord Luton's beleaguered party:

> "And now the sun had stretch'd out all the hills,
> And now was dropt into the western bay:
> At last he rose, and twitch'd his mantle blue:
> To-morrow to fresh woods and pastures new."

"That's the command," Luton said, "spoken from the grave. Tomorrow we head for the conclusion of our journey." Trevor, listening to these harsh, practical words, thought: How callous. But quickly became contrite: It was I who chose the poem. It was I who did not foresee the ending.

On through the silver night the *Sweet Afton* drifted, passing and ignoring one branch of the Mackenzie after another as the river fed off to the east. "We've got to find something leading in from the west," Carpenter said repeatedly, the edge in his voice betraying his unease, and when the hours from eleven at night through three in the morning passed with no sign of the Peel, even he began to lose confidence: "Could we have missed it?" The others frantically consulted their inadequate charts, as he prepared to turn back and research the west bank.

He was prevented from this mistake by the appearance on the near shore of a group of smallish dark men, apparently Indians, who leaped in the air and made wild noises, which, when Harry steered the *Afton* toward them, turned into the exciting words: "Peel! Peel!" With a deep sigh that revealed the tension under which he had been steering, Carpenter headed for the shouting men, and as the midnight dusk brightened into full arctic daylight Lord Luton's team left the broad and many-mouthed Mackenzie to enter its tributary—the narrow, unknown Peel.

They were in the new river only a few minutes when they came upon the ramshackle Indian encampment from which their guides had come; it was not a permanent village, nothing more than a collection of tents and improvised shacks to which a group of some three dozen Han Indians from the Yukon district had come to barter their furs with the Company men on the trading ships that would soon be probing such gathering sites. From the nervousness of the Indians, both Luton and Carpenter deduced that this might be one of their rare encounters with white men.

"They speak no French," Luton said. "Probably never traded with Hudson's Bay people. Or traveled with Métis hunters."

As he stepped forward and away from the *Afton,* the Han uttered screams, raced to gather their women, and fled far from their shacks. Dismayed that he had frightened them, Luton extended his hands, palms upward and empty, and moved slowly toward them, uttering reassuring words in French, hoping that someone among them would understand even one word. He accomplished nothing, for the Han continued to withdraw, but from the direction to which they were addressing their frightened looks he concluded that he was not the focus of fear, and when he looked back over his shoulder, he saw the cause of their anxiety.

Trevor Blythe, hungry for one last sight of the Mackenzie, had taken out the expedition's long black telescope, and after exploring the tangled mouths of the great river had turned it to look up the dark banks of the Peel. The Han, thinking the scope to be the white man's rifle with deadly power, assumed that Trevor would soon be shooting at them. They would have continued to flee had not Luton dashed back, taken the telescope, and held it sideways across his upturned palms above his head.

As he approached the terrified Han he began to laugh, not loudly or derisively but in accents of friendship, and when he had the first cautious Indians about him—all clad in the simplest of leather garments, with dirty matted hair and evasive eyes—he showed first one, then another how the telescope worked, and soon he had them pacified and genuinely friendly.

Everyone wanted to see the distant shore, the white birds on the mud flats, and before the *Afton* was allowed to move on into the Peel, there had to be a feast and dancing and the chanting of good-luck songs. It was a greeting of such amiability, so different from the austerity of the Blackfoot ceremonial at Edmonton, that Luton actually cried to Carpenter: "Harry, have we aught to give these good people?" and odd bits of cargo were distributed. Fogarty, with his peasant agility in solving simple problems, was soon talking in sign language with the Han, and learned that they had actually come from the Yukon or some other western river to the west as powerful as the Mackenzie.

"Is it far?" Luton asked, and the little men indicated that they had walked it in half of one moon, which caused Harry to say: "They must be talking of the Porcupine."

His pronunciation of that name excited the Indians, and with a jumble of signs they explained to Fogarty that, yes, it was the Porcupine, but beyond it there was this other huge river, and all members of the Luton party were both relieved and excited to learn that they were so close to the Yukon. They quickly made their departure, but as they poled their way up the Peel, for there would be no more easy downriver drifting, Luton asked his crew: "How is it possible that in a modern country like Canada, or the United States, there can still exist such hopeless savages? Little better than animals, really." Harry replied: "They knew where they were, and we didn't."

Two days later, as they sweated their way up the sluggish, unpleasant Peel, which seemed such a mean river after the clean, swift-moving Gravel, they were faced by one of those moments that determine human destinies, but it did not present itself with any sounding of trumpets or a glowing sunset at end of day. On the starboard side of the *Afton,* that is, the left bank of the Peel, they saw two men, heavily bearded and bare to the waist, engaged in sawing their small boat in half.

"What's the plan?" Carpenter called out as he headed his own boat for shore.

"Strippin' down so we can portage over the pass just ahead."

"What way you taking?"

"Rat, Bell, Porcupine. Quickest route to Dawson."

Lord Luton, hearing this conversation and not liking it, broke in peremptorily: "You're wrong about that. The Peel is much shorter."

"But not quicker," the men said, "not by a long shot. Join up with us, more hands, more speed."

Luton stared at them with distaste, prodded Carpenter, and said: "Let's move her up the Peel, Harry," but Carpenter felt that he must in obedience to common sense argue once more for what he knew to be the saner route, since all knowledgeable hands had recommended it.

Speaking quietly and using once again a formal mode of address to emphasize the gravity of his message, he said: "Milord, we shall never find a better spot to penetrate the Rockies than by the pass at the headwaters of this little river."

"Harry!" Luton snapped almost peevishly. "It's been decided. The pass at the headwaters of the Peel takes us much closer to Dawson," and he was correct. It would be closer, but over a route much higher and much, much more difficult.

He grasped the tiller and headed the *Sweet Afton* southward up the Peel. For half an hour he steered the rugged little craft in that direction, his jaw grimly clamped. At the end of this arrogant performance he handed the tiller over to Carpenter and said: "We're well started, Harry. Keep her steady."

As they left the Rat behind, Carpenter closed his eyes and for some moments did not breathe, knowing that a decision of terrifying importance to him and the others had just been made. Then he opened his eyes, sighed deeply, and saw ahead of him the uninviting Peel, a river of little grace or character whose once-sluggish current now ran far too swiftly for its banks, signaling that rapids lay ahead. Furling the sails and directing Trevor to stow them neatly, for they would no longer be of use, he reached for one of the long poles and started pushing the boat upriver.

By July 1898, a full year after having left London, Lord Luton's party was far into the Peel, all hands poling fourteen or sixteen hours a day and covering so many miles that even Carpenter was beginning to think that transit by this route might prove possible, but that dream was short-lived. Early one morning, when Trevor Blythe had been put on shore to run ahead to scout what the *Sweet Afton* would soon be facing, he came back ashen-faced, to shout from the shore: "Oh, Lord Luton! Worst possible news!" And as the three aboard strained to hear, he delivered the foul message that would characterize the remainder of their trip up the Peel: "Heavy rapids and canyon, no shoreline from which to drag." As the import of these dreadful words was absorbed, all hands began wondering what to do.

First they took Blythe back aboard, then they poled ahead to where the rapids ended their cascade down a fairly steep incline, and there three facts became inescapable. Harry, scrambling ahead, shouted back the reassuring news: "Enough water beyond the rapids to keep us afloat," but Trevor confirmed his earlier report: "Absolutely no shore footing from which we could pull." Luton recalled with a shiver the warning of one of the Schnabel brothers: "When there's no path, you catch your breath, step down into that cold mountain water, and hike right up the middle of the Rat . . ." At the reappearance of that fated name his breath really did catch, and he thought: Oh God! Should we have taken that little one after all? But he dismissed such self-recrimination, telling his men with a show of confidence: "We'll have to tow and push whilst wading, but we can't do that with a boat so big. Haul her ashore, break out the saw, and let's get started."

There was, of course, another option and a sensible one: don't cut the boat, turn around, drift back with the current, go up the Rat, and cut the boat there as everyone had advised. But since the others realized that Luton would not hear of this, the possibility was not discussed. Instead, the trustworthy little boat which had given such excellent service was hauled ashore, unloaded, and sawed in half, following exactly that red line painted by one of the Schnabels back in Athabasca Landing. When they saw how wee the half they proposed using was going to be, Carpenter said: "Not much sailing in this one. Pushing and pulling."

With good heart, now that the worst of their position was known, the four men laid out the driftwood they had been collecting, cut timbers from it, boarded and caulked the gaping hole left by the sawing, and carefully stowed their diminished cargo, discarding nothing. As a last gesture to the half not taken, Lord Luton saluted her and turned his face resolutely toward the waiting canyon and Dawson City, which lay only a hundred and ninety miles to the west.

A new routine was quickly set. Two teams were established: Luton and Fogarty in front hauling ropes, Harry and Trevor in back pushing. As might have been expected, Lord Luton was first in the water, and although he must have winced inwardly at the sudden coldness, not much above freezing, his face revealed nothing. "Heave, men! And with good heart, we'll make it."

That first day in the water was horrible, for the bouldered footing allowed no steady progress and the depth of the river in places plunged the men to their necks in icy water. Since they had to waste half their energy fighting to remain erect, forward motion was minimal, and all hoped for a sudden ending to the canyon so that they might find solid footing ashore and a decent chance to tow in an organized manner. But most of the day passed with no shore available, and Carpenter thought: This is going to be pure hell if night falls and we're stuck in here, but that fearful emergency was avoided, because the canyon did end and good footing was available on the left bank. By this time the men were so exhausted they could not avail themselves of it, and as night approached, they dragged their half-boat ashore and pitched their camp.

Before they fell asleep they conducted a fascinating conversation, for as men of sturdy will they were interested in such matters. "I say, Carpenter, how do you figure?" Luton asked. "Who had the more difficult task out there, we pullers or you pushers?" Without a moment's reflection Harry said: "You men," and when Luton asked "Why?" he received the correct answer: "Because we in the rear had the boat to lean on to steady our feet amongst the boulders," and Luton said: "I wondered. From now on we'll alternate at intervals."

Of course, when there was no canyon eliminating the shore, the four could make a respectable day's run, and then their hopes quickened as they visualized a short but demanding portage over some mountain pass and a swift descent into Dawson. But with appalling frequency, rapids, usually less formidable than that first one, impeded, and then the men had to grit their teeth, plunge into the frigid water, fight the boulders and haul-push their half-boat westward, but the worst punishment came when they climbed out of the water, drenched, and had to shiver in the increasing cold until they slipped awkwardly out of wet and into dry clothing.

One day in mid-August, when they still faced one hundred and sixty miles on the river, Trevor Blythe was in the pushing position when he suddenly awakened to the hideous fact that they could not possibly be able to cross the Rockies before oncoming winter froze the Peel and piled snowdrifts over all the passes. "Dear God," he whispered to himself as he struggled along the rocks. "Another winter holed up. And we have so little food to see us through."

He said nothing that day, but he did begin to scan the faces of his companions, trying to ascertain whether they appreciated the impasse into which they had quite literally stumbled and in which they were continuing to stumble day after taxing day. He could not deduce their inner thoughts or their fears, but he did notice they talked less and in the evenings were too exhausted to do anything but collapse in their crowded tent. The seminars were held no more. Now it was a matter of survival.

During the last week of August, Lord Luton broke the silence. At supper one night—beans and no meat—he said abruptly: "I suppose you realize we shall soon have to pitch permanent camp."

"No other way," Carpenter said. Fogarty remained silent, and Trevor, too, said nothing, relieved that at last their predicament was in the open.

By mid-September, when the upriver poling and dragging was at its worst, the men put on extra bursts of effort to get through this horrendous part of the Peel before the fall of snow and while they still had time to select a livable spot. They succeeded, breaking into an inviting plateau at the foot of the Rockies. During the second week of October, when the temperature was close to zero, they dragged the half-boat ashore, emptied it of the pitiful amount of gear they still had, leaned it against rocks to form a protection from the northwest winds, and began to search for trees or scraps of river-borne timber that could be used to build a kind of cabin, well aware that it would not duplicate the first, comfortable shelter they had enjoyed the previous winter.

As they worked, each man thought to himself at one time or another: Good God! This time even closer to the Arctic Circle! And each man swore that he would conserve his energy, eat meager rations without complaining, and do everything possible to maintain his health. And each prayed for inner strength.

As winter began, sixteen months since their departure from Edmonton, the men were in as good condition as could have been expected. Carpenter and Blythe had shin cuts acquired while hauling and all were markedly underweight, not from lack of food but from the endless hours of exertion. No one had any perceptible sickness, nor bad teeth, nor malnutrition, but all would have to face a most taxing winter, with temperatures lower than they had known along the Mackenzie and with a frightening lack of proper food.

This year there had to be new rules, as Lord Luton explained: "Latrine same as before. Daily run the same, and do not shirk. No one, and I mean no one, no one at all, is to eat anything except in the presence of us all. You must give me your word on that." And the men swore to share food equally and openly. "We shall pray that our distinguished poacher, Fogarty, will put his talents to good purpose." Plenty of hunting shells the group did have, thanks to the gift of

George Michael. Fogarty said that he would do his best, but he hoped Major Carpenter would assist, since he was a practiced shot.

Strangely, it was Fogarty who evoked the first revelation of the lurking terror which these men had so far successfully hidden. The latrine had been positioned as before, a respectable distance from the lean-to cabin, but the cold this winter was frightful, and Fogarty noticed that the other three were failing to visit it as often as he thought they should. One night he warned them about constipation: "In Edmonton they told me it was the curse of cold climates. Gentlemen, do not ignore those little messages from your bowels."

He was prepared to squat at the latrine for as long as necessary. "His bottom must be lined with bear fur," Harry suggested, but at the latrine Fogarty would stay. It was what he did when he returned that caused trouble, for always when he came into the warm room he sighed with deep satisfaction, saying the same four words: "Better out than in." Since this was true, and was also a kind of reproof to the others with less hardy bottoms, it occasioned resentment. No one did anything about it until one night, when the routine was lustily repeated, Lord Luton suddenly reached for his revolver and shouted, indeed, he almost screamed: "Say that one more time and I'll blow your brains out!"

There was an awed hush, during which each man acknowledged how desperate their situation was. No one apologized for what Luton had done, and he said nothing. Fogarty, aware at last of how offensive he had been, said: "I am sorry, Milord." And then he added as if nothing had happened: "I think I spotted where the caribou cross." Luton laid his revolver down and said calmly: "I hope so. We shall have to rely on you, Fogarty."

For several weeks the poacher failed to bring in fresh meat, and even when Carpenter accompanied him as second gun they returned empty-handed. Food now became the problem that superseded all others, and as the supplies purchased in Edmonton began to dwindle, everyone had to go on severely reduced rations, watching with deep apprehension as one can after another was carefully opened and scraped of every morsel. For some curious reason, which no one could have explained, the six cans of meat acquired by chance at Fort Norman were considered sacrosanct, not to be touched until the ultimate extremity. They stood neatly stacked in the corner, representing a fighting chance for survival. That pile became the religious icon that kept hope alive.

The savage deprivation had to have visible consequences: the men grew leaner, their countenances ashen as blood fled their faces, their movements more carefully considered. Also, their tempers frayed, but of this they were aware, so that they spoke to one another with a more careful courtesy, as if they were members of some ancient court in which formality was required. And then one day Trevor Blythe shattered the make-believe with a startled cry of real anguish: "Oh, Jesus! Look what's happened!" And he held forth in the palm of his left hand one of his back molars, unblemished and sound as a walnut but nevertheless ejected from his weakening upper gum.

"Scurvy," Luton said without showing his fear. "We must eat more carefully," but how this was to be accomplished he did not suggest.

One very cold afternoon as Carpenter and Fogarty were trying to find a stray caribou or the cave of some hibernating bear, Harry suddenly went lame, and when Fogarty inspected his left leg he saw that the open wound caused by the rocks in the Peel had not healed. This was bad enough, but when he pressed his fingers about the wound to see whether putrefaction had set in, he saw to his and Harry's horror that the prints of his fingertips remained indented in the graying flesh. Harry, never one to avoid reality, pushed his own fingers in, with the same result.

"Necrotic," he said.

"Is that what you told the young men about?" Fogarty asked, and Harry replied: "Yes. Scurvy."

"What can we do?" Fogarty asked, and he was told: "Catch us an animal. We heard fresh meat will cure it."

Of course, both Luton and Carpenter, as experienced explorers and students of British naval history, knew that this was not totally true; fresh meat did help combat scurvy because it strengthened the body and thus made it somewhat more capable of withstanding the attack, but they knew that this was merely a delaying tactic, not a cure. They were also aware of the remarkable work done in the previous century by Captain James Cook, who almost single-handedly eradicated scurvy as the curse of seafaring men. By almost forcing his crew to drink what they described as "a nauseating mix of things" containing ingredients like vegetables, seaweed, roots and the brine of fermented sauerkraut, he had sneaked into their diet the specific nutrient that would eliminate scurvy. Later experimenters said: "Cook had eight items in his mix and seven were totally useless, but somewhere in there he had lucked upon something which provided ascorbic acid, and that saved the day."

Luton and Carpenter knew that ascorbic acid in minute but life-saving amounts could be obtained from digging up a mess of roots, boiling them, and drinking the water. But what roots? Explorers never knew which particular ones carried the treasured acid, but a wide mix always seemed mysteriously to provide the necessary. But Luton's party could not dig for roots and grasses, for the arctic land on which they were camped was frozen so solid and for so long each year that normal roots could not thrive in it. Those that might have proved helpful were locked into the ground, frozen so deep that they were not attainable. Potential salvation was everywhere under their feet, but they could not get at it.

The condition of Harry Carpenter's leg was ominous but not yet fatal; a strong man like him, with tremendous inner courage and de-termination, would have a good chance of survival. So when Fogarty and Harry returned to the camp they both refrained from adding to Lord Luton's worries by informing him that a second member of his party had scurvy, but they did say that it was imperative to find meat. Luton, Carpenter and Fogarty went out to scour the countryside—Blythe was far too weak to join them—and although they shot noth-ing that day or the next, they could not allow their exhaustion to stop them, and on the third day they did shoot a small caribou, and with joy they butchered it and hauled it home.

It was a miracle. Harry said of it: "When that roasted meat hit my stomach, I could feel the proper juices rushing to all the starved veins," and Blythe said the same. They were self-deluded, of course, for not even fresh meat could halt the inroads of this terrible disease—only a replenishment of lost acids could accomplish that—but the salutary effect of the savory meat in their systems created such a sense of renewed well-being that Trevor believed his gums were strengthening and Harry was sure his necrotic leg had begun to mend.

But that was the last fresh meat they would enjoy for weeks. One night when the men were really starving, Lord Luton, as protector of the six cans of meat, announced almost merrily: "Gentlemen, we cel-ebrate!" and with exaggerated ritual he placed one of the precious cans on their rude table and watched approvingly as Fogarty slit it open with an ax, tossed the contents in a saucepan, and threw in odd bits of everything he could find. As they waited for it to heat, they became aware of the arctic wind howling at their shack, and for some reason not one of them could have explained, they began to hum and then sing softly the Christmas carols of their youth. When they came to that grand old English one not favored in other countries, "The Holly and the Ivy," Trevor Blythe's high tenor sounded so sweetly throughout the tent that one could imagine the sound of sleighbells echoing in the frigid air outside. They talked of home and family and of the grand Christmases they had known in England and Ireland. Then, one by one, each returned to his own sad silence, and only the thunder of the wind was heard.

Two nights after the caroling the others heard Trevor gasp, and when they looked in his direction he was holding in his palm two more of his big back teeth, flawlessly white and glimmering in the lamplight like the malevolent eyes of some ghost. Before anyone could commiserate with him, he said softly and with profound resignation: "I doubt I shall see spring."

"Now look here, Trevor," Luton began to bluster, but the young fellow said with the gentleness that always marked him: "Evelyn, will you please fetch my Palgrave?" and when the precious little book was found, Trevor asked: "Will you read some of the short poems?" In his strong baritone Luton read those wonderfully simple lines, those thoughts that seemed to represent the best that England had ever offered the world: "'My heart aches, and a drowsy numbness pains . . .'" and "'She dwelt among the untrodden ways . . .'" and "'Tell me where is Fancy bred . . .'"

As this essence of love and beauty and the longings of youth filled the cabin, Blythe sighed. Soon thereafter his breath became uneven and labored, and he whispered: "Evelyn, please read me the Herrick." Luton could not find the right poem, so Trevor with his trembling hands leafed through the pages for Number 93 and found the magical six lines:

> *"Whenas in silks my Julia goes*
> *Then, then (methinks) how sweetly flows*
> *That liquefaction of her clothes.*
>
> *Next, when I cast mine eyes and see*
> *That brave vibration each way free;*
> *O how that glittering taketh me!"*

When Luton finished reading, Trevor reached for Carpenter's hand and whispered in a voice so weak it could scarcely be heard: "When we reached home I intended speaking with your cousin, Lady Julia. Please tell her. And my *Treasury* . . . I want her to have it." Then he turned his ravaged body toward Luton: "Oh, Evelyn, I'm so sorry."

"For what?"

"For having let you down," this in a gray, deathly tone.

"Forget that!" Luton said heartily, trying to mask his emotion. "Sleep now and mend yourself."

He was long past mending. That remorseless killer, scurvy, had so depleted him, stealing his sources of strength and destroying his capacity to rebuild, that all he could do was look pitifully at his three companions and gasp for breath, even though he knew the cool, clean air would do him little good.

Fighting valiantly to maintain control, he reached out to clasp Evelyn's hand, failed, and watched with dismay as his fingers fell weakly onto the blanket. Knowing that he was near death, he tried with harsh rasping sounds that formed no syllables to bid farewell to his companions, fell back, and with one last surge of energy turned his face to the wall to spare them his distress. Thus isolated, this compassionate young man, so full of promise but with his love undeclared, his poems unwritten, died.

As before, the end of February was the time of hell and ice, except that this year there was no springlike break in the middle, and much of the misery it brought stemmed from the fact that the days were lengthening, visibly so, but the rate was slow and the persistence of the cold so deadening that it seemed a perversion, a teasing of the spirit. Spring was due but it did not come.

Camp routine continued as before. Lord Luton shaved, and tended his clothes, and protected his five cans of meat, and marched erect rather than bent over as the others did in order to keep whatever heat they had trapped in their bellies. He ran three laps in this winter's version of a track and he goaded the others to do the same. He ate sparingly, preferring that the others take larger portions, and he did everything possible to sustain the spirits of his two remaining partners. He was an impeccable leader, and barring that one dreadful night when he had threatened to shoot Fogarty, he never lost his composure. His party had fallen upon rough times and he intended leading the survivors to safety. Never, not even in his lonely, unspoken reflections, did he acknowledge personal culpability for the growing disaster; he viewed it as either a capricious act of God or the manifestation of the malevolent forces of nature.

Harry Carpenter was the regimental major. His big mustache had proliferated into a beard, but he kept it clipped, and when he sat in the cabin divested of the heavy clothes he had to wear when outside, he was a handsome man, not so rugged as before and somewhat drawn about the face because of scurvy, but still a proper officer whose upright bearing was relaxed rather than stiff. Had he stayed in India and become the colonel of his regiment, his men would have called him "Good old Harry," and here in the wastes of northern Canada he was the same. He did not run every day; he couldn't, but when he felt that Luton was silently chiding him he tried; after one lap he would return to the cabin, exhausted.

He was reading *Great Expectations* for the third time, not aloud this time, for Luton and Fogarty claimed they had not cared much for it the first time around and had more or less resented the waste of time during the second reading. He was sorry that he had confided to Fogarty his concern about his incipient scurvy, but now he wished he had someone with whom to discuss the matter; to do so with either Luton or Fogarty seemed quite impossible, and what was worse, improper. He suffered his debilitating disease mutely, supposing that Fogarty had informed Luton of the matter. Throughout the cabin, night and day, there was a conspiracy of silence regarding his affliction, and he allowed it to continue.

Fogarty resembled his master in his stolid acceptance of conditions. He ran with Luton on those days he was not searching vainly to find the meat that would ensure their safety, and he maintained that stubborn cheerfulness which made any good Irish servingman a model of his calling. Though not required to wait on his companions, he still found pleasure in heating Lord Luton's shaving water in the morning and in honing and stropping the razor. He helped Carpenter in a dozen ways and strove to maintain good spirits in the cramped quarters. He was appalled that they should be spending a second winter in such surroundings, and he watched almost breathlessly for even the slightest promise of spring: "Soon we'll be over the mountains, that I'm sure, and there'll be gold for the finding!" He was the only one who mentioned gold; the other two had never been obsessed with it and were now concerned only with survival.

As winter waned, so did Carpenter's reserves; each day he grew weaker, until once toward the end of the month he was unable to get out of bed in the morning, which now showed a clear difference from night. When Luton asked: "You joining us for a bit of running?" he grinned and said: "I shall sit this out in the tea tent," as if they were participating in a cricket match.

On the next day, when Fogarty returned from the latrine, he saw a pathetic sight: Harry Carpenter was on his weakened hands and knees, trying with the shovel, whose long handle he managed poorly, to grub away the surface of the frozen earth in what the Irishman knew was a search for elusive roots that might help stem his rampant scurvy. He was obviously not having any luck, but with the quiet determination that had always marked him he continued his futile scraping until he fell forward, exhausted, the heavy shovel falling useless beside him.

Fogarty considered for some moments whether he should run to Carpenter's aid, but some inner sense cautioned him that a man like this would want to solve his own problems and would, indeed, resent intrusion from another, so he withdrew out of sight, taking a position from which he could maintain watch over the fallen man. In due course Harry rose, took almost two minutes to steady himself, then walked slowly back to the hut, dragging the shovel behind him. When he saw Fogarty, he brought it sharply up and placed it against his shoulder as if it were a rifle and he on parade.

"I've been giving a touch to our track," he said as he walked past, but when Fogarty saw his ashen face he breathed a silent cry: Dear Jesus! He's going to die.

No matter how courageous and determined Carpenter was, he could not avoid brooding about the awfulness of dying in these bleak surroundings, where every means that might have enabled him to fight off his debility was missing: the medicines, the proper diet, the good doctors, the nursing, the supervised recuperation . . . How valuable these things were, how clear an indication that the society which ensured them was properly civilized.

However, his painful reflections did not always center on himself. He thought often of his cousin Julia, nineteen when last he saw her, and a young woman who would never be beautiful in the ordinary sense of that word; she did not even have what was described as a "flawless English complexion," but she did have what Trevor Blythe had recognized, a positively glowing inner fire that made whatever she said sound reasonable and whatever she did seem humane. "Best of her breed," Harry whispered to himself as he visualized her running freely across the lawn, to greet him after a safari in Kenya, "bubbling with life's infinite possibilities."

Then came the gloom, for he had in his life of moving about, especially among English families living abroad, seen a score of young women like Julia, radiant and of great power but not particularly marketable in the marriage bazaars, and if they failed in their twenties to find the one good man who could appreciate their inner beauty, they might find no one, and have to content themselves, in their forties, with playing the cello, reading good books and doing needlework.

When such thoughts assailed him he recalled Trevor's commission: "When we reached home I intended speaking with your cousin, Lady Julia. Please tell her." He was certain now that he would not be reaching home, that Julia would never know that a young poet of marked talent had loved her, nor would she receive the gift that would express this love. He became so obsessed with the thought that he would fail to fulfill this mission that for two days he chastised himself, then asked for one of the last precious pieces of paper, on which he tried to tell Julia of Trevor Blythe's death and of the young man's last request: that she be told he would have been coming home to marry her. But he had neither the strength nor the concentration to finish the letter, and as the pencil fell from his almost lifeless hand he realized the true significance of death and murmured in a voice too low for his companions to hear: "It means that messages of love will not be delivered."

That night Lord Luton, seeing the desolation of spirit which had overcome his chief lieutenant, cried brightly: "I say, men! Isn't it time we attacked another can of our Fort Norman supply," and as before, Fogarty chopped the can open and brought out the saucepan. This time he was able to throw in a small collection of roots he had grubbed from the thawing soil, and when stew was rationed out, it was twice as tasty as before and the three diners leaned back and smacked their lips, remarking upon what a civilizing effect a substantial hot meal could have upon a hungry man.

But Carpenter was so debilitated that his high spirits did not last the night, and in the morning he had neither the strength nor the resolve to leave his bed. Luton, sick at heart over the weakening condition of his friend, sat beside Carpenter and took him by the shoulders: "Look here, Harry, this won't do. It won't do at all." Harry, thinking he was being rebuked for purposely malingering and unable because of his illness to see that Luton was merely using the hale-and-hearty approach of the regimental marshal, took offense at his friend's chiding.

Hiding his distress, he rose on pitifully weakened legs whose sores had never healed but only worsened, put on his heaviest clothing, and said cheerfully: "You're right, Evelyn. I could do with a bit of jog," and walking unsteadily, he started to step out into the bitter cold, pausing for one fleeting moment to whisper to Fogarty. But what he said, Lord Luton could not hear.

The two men remaining in the hut agreed that spurring him to action had been salutary, but since they did not continue to monitor him as he ran right past the track, they did not see him slow down because of gasping pain near his heart, nor when he was out of sight, begin to take off his outer garments one by one. Heavy parka, gone! Woolen jacket with double pockets, thrown aside! Inner jacket, also of wool, away! Now his good linen shirt came off and next his silk-and-wool undershirt, until he stumbled ahead, naked to the waist in cold that had returned to many degrees below zero.

There was no wind, so for a few minutes he could move forward, but then his scurvied legs refused to function and his lungs began to freeze. Grasping for the branches of a stunted tree, he held himself upright, and in that position froze to death.

When Harry's return was delayed, Lord Luton said to Fogarty: "Good, Harry's whipping himself back into shape," but when the absence became prolonged, Luton said with obvious apprehension: "Fogarty, I think we'd better look into Harry's running." From the cabin door they stared at the track, but they saw nothing.

"Whatever could have happened?" Luton asked, and Fogarty had no reasonable surmise. They walked tentatively toward the running oval, and Fogarty spotted the red-and-gray parka lying on the ground and rushed forward to retrieve it. As he did so, Luton, coming behind, spotted the woolen jacket, and then the inner jacket and not far beyond the erect corpse of Harry Carpenter, already frozen almost solid.

When they returned to the shack, a distraught Evelyn could not accept the death of his friend as merely the kind of accident one could anticipate during a protracted adventure. In a voice trembling with anguish and self-doubt he asked: "What did he whisper to you, Fogarty?" and the Irishman replied: "He praised you, sir."

"What did he say?" Luton cried, his voice an agitated demand,

and Fogarty whispered: "He told me 'Keep Evelyn strong for crossing the mountains.'"

"Why would he have said that?" in a higher voice.

"Because he knew we were trapped . . . by those mountains Mr. Trevor wrote about."

Luton and Fogarty were to experience an additional horror in Harry's manly suicide. Unable at that moment to dig a grave, and not wishing to bring the corpse into the cabin, they collected his strewn garments and placed them like robes over the stiff body, which they laid in the snow. When they returned the next day they discovered what food the ravens of the arctic fed upon.

March was especially difficult, for with the coming of the vernal equinox, when night and day were twelve hours long at all spots on the earth, the two survivors had visible reason for thinking that spring was already here, and desperately they wanted the snow and ice to melt so they could be on their way. But this did not happen, for although the days grew noticeably warmer and those fearful silent nights when the temperature dropped to minus-sixty were gone, it still remained below freezing and no relaxation of winter came.

It was a time of irritation, and one day when Luton was beginning to fear the onset of scurvy himself, he railed at Fogarty: "You boasted last year that you were a poacher extraordinaire. For God's sake, let's see you bag something," and Fogarty merely said: "Yes, Milord," but was unable to find anything to shoot.

Even in the closeness of the cabin, Lord Luton maintained separation by caste. Fogarty was a servant, an unlettered man who had been brought along to assist his betters, and never did either man forget that. During two winters, each more than seven months long, Luton never touched Fogarty, although Fogarty sometimes touched him when performing a service, and it would have been unthinkable for Luton to have addressed him by a first name. And had Fogarty referred to His Lordship as Evelyn, the cabin would have trembled as if struck by an earthquake. From these strict rules, hammered out over the centuries, there could be no deviation. If Fogarty had to address Luton directly, it was "Milord" and nothing else; Luton would have considered even "sir" too familiar.

And yet there was mutual respect between these men. The Luton party had started with five, and now only two were left, and at times

Luton had entertained but never voiced the judgment that if in the end there was to be only one to reach Dawson, it would probably be this happy moonfaced Irishman. "Damn me," he muttered to himself one day as he watched Fogarty running his laps on the oval track where mud was beginning to show. "Peasants have a capacity for survival. I suppose that's why there's so many of 'em."

In fairness to Luton, he never demanded subservience of a demeaning kind. The original rule still prevailed: "Fogarty is the servant of the expedition, not of any individual member." And in a dozen unspoken ways he let the Irishman know that the latter's contribution was both essential and highly regarded. It was an arrangement that only two well-intended and thoroughly disciplined men could have maintained under these difficult conditions, and they knew that if they remained obedient to it, they had a fighting chance to bring their odd combination safely to Dawson and its gold fields.

Despite their shared determination to avoid any differences of opinion that might exacerbate tempers already in danger, each had a strong individual attitude toward what should be done with the four remaining cans of meat. Lord Luton, as the descendant of gentlemen for fifteen generations and noblemen for nine, insisted upon living by the code of the endangered aristocrat: "Decency says we must save the cans till the very last. Stands to reason, Fogarty, it would be unconscionable to devour them now, when they may be required in some great extremity."

Fogarty, on the other hand, was descended from some of the shrewdest, self-protecting peasants Ireland had ever produced, and like the sensible pragmatist he was, he saw even the precious cans of meat only as means to some worthy end, and if there was a good chance of getting to Dawson alive, he would use them now, when they were obviously needed: "I say, with all due deference, Milord, we ought to chop one of them open right now and fill our bellies."

"We'll have none of that, Fogarty. Those cans are for an emergency."

At this very moment, in a small Scottish hamlet many thousands of miles distant from this segment of the Arctic Circle, a sentimental little Scottish writer, James Barrie (later Sir James), was brooding over a winsome idea for a stage play, one which would later fill theaters of the world with joy and chuckles. *The Admirable Crichton* dealt with a situation somewhat like the one in which Luton and Fogarty found themselves: a spoiled and pampered family of the English gentry is marooned on a tropical island along with a trusted retainer, their butler Crichton, and as the family falls apart in this crisis, displaying a lack of both common sense and will power, Crichton reveals himself as a master of every emergency. Only his courage, inventiveness and inexhaustible good sense save the family, but when rescue comes, he, of course, reverts to being their servant. It was neat, amusing and reassuring, and people loved it, especially the upper classes who were the butt of the joke.

That was not to be the case on the frozen banks of the Peel. Lord Luton did not reveal himself as a giddy fop; he was tougher than walrus hide. Nor did Fogarty suddenly step forward as all-wise or possessed of the masterful characteristics that Luton lacked. Fogarty was a good factotum, and Luton was more than able to care for himself, but gradually through the pressure of circumstances and the necessity for decisions of great moment, the two men seemed to reach a status of equality, each complementing the other and necessary to the partnership. This was never better exemplified than during the days following the equinox when they had to make up their minds as to how they would operate in the more fortunate weeks they could be sure were coming when summer returned. All depended upon one crucial decision: "Since we're through the canyons, shall we put the half-boat back in the water and pole our way to the headwaters and then hike over the mountains, or shall we abandon the boat here and start walking immediately?" They whipped this back and forth, with Luton now asking Fogarty for his opinion, because at long last the noble lord was beginning to suspect that his earlier obstinate decisions might have been largely to blame for the deaths of Blythe and Carpenter.

Pleased that finally Luton sought his advice, Fogarty would propose: "Let's keep the boat, Milord, because with it, we can carry more stuff," and Luton would respond: "But if we head out swiftly on foot with the simplest backpacks, we can certainly make it before another winter."

At the next discussion, Fogarty would defend the backpacks and Luton the retention of the boat, and in this way each calculated danger or emergency was voiced and assessed. It was Luton who had the courage to investigate one of the most painful situations: "Fogarty, we've seen men die . . . from causes they could not control. If only one of us survived, which way would be better?" Without hesitation Fogarty replied: "If he lived and was alone, he'd have to leave the boat, because otherwise . . . ." and that settled the matter: "Since we're both going to live, we'll keep the boat until the last practical moment."

The choice having been made, the two men spent much of April deciding in minute detail what would be carried by boat to the headwaters and which articles would be taken forward in each of the backpacks. They must take the tent, and the tools for survival and all available food, which was not much. Looking at the dried beans and the other edibles that kept the body alive but allowed the extremities to die, Luton again felt intimations of scurvy—a loosening tooth, a sensation of numbness in his toes. When Fogarty was absent he saw with horror that when he pushed his forefinger into the flesh of his right leg, the indentation remained.

At this moment in the twenty-first month of the doomed expedition, he almost lost heart, but when he heard the approach of Fogarty he stiffened and presented his servant with the obligatory posture of a gentleman still in control: "Fogarty, we really must see if we can get ourselves some meat." That was all he said, but the Irishman knew that Lord Luton was not going to make it through the mountains unless he, Fogarty, brought home some game.

He thereupon started the most significant hunting journey of his life, traveling each day up and down the frozen Peel looking for anything that moved, and each night when he returned empty-handed, to the terrible disappointment of his waiting companion, he could see His Lordship's shoulders not sag but stiffen with determination: "Good try, Fogarty. I'm sure you'll get something yet."

Luton's journal now lacked the easy flow and broad philosophical base that had characterized it the preceding winter, when five able men were really exploring life in a cramped cabin in the arctic. One night, after Fogarty had once more returned empty-handed, Luton wrote in disjointed, trembling phrases:

> Again no meat. Pushed right forefinger in leg, mark remained hours. Am slipping. If I must die terrible isolation pray God able to do it with grace of Trevor Blythe, courage of Harry Carpenter. Right now pray Fogarty finds caribou.

Shortly after this admission of despair, Luton left the cabin and tried to run his customary laps, but as he used the oval which Harry Carpenter had tramped into the snow, he began to see images of that good man whom he had brought to his death, and of Philip lost in the Mackenzie, and of the poet Trevor Blythe, perhaps the greatest loss of all. He started to stagger and duel with phantoms, so that Fogarty, who was watching from the cabin, having learned from Carpenter's suicide, saw that his master was in difficulty.

Running to help, he heard Luton cry to the phantoms: "I am strangled! I am cursed with grief! Oh God, that I should have done this to these men through my ineptitude!"

The Irishman, who was not supposed to hear this confession, jogged methodically behind Lord Luton, overtaking him on a turn, where he said in his best matter-of-fact voice: "Milord, we'll be in sore trouble if we don't chop more wood." Luton, rattling his head to drive away the cruel images, said: "Fetch the axes," and as they exorcised their terror through sweating work, Luton's head cleared and he said: "Fogarty, unless you bag us something . . ." and Fogarty knew immediately what he must do: they were starving and to allow this to continue when the four cans of meat were available was stupidity.

Ignoring orders and grabbing the ax before Luton could stop him, he strode back to the cabin, took one of the sacrosanct cans, chopped off the top, and placed the meat in a saucepan, adding one of the last onions and handfuls of his arctic roots. When the stew was bubbling, he ladled out a bowlful and set it before Luton, who looked down at it, breathed its ravishing aroma, and with a fork neatly picked out one small piece of meat after another, never wolfing it down and never berating Fogarty for disobeying him.

Refreshed by the unexpected food, he slept soundly, rose early and shaved as usual. Refusing to acknowledge even to himself how close to surrender he had been the night before, he dressed in his meticulous way, took down his gun and a pocketful of George Michael's shells, and said: "Time comes, Fogarty, when a man must find his own caribou," and off he marched, thinking as he went: This may be the final effort. My legs. My damned legs.

Fogarty, of course, trailed behind, and during that long cold day whenever he tired of climbing the snowy hummocks, he knew that this was for Luton the do-or-die effort, and he had not the heart to stop him. It was good that he didn't, for toward evening when he joined up with Luton, the pair came upon spoor which excited them to the trembling point. A herd of the large deer called wapiti, moving north for the summer, had recently crossed this way, leaving fresh signs.

The animals could not be impossibly distant, both agreed on

that, so the chase began, the men following the signs with desperate intensity, but when the silvery night fell, the wapiti had not yet been overtaken. There had to be a great temptation for them to go back to the safety of their cabin, but without speaking, Luton pointed to the spot where they stood, indicating that here he would shoot his deer or die, and Fogarty, feeling deep affection for the austere man, nodded. Through the early hours of the shortening night they remained in position, each man striving to catch a little rest against the demands of the coming day. At midnight, when the waning moon stood high, Luton thought he heard a movement to the east: "I'm going to scout over that hill. Watch sharp if I rouse anything and it comes this way."

When he had crept quietly to the crest of the hill covered with sparse snow, he broke into a sweat, for below him in a cleared space grazed five wapiti, incredibly beautiful, and big, their huge antlers gleaming in the moonlight. Should I try to call Fogarty? he asked himself. Rejecting that idea lest the animals be alerted, he tried to control his shaking wrists and mumbled: "I do it myself or I die along this cursed river."

Moving like a ghost, for he was nearly that, he closed upon the unsuspecting animals, saw once more how glorious they were, bowed his head in silent prayer, then raised his rifle slowly and squeezed the trigger. Fogarty, hearing the shot from behind the hill, cried: "Good God! He went off to shoot himself!" And when he clambered up the hill, he saw four or five deer running free across the tundra and a dreadful panic gripped him. But then he saw Lord Luton leaning on his gun over the body of a dead animal whose great antlers shone in the moonlight.

When Fogarty rushed up to the lifeless beast, he nodded deferentially to Luton, who nodded back. Both men then began gathering brush, and after Fogarty had built a substantial fire, he dressed out the big deer. By unspoken agreement he ripped out the liver, and that was the first portion of the meat they roasted on sticks over the flames. Jamming it down their mouths half raw, they allowed the blood to trickle down their chins, and they could almost feel the life-saving juices running into their own livers and down the veins of their legs, which only a few minutes before had been doomed.

But Fogarty, who had been listening to all the talk about scurvy, was not deluded into thinking that Luton had been cured; he had been no more than temporarily strengthened, and in an effort to capitalize upon this temporary improvement, the Irishman adopted as his credo Harry Carpenter's final commission: "Keep Evelyn strong for crossing the mountains" and he directed his efforts toward that seemingly impossible goal.

Adopting a routine he would doggedly adhere to throughout the remainder of this devastating journey, he went out three or four times each day with a spade and a digging stick made from one of the wapiti's antlers and began digging in all those thawed places where the looser soil and gravel of the upland terrains had proved hospitable to roots. He dug for half an hour at a time, probing downward through thin ice and into stony soils which contained networks of roots, some capable of producing low trees, others attached to shrubs and some merely connected with grasses. But like others who had saved their lives in this way, he accepted whatever the earth provided, shook off the dirt, and carried it back to the hut, where he kept a pot simmering in the ashes.

With his precious roots, gathered at such great expense of labor and affection, he concocted a witches' brew that in some mysterious way contained the precious acids. As he and Lord Luton drank this acrid broth as an act of faith, believing that it would cure Evelyn and prevent Fogarty from becoming afflicted, the magic worked. With deer meat to make the muscles stronger and acids to revitalize the blood and the body's protective systems, the day came when Luton was able to bare his legs for Fogarty and allow the Irishman to press his thumb into the flesh. To the joy of both men, the flesh proved firm and resilient; no longer did it remain indented in the gray mark of death; it sprang back in the reddish sign of health.

But still Fogarty continued grubbing and replenishing the vital powers of his master, until the spring day when Luton said: "Fogarty, I do believe we're both strong enough to tackle the Divide." So the half-boat was loaded, the deadly campsite was abandoned, a final farewell was said at the rude graves of Harry and Trevor, and the two men, their legs strong, resumed their journey up the Peel, poling and pulling as before.

Now there were no rapids to be forded in icy water, and in time they reached a place where the Peel branched, one tributary leading to the west, the other to the south, and the two men debated at their camp that night which course to follow. The maps were consulted once more, as if each man had not already memorized their every detail. At last Luton stood stiffly, and placing them on the ground, anchored them with a large stone and said: "They have served us well, but we are beyond them now," and he left them. Then he added: "I fear we would be headed to America if we press west. We shall steer to the south." Their compass direction would remain south-southwest until, at some point farther along, they intercepted some west-flowing river, several of which had to lie beyond the mountains.

As Luton and Fogarty muscled their half-boat up the remaining miles of the Peel, they reached the upland where the final tributary of that river contained so little water that it could not keep their craft afloat. They had to bid the *Sweet Afton* farewell; as a whole boat it had served them well on the Mackenzie River, and had its half been steered up the correct sequence of Canadian streams, it would have long since deposited them at the gold fields safely. They were sad at leaving it beached at the foot of the mountains they must now attack, and Lord Luton said as he patted its gunwales: "Proper boat properly built. No fault of yours." After a formal salute, he and Fogarty were off to tackle the Rockies.

For two days they struggled in their attempts to find an easy procedure for carrying everything on their backs, and many ingenious stratagems were explored as they packed and repacked their gear. After numerous promising solutions proved futile, each man hit upon some adjustment which suited him best, and when Fogarty hefted his burden, feeling it pressing down upon his shoulders, he told Luton: "Every packhorse I treated poorly for his lazy ways is laughing at me now."

Their goods were divided into four properly tied bundles: two forty-pound rucksacks, one for each man, and two much smaller knapsacks which they could carry in one hand or under an arm. In allocating them, Lord Luton was meticulous in seeing that he received the heavier of the pairs, and it was always he who stepped out most boldly when the day's journey began, but Fogarty, trailing behind, monitored him carefully, and during the course of the day he would wait for a halt, after which he would slyly appropriate to himself the heavier burdens, and in this manner they approached the mountains that separated them from the gold fields. Luton, of course, realized what his ghillie was doing, and normally as a gentleman and head of the expedition, abbreviated though it was, he would have protested, but even though he had recovered from his attack of scurvy, it had left him so debilitated that he needed the assistance Fogarty provided and was grateful for it. But each morning, when they set out afresh, Luton would heft his own packs and cry as before: "Let's get on with it, Fogarty!" and he would forge ahead in full vigor.

The land they were entering sloped upward to a range of low rounded mountains from which in some ancient time loose boulders and scree had tumbled in vast drifts. As they scrambled up, in places skidding back in one minute what ground it had taken ten to gain, Luton said: "Mark it, Fogarty. These mountains are very old," and when Fogarty puffed: "How can I see that?" Luton explained: "Erosion, snow in winter, wind in summer, has worn their jagged tops away," and the Irishman replied: "Then they should be called hills, not mountains." Luton accommodated him by saying: "When we cross over to the next range you'll see real mountains. New ones. All craggy and pointed peaks. Then the climbing becomes a test."

As they descended the gentler western slope they caught their first glimpse of the splintered, craggy mountains behind which Dawson lay. But between where they stood and that stern jumble of waiting peaks and ragged troughs lay a wide valley so bleak that each man shuddered to think that he must first cross this unforgiving arctic tundra. This was desolation, as alien as any land Luton had seen in his many travels, a land without even the slightest sign of hope.

In those first moments of inspecting the intermontane wilderness and the mountains beyond, Luton saw three aspects that terrified him: there was no defined path through the wasteland, nor even a continuation of the fragmentary trail that had led them from the Peel to the mountains; the bleak area was speckled with a plethora of little lakes indicating that boggy swampland probably lay between, linking them together; and the distant mountains gave no hint of any pass. The prospect was so forbidding that he halted to assess the chances of even reaching the opposite mountains. The clear path they had followed up the Mackenzie River and along the gloomy Peel had deserted them. As he surveyed the terrain he and Fogarty must now try to cross, Luton beckoned the Irishman to his side and said: "We did not anticipate this. Mr. Harry, who studied the maps so carefully, did not . . ."

His voice betrayed the anxiety he felt at standing on the edge of this desolate land, but then he sniffed, cleared his throat as if beginning a new day, and said: "Stands to reason, doesn't it? If we've been following a footpath, and we have . . . you certainly saw that . . . well, the path must come from somewhere. It must be from Dawson City lying just beyond those far mountains. Our job is to cross this wretched vale and climb them," but Fogarty cautioned: "Milord, they are too sheer. We cannot cross them unless we happen upon a low pass to take us through, and I can see no pass. We must follow the valley westward until we spy a break in their wall," for the Irishman knew that Luton's strength would not endure the scaling of such precipices, and feared also that his own vigor might be too much spent. Luton remained quiet for a moment, then said: "No! There's got to be a safe route through there and it's our job to find it. Eyes sharp, Fogarty!" and they left the relative security of the low mountains to plunge into this hostile wasteland.

As evening came on that first day it was clear to both men that they were lost on this trackless plain. A mist had obscured the distant mountains so that no fixed beacon drew them onward, and the interminable lakes, little more than collected swamps with marshy edges, obliterated whatever tracks there might have been between the two mountain ranges. They slept only fitfully that night, assuring each other: "Tomorrow we'll find the way," but neither man believed they would.

The next day, their first full one in the barren tundra, was a horror of wrong choices and blind guesses as the light mists of the previous night turned to heavy cloud and pelting rain. At times they seemed to go in circles, or get bogged down in swamps much deeper and tenacious than before, so that any hope of completing an orderly transit of the valley vanished. Fogarty, always the realist, said at dusk when the rains ceased and the clouds in the east lifted: "Milord, we are close still to the hills we left yesterday. I can see where we came out of them. I know where the trail back is, and if we start right now, we can retrace, go down the Peel, and get back to Fort Norman before another winter."

Luton, poking about among the bogs to find a place to catch some sleep, stopped his search, turned to glare at Fogarty, and said very quietly: "I did not hear what you just said. Tomorrow, bright, I shall explore some distance in that direction. You'll do the same in the opposite, each of us keeping the other in sight, and we shall try to intercept the missing path. It has got to be here. It stands to reason."

So on the second full day, when the thick clouds closed in once again and the escape route back to the Peel was no longer visible, the two men scouted exactly as Luton had devised, he to the north flank, Fogarty to the south, until each was almost lost to the other. Finding nothing, they would shout, wave arms, and reconvene in the swampy middle, march forward, then launch a new probe outward. They accomplished nothing, and at dusk had to acknowledge that they were truly lost.

But not hopelessly so, for Luton said grimly as they ate their meager rations: "There has to be a path through this morass. Tomorrow we find it and hurry down to Dawson."

On the third day of fog and rain they succeeded only in penetrating ever deeper into this hellish vale of lakes and hummocks and ankle-deep swamp. At dusk Lord Luton could no longer deceive himself: "Fogarty, for the first time I fear we are getting nowhere."

"Milord, I'm sure I could find the way back to those first hills."

"They're mountains," Luton said almost primly, "and we shall not see them again."

"You mean to press on?"

"I do." He said this so simply and with such finality that any gentleman would realize that no adverse comment would be entertained, but Fogarty persisted in his blunt way: "So you mean . . . ?"

Before he could phrase the question, Luton said: "Fogarty, when a man sets forth upon a journey, he completes it."

"And if he can't complete it? If there's no way on God's earth he can complete it?"

Luton did not respond, and that night he slept apart from the Irishman. At dawn they rose with new hope, as the heavy mists had thinned. But even before they made their start the two travelers were thrown together in self-defense, for they were about to be assaulted by one of the most terrible of arctic enemies. It began with a low humming sound, which Luton heard first but could not easily identify. The enemy scouts, after an exploratory pass, flashed back a signal to their waiting army, and within moments a devastating horde of buzzing creatures descended upon the men, launching an attack that terrified them.

"Fogarty!" Luton shouted with unlordly vehemence. "Mosquitoes!" and before the Irishman could protect himself, thousands of the arctic terrors had engulfed him.

The first minutes of the attack were horrifying, because no one unfamiliar with the arctic wastelands could imagine what an assault of this nature was like. Many lands are famous for their mosquitoes, but their breeds are positively docile compared to those of the arctic, and Lord Luton had led his partner into the heart of a breeding area:

the swampy land of little lakes which provided endless wet grounds for the winged tormentors.

Before the two men had a chance to break out their mosquito netting—to have traveled along the Mackenzie without it would have been suicide—they were blackened with the insects, and the biting was so incessant and painful that had they not quickly found protection under the nets, they might well have been bitten to death by nightfall, so tenacious was the attack. When the two men finally arranged themselves under the green netting, they were able to survive, even though thousands of the insects swarmed over them, battling to find even one opening in the clothing through which they might gain entrance to the target within.

Within minutes of the opening assault, the ankles of the two men were a mass of inflamed bites, and not until Luton showed Fogarty how to tie cords about his pant legs were the terrifying beasts kept away. It was a long and terrible day, and the men were so busy protecting themselves that any thought of trekking farther toward the western mountains, wherever they might be, was preposterous. When night finally came, and a smudge fire was coaxed from damp twigs to keep the insects at bay, Luton and Fogarty had to sleep side by side to share and tend the fire, and before they fell asleep, Luton said: "This was not a good day, Fogarty. A few more of these . . ."

"I'm sure I can still find the Peel . . ."

At the mention of that repugnant river Luton shuddered and said: "We're engaged in a challenge, Fogarty, and the more hideous it becomes . . ." The Irishman, formulating his own finish to the sentence, thought: He intends to move forward until we perish. Making the sign of the cross, he vowed: And I shall stay with him till he does. But then he added: The minute his eyes close for the last time, back to the Peel and Fort Norman.

The next day was the worst the two men would know, for with the coming of dawn and the dying of the smudge fire, the hordes struck with renewed fury, attacking any centimeter of exposed skin. They simply engulfed an area, sinking their proboscides deep into the skin, and their bite carried such a potent irritant, that once they struck, Luton and Fogarty had almost uncontrollable desires to scratch, but if they succumbed, they exposed more skin, which was immediately blackened by new hordes. "My word, this is rather frightening," Luton cried as he adjusted his netting to keep the little beasts from

his face and eyes, but Fogarty expressed it better when with ghoul-
ish humor he muttered as they attacked him in a score of different
places: "Stand fast, Milord, or they'll fly off with you."

The two men found macabre delight in chronicling the ingenuity
of their foe. Luton said: "Look at this rivet on my glove. You'd think
not even a gust of air could force its way in there, but they do." Belatedly, Fogarty found that the insects were assaulting his face by forcing their way through a minute hole in his net; they had detected it in
the first moments of their attack. No opening, no gap in clothing
could be so insignificant but what these murderous creatures ex-
ploited it. And they were murderous, for tradition in the arctic was
replete with stories of unprotected men who had been caught in summer and driven to suicide by millions of mosquitoes which assaulted
them without respite. There were many cases in which caribou or
horses had been killed by overwhelming and relentless attacks.

In all of nature there was no comparison with the arctic mosquito; mercifully, it appeared only for a few weeks in late spring and
summer, but when it did men shuddered and animals sought high
ground where breezes would keep the pests away.

On this hideous day the two men were not to find their escape on
high ground, for there was none that they could see, only the remorseless tundra swamp populated by myriad mosquitoes which
maintained their attack in unbroken phalanxes. At one point in the
early morning Lord Luton was so beleaguered by a black swarm—
perhaps five hundred thousand coming at him in waves that darkened the sky—that he clawed at his face in despair as hordes broke
through a tear in his netting. In that moment he realized that if the
assault were to continue with such fury throughout the day, he might
indeed go berserk as caribou were said to do when the mosquitoes
pursued their relentless assault.

Fortunately, Fogarty spotted the break in Luton's protection and
repaired it with grasses that he wove through the surrounding inter-
stices, and in this way Luton was saved, but neither man had much
hope that if such conditions persisted for several days, they could
survive, especially since they had only limited food and no clear understanding of where the western mountains lay.

They did have drinking water, of course, and Fogarty suggested:
"Milord, that was a sad attack you suffered. Fill your belly with
water. It gives a man courage to feel something down there . . . anything." But when the Irishman led Luton to one of the pools and

they bent down to drink, they found the surface covered with millions of black and wriggling larvae that even as they watched were transforming themselves into mosquitoes. The insects rose in swarms from the lake to enjoy their brief two or three weeks chasing across the tundra in search of any living thing that carried blood. Finding Luton and Fogarty delivered right into their cradle as it were, they swarmed upon them so mercilessly that drinking became impossible, and in this extremity Lord Luton very nearly lost control: he shivered, he fought the attacking hordes with shadowy movements of his hands as if he were a doomed boxer, and looked helplessly at Fogarty.

But before he could speak and reveal his near-disintegration, he saw behind the Irishman an animal moving, or was it a pair of animals? Believing that he was to be attacked from yet another quarter, he ran back to retrieve his gun, and would have fired at the creatures had not Fogarty anticipated his wild action and knocked the gun aside, so that the bullet sped harmlessly through the horde of mosquitoes rising from the lake.

"Milord, they're Indians!" and when Luton lowered his gun he saw two Indians of the Han tribe whose representatives he had seen at the mouth of the Peel. Toward them walked a robust man, dark-faced and with black hair neatly cropped above his eyes, and a lively little woman adorned with strands of seashells around her neck and with intricately beaded shoes upon her feet. They halted a few yards before the two men and dropped to their knees. From their manner of probing into everything and even inspecting the knapsacks, Fogarty concluded that they had come, with friendly intentions, across the tundra to see whether the white men were lost and needed help.

Luton, with a bounding joy which cleared his tormented brain, rushed toward the startled Indians, shouting to Fogarty: "You see! There is a track through this wilderness! They've come to show us!" But when he reached the Indians he stopped short, as if a mighty hand had been thrust in his face, for the Indians were engulfed in a most putrid stench. However, when Fogarty came close he burst into laughter and pointed to the man's face: "Some kind of animal grease, probably rotting. Keeps away mosquitoes, but it does stink."

Luton was correct in guessing that the Han had come to help; they had seen the wanderers from a distance and had deduced that they were lost and in grave trouble. Their tribe made their summer camp along the edge of this inhospitable land and various members had made the long excursion to the Hudson's Bay establishment at

Fort Norman, where they had traded furs for the rifles, axes and iron cooking pots they treasured. They were not engaged in such travel now, for it would have been unlikely that any Han man would take his wife on such a trip, trading among strangers, especially when the latter were white. They were in this harsh land only to hunt the arctic hare, but this intent was discarded now, for to succor men who were obviously lost was another matter.

However, Lord Luton could conceive of no way to converse with these people who had no command of English and no proficiency in any language other than their own, and he was angry with himself at being unable to explain to them the extremity in which he and Fogarty found themselves. But the Irishman was encountering no difficulty in discussing his predicament with the Indians, for with vigorous and imaginative gestures he described Fort Norman, and the Mackenzie River, and the Peel with its ugly rapids, and the journey through the western range, and the mosquito attacks.

When this was understood, with the Han nodding in enthusiastic agreement and adding comments of their own, also in sign language, Fogarty turned his attention to the gold fields at Dawson, and he had dug only half a gold mine with his lively gestures when the Indians indicated that, yes, they understood about the find on the Klondike because several of their men had worked there and others had acted as guides from the headwaters of what had to be the Porcupine or some similar river into Dawson. Yes, they knew the mosquitoes were horrendous at this time of the year. Yes, there was some game among these many lakes. And what was most important of all, yes, they would guide the two men through the myriad lakes and the endless swamps along the paths which gained high ground where the mosquitoes were less ferocious.

When Fogarty gestured a question about a route directly through the distant mountains, the Indian man shook his head and pointed insistently along the valley, indicating that if they kept to the lower elevations, they would at the far end of the valley reach a spot from which two relatively easy passes led through the mountains. Then he turned toward the nearby range Luton had proposed to climb, and started to scrabble in the air as if hauling himself up sheer rock and then collapsed suddenly on the ground. His stunned audience realized that they would have perished had they attempted to climb those heights; fallen to their deaths down some monstrous chasm.

That night the two Indians took from sacks about their waists odd bits of dried meats they carried with them when traveling the tundra, and after assuring the strangers that they were going to make a kind of stew in an iron pot they carried, they went to the shore of the very lake that Luton had refused to drink from because of the mosquito larvae and dipped up a copious supply of the water. Fogarty, seeing that the water was still crawling with future mosquitoes, indicated that perhaps the Indian would want to skim off the violently swimming creatures, but the woman shook her head vehemently, indicating that the larvae, when properly boiled with bits of venison, were not only palatable but also nourishing.

After they had eaten, the Han built a smudge fire, using an aromatic grass they had gathered that repelled the insects most effectively, and the men slept well, with Luton whispering to Fogarty before they fell asleep: "They've saved our lives. We must pay them well."

It was what happened the next day that shocked Lord Luton, making him not a scorner of the primordial Han but a devotee, for after leading them to a footpath and pointing out the pass through the mountains, they insisted that the two strangers leave the path, which Luton was reluctant to do, and visit a site on a little rise beside a clear lake. There Luton and Fogarty found three mounds, each the size of a grave, and where the headstones might properly have been, rested three small piles of stone.

"Who?" Fogarty asked in sign language, and so clearly that it could not be mistaken, the little Han woman indicated that the three corpses had been white men like himself, that they too had become lost, and that they had perished from mosquito bites and madness and starvation. To indicate madness she rotated her forefingers about her ears, crossed her eyes, and staggered to her imaginary death.

Luton was tremendously affected by this account: "Damn me, we've got to give the poor souls a Christian burial," and to Fogarty's astonishment, Luton stood bareheaded facing the graves and recited long passages from the Book of Common Prayer, saying at the close: "Heavenly Father, accept belatedly the souls of these good men who perished in their Wilderness of Gibeon."

It required three days for the Han couple to lead their guests across the desolate plateau to the first rises of the jagged mountains, and when they had deposited them safely, they indicated that from this spot two well-marked tracks led to Dawson; they would accompany the men no farther. That evening as the four travelers shared their last frugal meal, Lord Luton addressed his saviors in flowing and gracious words they could not possibly have understood: "Beloved friends, guides and helpers, when I first saw your people engulfed in the strangeness of Edmonton, I saw you as savages. When you helped us find the mouth of the Peel, I chuckled at your confusion about the telescope. And even when I saw you coming as our saviors as I knelt by that fetid mosquito lake, I tried to shoot you as if you were animals. I was vain and blind and arrogant, and I pray you will forgive me, for I owe you my life."

They could make nothing of his words, of course, but Fogarty repaired that deficiency by indicating that he, Luton and the Indians had shared the same camps and the same food. They had marched together, had fought the mosquitoes, had prayed together at the graves, and had crossed the land of death. This sharing had made them brothers, and as members of mankind's common family they would place their final beds side by side. Before they fell asleep Luton whispered: "I've almost grown to like their stench. Reminds me of salvation from mosquitoes and that wilderness of lakes."

Next morning they faced an impasse, for although the travelers were safely through the desolate land, where assistance from the Han was vital, they still faced a taxing journey to Dawson, and they must now choose which of two radically different routes to follow. Each path, as the Han indicated, had been well marked by the passage of many Indian feet in centuries past and even by some white men's traces in recent years.

The first was the easiest and most inviting: a northwest trail which led over relatively low mountains to the Yukon some miles down the river from Dawson, where the travelers could catch an American boat that would carry them upriver to the gold fields. The alternate path led off to the southwest, plunged immediately up into the higher mountains and quickly led down into Dawson; it would require real climbing. But there was one more significant difference: the route to the right edged toward the American portion of the north; the way to the left stayed completely within Canada, and although Luton could not verify that this would be the case, for his discarded maps had lacked accuracy, he still was so determined to avoid America that he said resolutely: "We'll take the mountain route."

When the Han saw the two men actually start for the more dif-

ficult climb they protested, showing by labored steps and bent backs
that the route being chosen was bad, then springing easily along the
lower pathway and even indicating a boat on the river. For the first
time in their days together, Fogarty was unable to devise any hand
symbols which would explain to the Indians that Lord Luton was
driven by an obsession to complete this tortured journey on Empire terrain and to avoid even in the last painful moments any tres-
pass on American soil. Indeed, the Irishman found it difficult to
explain to himself why Luton was choosing the more difficult route,
but in a restatement of the decision he had made that night as they
plunged blindly into the pathless tundra, where they would surely
have perished had not the Indians saved them, he now told the Han
in words neither they nor he could comprehend: "He leads. I go,"
and he resolutely followed Luton onto the path leading to the high
mountain.

Now came the moment of farewell, one that moved Luton profoundly, for he had developed a bond of deep affection for these two
Indians who had saved him from the mosquitoes and the feral tundra
and who had gone so far out of their own way to guide him to safety.
He saw them now as remarkable human beings, living at their own
level of civilization and doing it with competence, for they knew their
vast wasteland as well as he knew his London, and such mastery he
could respect. But he really did not care to embrace them as brothers
any more than he would have wanted to clutch Fogarty to his bosom
in gratitude for what the Irishman had done, so stiffly he stood before
the two small brown people and bowed, saying: "I shall remember
you with affection all the days of my life." Then he handed each a
pair of Canadian bills, which he delivered with another bow.

For one frightening moment he feared that the Han woman was
going to clutch his hands in gratitude or even throw her arms about
him, but her intentions were quite contrary. She placed her hands not
in his but in the air close to her ears, where she revolved them as she
made funny faces and wobbled about to indicate that Luton, in
choosing the more difficult route, was out of his mind. As she danced
her pantomime of insanity, Fogarty muttered to himself: "I think
he's crazy, too," but unlike her, he had to follow Luton as His Lordship attacked the final range that rose between them and the gold
fields.

• • •

The first half-mile into these newer mountains with their sharp peaks and deep gorges proved that the concluding segment of their journey was not going to be an easy one, for although the range was not excessively high—little more than six thousand feet—it was rugged, and at times the well-marked track could be so steep that real effort was required to master it. Indeed, the climb proved so demanding that the two men reacted as other climbers had throughout history: the more their path led upward, the more encouraged they were to dispose of trivia they felt they no longer needed, and this impulse was intensified by the realization that they were closing in upon their goal. So quietly they began to cast aside the burdens which, though once of vital importance, they now calculated they could do without: a hammer, a valuable rope, two books without covers, one of the axes, a score of things once treasured but now too heavy to lug.

There was one bundle, however, of concentrated weight which Lord Luton alone carried, the remaining cans of meat, for since Fogarty had once opened a can without permission, he could not be trusted to guard these, for Luton knew that upon their rich contents might depend the safe conclusion of his expedition. Once as they started the day's climb, Fogarty hefted the rucksack containing the cans and said: "Heavy, Milord, too heavy," but Luton said as he took the burden himself: "Not if our salvation depends upon it."

The angle of upward climb was sharper than Luton had anticipated, a steady, grinding ascent up a barely discernible rock-strewn trail, not precipitous like the Alps, but fearfully exhausting for climbers in their debilitated condition. Luton could feel the heavy weight of the meat cans pulling him back, but in a curious way this added burden inspired him, for whenever he became aware of its familiar weight he assured himself: Well, we won't starve on the mountain.

But as the trail grew steeper, Fogarty, struggling along behind with his own burden, saw Luton's steps begin to waver and his pace to slow; at times it would look as if he was in danger of plunging forward onto his knees, so exhausting was his pack. Then the Irishman would quietly maneuver to take the lead, from where he would search for a resting spot, and when he sighted one he would cry out as if it were he who was at the end of his tether: "Milord! This one looks inviting. I'm near spent," and he would throw down his pack as if he could proceed no farther.

This enabled Luton to play the game of wanting to forge ahead but agreeing grudgingly to a pause for his companion's sake. After a rest, which each man needed, Luton would be the first on his feet, as if he were impatient to get on with the climb, but almost without betraying that he was doing so, Fogarty would hoist Luton's heavy rucksack onto his own back, and the two would resume their climb.

Now the miracle of the arctic abetted them, for the days of late spring were practically endless, more than twenty hours long during which they could climb as they wished. They kept pushing painfully upward through the silvery dusk, stopping for rest and even unplanned sleep, then rising again, as if it were dawn, to strike for higher ground. However, real night, shadowy though it was, did eventually come upon them, forcing them to face the problem of what to eat, and this caused tension.

"We can't go on climbing like this without something to eat," Fogarty said on the second night, staring at the rucksack in which Luton kept the remaining cans of meat. Luton replied: "It's up to you. You're the hunter. For God's sake, get going," and desperation glared in his eyes. Luton absolutely refused to discuss the possibility of slashing open one of the cans: "No! No! We must still have scraps of that meat the Indians gave us," and they searched their bags for fragments of food, chewing on them in triumph when they found a few edible morsels.

When they neared the top of their exhausting climb, Fogarty succeeded in bagging an adventurous goat, a remarkable feat considering the wariness of that beautiful animal. And on each occasion when they built a fire with such twigs as they had gathered during that day's struggle, and they could smell the meat beginning to roast, Luton said generously: "Excellent shot, that one, Fogarty. Never seen better."

The upward climb was merciless, but no matter how steep the rude pathway sketched out by earlier travelers to and from the gold fields, the pair were consoled by the knowledge that the Yukon could not be far distant, and they did not allow their spirits to flag. At the close of one extremely difficult climb, when Fogarty who carried the slightly heavier load was exhausted, and there was no more goat meat, he went boldly to Lord Luton's rucksack, ripped open the package of cans, took one out and chopped it through the middle, handing Luton one half. Since the meat had been well cooked by steam before packing, they could eat it as it was, but they did so in grim silence, for Luton felt himself aggrieved. At the conclusion, knowing that he must in decency say something lest they go to sleep embittered, he observed: "Up here we aren't bothered by mosquitoes."

This wasn't good enough for Fogarty: "Milord, I almost staggered today. My rucksack is far too heavy. We must finish with those cans and you must help me with my burden."

Very quietly, and with not the slightest show of temper or resentment, Luton replied: "You are right, Fogarty. We need the nourishment and you need help, but if you try to touch these cans I shall shoot you."

Fogarty did not blink. Putting a finger to his forelock, he said easily: "That's the second time you've threatened that. Once for me crapping, now for me eating. I do seem to run into danger of me life because of me digestion." He said this with such easy good humor that Luton did not resent the familiarity which would have appalled him a month ago.

On the next evening Fogarty ended the day's climb so famished that he feared he might topple over, and he pleaded: "Milord, let us open another can," but Luton was adamant: "We shall hoard them against the day we face a desperate crisis," and Fogarty asked weakly: "Will my death be considered such a crisis?" Luton replied: "I am determined that we shall reach Dawson, you and I. And these cans may be the agency that enables us to do so." Ostentatiously he used the rucksack containing the cans as his pillow, and fell asleep with the rifle across his chest.

They struggled up the last rocky tor, sustained only by their primordial courage, which all men can call on in extremity but which only a few are ever required to exercise. Fogarty, gasping up the final slope, was in the van, with Luton's extra pack draped about his shoulders, when he saw with mute joy that the apex had been reached. Staring down the forested valley that awaited to the west, he turned and said quietly: "From here on, Milord, it's all downhill."

Luton affected not to hear, nor did he look ahead to the route that lay revealed before them; he stood with his back turned to his destination, his gaze reserved for the dreadful steeps they had climbed with such pain. As he stood there exhausted, his back bent, even though Fogarty was bearing half his burden, his thoughts wandered down the slopes, beyond the horizon and the hidden Peel River, to the lonely shack in which Trevor had died and from which Harry had walked to his death. It was impossible for him to experience any sense of triumph in having conquered the mountains.

But then Fogarty tugged him away from the doom-ridden past, turning him to face the more promising future, and when he had Luton's attention he repeated his encouraging words: "From here on, all downhill." Luton, ignoring Fogarty's efforts to inspirit him, continued looking back at the brutal path they had taken, and his shoulders sagged so perceptibly that the Irishman wondered if Luton was weeping. Then, with a sigh that caused Fogarty to shudder, the noble lord said: "There must have been a simpler way through the tangled rivers and the mountains but we were not allowed to find it." Even at this near-conclusion to their terrible ordeal he resisted accepting responsibility for the fatal choices taken: it was still implacable nature that was to blame.

But as he spoke these words by which he absolved himself, he felt intuitively that he really must present a more resolute impression to his servant, so he straightened suddenly, hoisted his heavy main pack, recovered his secondary one from Fogarty, and stepped boldly into the lead, uttering a command that fairly rang with enthusiasm and authority: "Let's get on with it, Fogarty! Dawson's got to be hiding behind that bend." Off they strode on the last leg of their journey, elated to know that they had at last penetrated the mountains that had opposed them from the beginning.

Then on a memorable day in June, Fogarty in the lead position went around a bend and shouted: "Milord, there it is!" When Luton hurried up he felt dizzy and had to shake his head to clear his eyes, for below him, on a narrow ledge of land fronting a great river, stood the tents and false fronts of what had to be Dawson City. Seeing it nailed down in reality, and not a chimera, the two men stood silent. They had defeated scurvy and temperatures of minus-sixty, and rapids up which their boat had to be hauled by bare hands, and murderous mosquitoes, and they had reached their destination after twenty-three months and nearly twenty-one hundred miles of hellish travel.

Neither of the men exulted or gave cries of victory, and neither revealed what prayers or thanks he did give, but Lord Luton, in this moment of extraordinary triumph, knew what any gentleman must do. Instructing Fogarty to conceal their camp in the treed area that sloped away from the river, lest anyone down in Dawson see them before they were prepared, he said: "Fogarty, we'll enter in style." For two days he kept himself and the Irishman less than a mile from their destination while they cleaned their gear, dusted their clothes, and made themselves generally presentable. From a tiny military kit which he carried, Luton produced a needle and thread, and for much of the second day he perched on a rock mending the tears in his jacket. Fogarty's beard presented a problem. "It must come off," Luton insisted. "It would look improper for me to present myself clean-shaven while I allowed you that wandering growth. Would look as if I didn't care."

"I'd like to keep it, Milord. It was most helpful with the mosquitoes." But there was no reprieve, and during most of the second afternoon, Fogarty heated water, soaped his heavy beard, and hacked away at its edges, wincing when the pain became unbearable. Finally he threw down the razor: "I cannot," whereupon Luton retrieved the razor and cried: "Well, I jolly well can." And for the first time during this long journey Lord Luton touched his manservant voluntarily.

Perching him on a log and covering his heavy beard with as much lather as their last shreds of soap would produce, he grabbed Fogarty by the head, pulled his face upward toward the warm June sun, and began almost pulling the hairs out by the roots. It was a process so painful that finally Fogarty broke loose, leaped to his feet, and cried: "I'll do it meself!" and the rest of that day and into the evening, using the tired old razor which he stropped at least fifty times, he fought the battle of the beard, exposing always a bit more clean Irish skin. At bedtime he looked quite presentable, a lean, capable, rosy-faced man who, as much as Lord Luton, had held the party together.

That night when Fogarty was not looking, Lord Luton took from his pack one of the two remaining cans of meat, placed it on a flat rock, and laid the hatchet quietly beside it. When Fogarty finally spotted it, he was overcome, and after a painful joyous pause in which neither man spoke, the Irishman lifted the hatchet by its cutting end and pushed the wooden handle toward Luton: "It's your can, Milord. You got it here and you shall do the honors."

When the can was neatly severed, Fogarty ransacked the gear for whatever scraps were still hiding and made one final stew, which he served elegantly to his master: "One spoonful for you, one for me, and, Milord, never on this entire trip did any of us break that rule about eating. We never ate secretly nor at expense to the others." When Luton made no response, the Irishman added: "And you arrive as you said you would, with your meat to spare. You got us here." Only then did Luton speak: "It's like dear Mr. Trevor said that night in the tent. A good poet always has in mind the closing lines of his poem. So does the leader of an expedition. He intends to reach his target." He fell silent for just a moment, but then his voice hardened: "Scurvy or arctic freeze, pushing or pulling, he does reach his target."

Real trouble arose at dawn when Fogarty wanted to throw into a nearby ravine the unnecessary gear that he had lugged so laboriously and which was now useless. "Let's toss all this in the ditch, with the last bloody can of meat!" he cried, but before he could do so, Luton restrained him with a warning cry, and when Fogarty turned he could see His Lordship's face was gray with anger.

"Fogarty, we have come so far, so very far. Let us today march into Dawson as men of honor who remain undefeated," and to Fogarty's bewilderment he spread on blankets what gear their rucksacks could not contain and gave a demonstration of how it should be properly packed, with the corners neatly squared.

When all was in readiness, Luton supervised the placement of Fogarty's pack on his back and then inspected the Irishman's clothes, brushing them here and there: "Let us enter that sprawling mess down there as if we were prepared to march another hundred miles," and when Fogarty said truthfully: "Milord, I could not go another hundred," Luton said: "I could."

At eight in the morning of 21 June 1899, Lord Luton, tall, erect and neatly shaven, led his servant Tim Fogarty, who marched a proper three paces behind, into Dawson City as if they were conquerors. When Superintendent Samuel Steele of the Mounties heard that Luton had arrived, he hurried down the false-fronted street to meet him, bringing several packets of mail and a list of inquiries from London. But Luton could express no interest in such things; his only concern was to dispatch immediate telegrams to the families of his three dead companions. Each message concluded: "His death was due to an act of God and to human miscalculations. He died heroically, surrounded by his friends."

Satisfied that he had discharged his obligations, he was about to leave the rude shack that served as telegraph office when Fogarty said quite forcefully: "I'd like to inform my people, too." Luton, striving to mask his astonishment at a servant's presumption, said: "Go ahead," but Fogarty said: "I have no money, Milord," Luton asked: "All that money you earned cutting hair? Four customers, almost two years." Fogarty looked squarely at the man who'd brought him so far from Ireland and said: "I'm keeping that money, as I may need it to buy me a gold mine." Luton smiled icily at the cheekiness of his ghillie and told the clerk: "I'll pay for one more. To Ireland." Fogarty, after careful calculation, sent his wife seven words: ARRIVED GOLD FIELDS ALL WELL WRITING SOONEST.

While Fogarty was drafting his message, Steele informed Luton that a generous supply of funds had been received from London "to be delivered to Lord Luton's party, should it ever arrive." The sender, the Marquess of Deal, had expected his son to reach Dawson in the summer of 1898; he was a year late.

Steele's message reminded Luton of the package of mail he still held, and he tore open a thick envelope addressed in his father's strong hand and quickly read the first page. His back stiffened, and Steele inquired if the letter had brought bad news. Luton stared at the man as if he were not there, folded the page, and slid it back into its cream envelope. His older brother, Nigel, dead in a hunting accident on their Irish estate. Luton's stern, imperial face betrayed no hint of the conflicting emotions sweeping over him: shock at his new responsibilities as heir to the marquisate; grief at news of his brother's death, for he had loved and respected him; and confusion regarding his cheerless victory in having at last reached Dawson despite intolerable defeats along the way. Head bowed, he mumbled: "Mostly it was bitter gall. But there were moments. And every man on our team did behave well. They really did, including Fogarty."

When Steele asked: "Will you be heading for the gold fields?" Luton stared at him in amazement and said nothing. Gold was not on his mind or even in his consciousness; he could not recall how he had ever become interested in it, and certainly it was no concern of his now. Later, when Steele related the story, he said: "He looked as if he had never heard the word. But then most of the people who reached Dawson from Edmonton never went to the gold fields. They seemed content merely to have got here alive." Steele's people later compiled this summary of the Edmonton traffic:

There left that town in the years 1897–1899 some fifteen hundred persons, men and women alike, Canadians and foreigners with no distinction. More than half turned back without ever reaching the Klondike. At least seventy perished en route, and they among the strongest and best prepared of their societies. Of the less than a thousand who reached the gold fields there is no record of anyone who found gold and only a few cases in which claims were actually staked, invariably on non-productive streams. Most who did succeed in arriving here turned right around and went home without trying to visit the fields, which they knew had been preempted, the most famous case being that of Lord Luton, the future Marquess of Deal, his older brother Nigel having died.

Luton achieved local immortality by the boldness of his actions that day in Dawson. He arrived with Fogarty at eight, received his accumulated mail at nine with indifference, not even bothering to open most of the letters, sent his cables, and at ten, after having given depositions concerning the deaths of three members of his party, spotted the old stern-wheeler *Jos. Parker* anchored at the waterfront. Inquiring as to its destination, he was told: "The young feller at Ross and Raglan can explain."

Hesitating not a moment, he marched down the muddy street to the store and demanded two passages to Seattle. A bright young clerk said: "Boats from here have too shallow a draft. Ours goes only to St. Michael."

"What do I do then?" Luton asked severely, and the clerk replied: "Oh, sir, one of our fine, new steamers bound for Seattle will be waiting to pick you up the moment you arrive." As Luton signed his name to the manifest, the young man said: "Evelyn, that's a funny name for a man," and the noble lord stared down at him as if from a great height.

As he started to leave he grumbled to himself: "I came through Edmonton to avoid America. Now I'm heading into the heart of the damned place." He shook his head: "The only other course is to return the way I came, but that would be insanity."

Turning to Fogarty, he held out a ticket for the steamer, but he did this with a gesture so impersonal and demeaning as if to say: "Here it is, come aboard if you wish," that the ghillie ignored it, and to Luton's surprise, said rather blithely, "No, Milord, I came to find me a gold mine and I shall."

"You mean . . ." Luton fumbled, "you're not coming?"

"No, Milord," Fogarty said brightly. "We've come to a free land and I aim to run me own gold mine . . . me own way."

There was no rancor in what he said or how he said it, and that afternoon when the flustered nobleman started for the gangway that would separate him forever from Fogarty, the Irishman demonstrated his good will by offering to carry Luton's two small pieces of luggage, one containing new clothes he had purchased in Dawson, the other the rucksack he had carried so far and with such uncomplaining determination. "No," Luton said, returning the rucksack, "this is for you. To help you on the gold fields," and he strode on ahead as was his custom.

But as he approached the steamer he knew that he could not in decency part from this faithful helper without some gesture of appreciation toward the man who had saved his life by grubbing for roots. Reaching out with his lean left arm, he grasped Fogarty's left shoulder and said in a voice so low that no passengers could hear: "Stout fellow, Fogarty," and started onto the boat, indicating that the Irishman had been dismissed.

But Fogarty, as if already imbibing the spirit of raucous freedom that animated Dawson, reached out and grabbed Luton's arm, swinging him about: "I have a name, Milord. Me friends call me Tim. And I have a little something for you." Rummaging in the rucksack Luton had just given him, he produced the treasured final can of meat and with proper deference handed it to Evelyn: "You guarded this faithfully during our long trip. I'm sure you'll want it for remembrance."

Luton, neither flinching nor showing color at this forwardness of his erstwhile servant, accepted the can with a slight bowing of his head as if expressing gratitude, then said evenly: "It served its purpose, Fogarty. It got us here. And now, as you expressed it so eloquently, 'Let's toss this in the ditch . . .'" and with an easy swing of his arm, as if he were once more bowling in county cricket, he tossed the can far out into the waters of the Yukon. Then, turning on his heel without a gesture of any kind, he stalked toward the waiting ship. But he was not destined to board it on this first try, for as he stepped onto the gangway he was stopped by a rough voice accustomed to giving commands, and when he turned he saw Superintendent Steele, who was saying: "Lord Luton, this young woman came pleading to my office. Said she had come to see you," and he pushed forward the one woman in all Canada that Luton was least eager to meet.

It was Irina Kozlok, the North Dakota castaway he had rescued from that bleak shore along the Great Slave Lake, the one who had caused him such anxiety as they drifted together down the Mackenzie in the crowded *Sweet Afton.* What could she be doing in Dawson? And how in God's name had she got here?

In his first agitated glance he saw that she was as trim and self-assured as ever, with her freshly laundered military uniform, her heavy boots and her neat little kepi still cocked at a jaunty angle so an ample supply of silvery hair shone below. Against his better judgment he had to concede: Gad, she keeps herself appealing. What kind of story will she tell this time?

Before Luton could speak, Fogarty saw her, and with an almost indecent yell rushed forward, grabbed her by her slim waist, swung her in the air, and gave her a resounding kiss before he plumped her back on her feet: "How did you get here, Madam North Dakota?"

Half ignoring Fogarty, she straightened the suit he had rumpled and addressed the man she had been so eager to meet: "Like I told you that day on your boat, Lord Luton, I was always determined to reach the gold fields, and as you see, I did." She said this with just enough of her old icy force to make her point, but having done so, she quickly softened and said: "I never forgot how you rescued me from certain death . . . how out of Christian generosity you paid my fare back to Edmonton . . . how in fact you enabled me to do the things I've done."

She said this with such an engaging accent, with such an appropriate smile that Luton was almost forced to think: Now that she's not endangering a young Bradcombe, she's really not such a bad sort, and he shuddered to think that he had once considered pushing her off his boat in the dark of night. To make amends, he asked with unfeigned interest: "How'd you get here?" and she was glad of the invitation, because she desperately wanted to tell him of the sequel to their exciting but abortive acquaintanceship.

"That big ship you put me on, and thank you again for paying my fare, steamed its way up the river just as ice formed behind us. I got into Edmonton in October, I guess it must have been, and just like you advised, everyone wanted me to go back to North Dakota. But I'd have none of that. I got me a job as waitress. Last autumn in Edmonton anybody could get a job."

"What miracle happened to get you here?" Luton asked, and she said almost demurely: "There was a big Australian who had dug for gold in his country and was eager to try his luck on the Klondike, but like all sensible ones he hadn't rushed north when your team and mine did. He sat the winter out in a warm boardinghouse in

Edmonton. He came to our restaurant for his meals, and what with one thing and another we got married. That's him, standing over there. He jokes that he's the only man in Alaska with no neck, but he's fierce in a fight." Then she added one of those extraordinary touches that distinguished her, amusing, revealing and just a bit self-deprecatory: "An unmarried woman in Edmonton, especially a widow with no children working in a public place, I do believe I received six proposals of marriage a week, and Verner had three big fights before he drove the others off. It was dreamland, Lord Luton, and it seems so long ago."

Then, putting her own affairs aside and grateful for the domestic felicity she had attained, she asked: "Where are your other three? That delightful young fellow who cared for me so thoughtful? Wasn't his name Philip?"

When Luton could not bear to answer, Fogarty said gently: "Drowned. Those boots you warned him about. They dragged him down."

Uttering a cry of grief, she covered her face and soon was sobbing: "I told him he was too young to go." Then she recovered her poise and asked: "Carpenter, the nice one?"

"Dead. Scurvy in the second winter."

"You spent two winters? How about the one who quoted poetry?"

"Dead."

"Oh my God! What happened to you men? Did you miss the easy route or something?"

Neither Luton nor Fogarty dared answer that terrible question, but after a moment Evelyn asked: "And you? How did you negotiate the Mackenzie? On your second try, that is?"

"Come early spring we're back at Athabasca Landing, same four Germans sell our group, three couples, a new boat, bigger and stronger this time, and the rest was easy."

"Easy?" Luton asked in a distant, displeased manner.

"Yes. That fall when you put me on the big boat, ice chased us up the river. In the spring in our boat, we chased it down. Like everyone advised us, we found the Peel, then the Rat, where we cut our boat in half along the line the Germans had painted on it, and we hauled it inch by inch—what hellish work—over the Divide, but when we reached that other little river . . . what do you call it?"

"The Bell," Luton replied in a drained whisper.

"Once we hit it, no more trouble. It fed into the Porcupine, and after being careful to turn right at that junction we sailed so fast, first thing you know we were on the Yukon, where we bought six tickets for that steamer right there, the one you were boarding, which whisked us into Dawson in a proper hurry."

"How long did it take?" Luton asked, and he listened almost benumbed as she calculated: "Well, we left Edmonton earlier than most, maybe twentieth of May, so we could beat the crowd to Athabasca and get one of the good boats. The rest, pretty normal except that portage was no fun. We got into Fort Yukon, where we bought our tickets for Dawson . . ." Losing count, she beckoned for her husband to join them, and the big Australian, a veteran of gold fields, ambled over. "Verner, what date did we reach Dawson last year?"

"Eighth of September. Everyone said it was one of the speediest trips. So it would be twenty May till early September, fifteen, sixteen weeks." He said this in such a barbarous Australian accent that Lord Luton almost winced to think that this man, and a million like him, were full-fledged members of the British Empire.

"What are you doing now?" Fogarty asked, and the couple, taking turns, explained: "We arrived here too late to hit that big strike on the Klondike, but so did most everyone. Anyway, Verner said he was tired of mining. We operate what you might call a pawnshop, buy and sell anything," and Irina added: "You can make surprising money if you're sharp." Luton gasped inwardly: A pawnshop. This couple is right out of Dickens. But Fogarty cried: "That's wonderful! You have your own store and all?" and Irina said: "We do. Verner built it. We used the timbers from six Yukon riverboats abandoned by those who couldn't wait, they were so eager to be off to the diggings. We bought two for one dollar American each."

But now, in her moment of triumph, Irina, like the responsible woman she had always tried to be, wanted to repair ancient damage, and she asked: "Lord Luton, could we please sit over there?" When they were apart from the others, but still within the shadow of the steamer that would separate them forever, she said quietly: "You never liked me, and I didn't like you. But I did understand you, and I pray you understood me. You were a man frightened by the onset of winter, I was a lone woman who had just survived a terrible tragedy."

Luton started to speak, but she held up her hand, and when it was in the air she used it to brush off her cap, so that her wealth of silvery hair fell free to frame her face: "No, let me finish, then you. I knew your problem. You were terrified that your nephew would fall completely in love with me. As a proud man from a proud family you couldn't allow that. You would do anything to prevent it and so would Mr. Carpenter, because you understood how such an affair . . . the woman six or seven years older . . . it could unbalance a young man for life. You knew that, but so did I, Lord Luton. I would never have allowed it to happen . . ."

"But you encouraged it. Harry and I could both see that."

"I was not thinking of Philip," she said contritely. "I was thinking of myself. I had suffered terrifying loss. At the end of the world. With no one. With not one penny there or back in Edmonton. Lord Luton, I needed assurance. I needed the affection of some other human being. In that cold, cold land I needed warmth." Covering her face, she wept silently for several moments, then said as she wiped her nose with her sleeve: "He was such a dear boy, so good, so promising. I share your grief at his loss."

Luton, a man who had in the last year also suffered defeats few men experience, needed to exorcise himself, and confessed: "At one point I was so distraught I contemplated shoving you overboard in the dark of night. Harry prevented me. He thought I was joking, but I wasn't."

Irina stared at Luton, who averted his eyes, and she wondered what alchemy the deaths of his friends had wrought on his soul that he would now admit this monstrous thought to her, his intended victim. A few moments later she asked: "Why did things go so wrong that three of your team died?"

"Nature dealt us a series of dreadful blows . . . much like the storm that sank your first boat on Great Slave." He was still unwilling to admit that he had abetted an uncharitable nature, had indeed invited her retaliation for his blunders: "You could call it rotten luck." Then, to his own surprise, he asked: "Have you ever known anyone who stood this close to death from scurvy . . . the slow rotting away of the human body?" And he held his thumb and forefinger only a millimeter apart.

"So now it's back to England and a castle somewhere, I suppose?"

"Yes, I do now have a castle and many new responsibilities."

A gush of tears overwhelmed her, and at the end she said: "I can see the faces of each of your three men, of my own three farmers. They will be with us forever."

When Luton said nothing, she concluded: "On the first time we parted, you refused to accept my kiss of thanks. Don't refuse me again." He rose, stood very erect, and striving to mask his distaste, he allowed her to kiss him but she had to stand on tiptoe to do it. Then he asked: "What will you do when the gold runs out?" and she shrugged her shoulders as she replaced her kepi: "Who knows? Verner might rush off to another gold field. Who can guess what we will do? We are voyagers headed for destinations we cannot see. But like traveling the Mackenzie, if you get thrown back the first time, you keep trying."

Signaling to Fogarty and her husband that she was ready, she joined them and watched Lord Luton briskly climb the gangway and turn at the railing of the *Jos. Parker* to salute her in farewell. "Where are you heading?" the big Australian shouted, and he called down: "Back to civilization," and with a kind of sardonic amusement Evelyn lingered there, watching the three as they walked jovially away: There they go, an upstart Irish peasant trying to be better than he is, a hulking Australian with no neck nor any command of good English, and a Yankee farm girl of no background whatever. He shook his head in a gesture of surrender and mumbled: "Barbarians take over the world while proper men huddle like bears in icy caves."

But that cynical comment was not to be Lord Luton's final evaluation of his well-planned expedition to Dawson. It could not be; he was too good a man for that. As he watched Irina Kozlok disappear from view, swinging along with her mates in a free and easy stride, her fine uniform glistening in the sun, her kepi properly cocked, he suddenly uttered an anguished cry that startled others lining the rail, and he felt no embarrassment in disturbing them in this highly improper way.

"Oh God!" he cried, his heart torn with anguish, his brain finally prepared to face the truth. "She spent fifteen weeks going the right way. I spent one hundred going the wrong, and I lost three companions in doing so." He trembled, still looking at the space she had just vacated, and then like some penitent anchorite in his medieval cave he mumbled, his proud head bowed at last: "Merciful God, let the souls of those precious three men forgive me."

FOUR

REQUIEM

THOUGHTFUL BIOGRAPHERS OF THE NINTH MARQUESS OF DEAL, which title he inherited in 1909, judged that his disastrous expedition to the Klondike had not been all loss:

He spent twenty-three months covering the two thousand and forty-three miles getting to Dawson and remained only a few hours, but it was this prolonged and dreadful experience, in which he lost three of his party, including his sister's only son, that put steel into the heart of the Marquess. When Lloyd George tapped him in 1916 to whip the British industrial effort into line so that Britain could muster its full strength against the Kaiser, he was as well prepared as a man could be to discipline the private sector.

A blue-blooded nobleman and a man who in the privacy of his club had dismissed Lloyd George as "that insufferable little Welshman, no gentleman at all," he rallied to his assignment, became one of Lloyd George's most trusted adherents, and performed wonders in helping to throw back the German might. In dealing with refractory industrialists who came to him complaining that they simply could not accept the difficulties involved in this wartime measure or that, he never referred to his two years in the Arctic, but he did look the man in the eye, stare him down with what was known as "Evelyn's silent-sneer" and ask: "Difficulties? Do you know what difficulty is?" and because everyone knew of his experiences in the Arctic, he got his way.

But that was not the characteristic which enabled him to become one of the most effective ministers of war, for as Lloyd George remarked in one of his cabinet summaries: "The Marquess of Deal could reach a decision quicker than any man I ever knew, defend it with brilliant logic and ram it down the throats of all who opposed. But if his opponent marshalled relevant facts to support his case, Deal was prepared to listen and even reverse himself, acknowledging with disarming grace: 'I could have been wrong.' I asked him once: 'Deal, how in God's name can you be so over-powering when you first thunder out your decision, then be so attentive when the other fellow argues his case? And how did you school yourself to surrender so graciously if his arguments prove superior to yours?' and he gave a cryptic answer: 'Because I learned in the Arctic it's folly to persist in a predetermined course if in your heart you suspect you might be wrong.' I do believe his willingness to listen to others, to bend his will to theirs, anything to keep production humming, helped us win our war against the Boche."

Among the few personal items Lord Luton carried back to England was Trevor Blythe's battered copy of Palgrave's *Golden Treasury*. He would complete Harry Carpenter's mission and bring Trevor's message of love and his precious book to Lady Julia. But before making the presentation he had put together in an elegant limited edition for family and friends a slim volume consisting of three parts: a selection from those Palgrave lyrics Trevor Blythe had read during the night sessions near the Arctic Circle, extracts from his own journal of the expedition, and, most precious of all, disjointed fragments of a poem cycle Blythe had intended to call *Borealis*.

In selecting the Palgrave poems, Luton chose those which he and the others had especially prized, and that collection is here reprinted in part. The editors express gratitude to the tenth Marquess of Deal for allowing access to this treasured family heirloom, which is now part of the library collection at Wellfleet Castle.

In justifying his choices Luton explained: "Three of us were not yet married, so it was understandable that we would find great pleasure in the love poems, and Trevor read to us some of the most beautiful, none better than this first one which we all cherished."

LXXXIX
Go, lovely Rose!
Tell her, that wastes her time and me,
That now she knows,
When I resemble her to thee,
How sweet and fair she seems to be.

Tell her that's young
And shuns to have her graces spied,
That hadst thou sprung
In deserts, where no men abide,
Thou must have uncommended died.

Small is the worth
Of beauty from the light retired:
Bid her come forth,
Suffer herself to be desired,
And not blush so to be admired.

Then die! that she
The common fate of all things rare
May read in thee:
How small a part of time they share
That are so wondrous sweet and fair!

E. WALLER

LI
Cupid and my Campaspe play'd
At cards for kisses; Cupid paid:
He stakes his quiver, bow, and arrows,
His mother's doves, and team of sparrows;
Loses them too; then down he throws
The coral of his lip, the rose
Growing on's cheek (but none knows how);

With these, the crystal of his brow,
And then the dimple on his chin;
All these did my Campaspe win;
At last he set her both his eyes—
She won, and Cupid blind did rise.
O Love! has she done this to thee?
What shall, alas! become of me?

J. LYLY

XCII

A sweet disorder in the dress
Kindles in clothes a wantonness:—
A lawn about the shoulders thrown
Into a fine distractión,—
An erring lace, which here and there
Enthrals the crimson stomacher,—
A cuff neglectful, and thereby
Ribbands to flow confusedly,—
A winning wave, deserving note,
In the tempestuous petticoat,—
A careless shoe-string, in whose tie
I see a wild civility,—
Do more bewitch me, than when art
Is too precise in every part.

R. HERRICK

CI

Why so pale and wan, fond lover?
Prythee, why so pale?
Will, if looking well can't move her,
Looking ill prevail?
Prythee, why so pale?

Why so dull and mute, young sinner?
Prythee, why so mute?
Will, when speaking well can't win her,
Saying nothing do't?
Prythee, why so mute?

Quit, quit, for shame! this will not move,
This cannot take her,

If of herself she will not love,
* Nothing can make her:*
The D—l take her!

SIR J. SUCKLING

XC

Drink to me only with thine eyes,
* And I will pledge with mine;*
Or leave a kiss but in the cup
* And I'll not look for wine.*
The thirst that from the soul doth rise
* Doth ask a drink divine;*
But might I of Jove's nectar sup,
* I would not change for thine.*

I sent thee late a rosy wreath,
* Not so much honouring thee*
As giving it a hope that there
* It could not wither'd be;*
But thou thereon didst only breathe
* And sent'st it back to me;*
Since when it grows, and smells, I swear,
* Not of itself but thee!*

B. JONSON

LXXXII

Gather ye rose-buds while ye may,
* Old Time is still a-flying:*
And this same flower that smiles to-day,
* To-morrow will be dying.*

The glorious Lamp of Heaven, the Sun,
* The higher he's a-getting*
The sooner will his race be run,
* And nearer he's to setting.*

That age is best which is the first,
* When youth and blood are warmer;*
But being spent, the worse, and worst
* Times, still succeed the former.*

Then be not coy, but use your time;
* And while ye may, go marry:*

For having lost but once your prime,
  You may for ever tarry.

R. HERRICK

"But the harsh times, the terrible times came when we needed not the reassurances of love but these stern reminders of what the essential character of a man ought to be. Then we turned to those oaklike definitions of how a true Englishman should behave in adversity; poems that sound like bugle calls at night with barbarians at the gate. My heart elates as I recall them."

CXXIV

How sleep the Brave who sink to rest
By all their Country's wishes blest!
When Spring, with dewy fingers cold,
Returns to deck their hallow'd mould,
She there shall dress a sweeter sod
Than Fancy's feet have ever trod.

By fairy hands their knell is rung,
By forms unseen their dirge is sung:
There Honour comes, a pilgrim grey,
To bless the turf that wraps their clay;
And Freedom shall awhile repair
To dwell a weeping hermit, there!

W. COLLINS

LXXI

When I consider how my light is spent
Ere half my days, in this dark world and wide,
And that one talent which is death to hide
Lodged with me useless, though my soul more bent

To serve therewith my Maker, and present
My true account, lest He returning chide,—
Doth God exact day-labour, light denied?
I fondly ask:—But Patience, to prevent

That murmur, soon replies; God doth not need
Either man's work, or His own gifts: who best
Bear His mild yoke, they serve Him best: His state
Is kingly; thousands at His bidding speed

And post o'er land and ocean without rest:—
They also serve who only stand and wait.

J. MILTON

LXXIII

It is not growing like a tree
In bulk, doth make Man better be;
Or standing long an oak, three hundred year,
To fall a log at last, dry, bald, and sere:
  A lily of a day
  Is fairer far in May,
  Although it fall and die that night—
  It was the plant and flower of Light.
In small proportions we just beauties see;
And in short measures life may perfect be.

B. JONSON

CCXLVI

I met a traveller from an antique land
Who said: Two vast and trunkless legs of stone
Stand in the desert. Near them on the sand,
Half sunk, a shatter'd visage lies, whose frown
And wrinkled lip and sneer of cold command
Tell that its sculptor well those passions read
Which yet survive, stamp'd on these lifeless things,
The hand that mock'd them and the heart that fed;
And on the pedestal these words appear:
"My name is Ozymandias, king of kings:
Look on my works, ye Mighty, and despair!"
Nothing beside remains. Round the decay
Of that colossal wreck, boundless and bare,
The lone and level sands stretch far away.

P.B. SHELLEY

LXXXIII

Tell me not, Sweet, I am unkind
  That from the nunnery
Of thy chaste breast and quiet mind
  To war and arms I fly.

True, a new mistress now I chase,
The first foe in the field;
And with a stronger faith embrace
A sword, a horse, a shield.

Yet this inconstancy is such
As you too shall adore;
I could not love thee, Dear, so much,
Loved I not Honour more.

COLONEL LOVELACE

"And then there was that little song by the master voice of our tongue. Its words were simple and some lines almost comic, but they bespoke the pure joy of being alive. We treasured them, reciting them often to one another when temperatures plunged."

XXVII

When icicles hang by the wall
And Dick the shepherd blows his nail,
And Tom bears logs into the hall,
And milk comes frozen home in pail;
When blood is nipt, and ways be foul,
Then nightly sings the staring owl
Tuwhoo!
Tuwhit! tuwhoo! A merry note!
While greasy Joan doth keel the pot.

When all aloud the wind doth blow,
And coughing drowns the parson's saw,
And birds sit brooding in the snow,
And Marian's nose looks red and raw;
When roasted crabs hiss in the bowl—
Then nightly sings the staring owl
Tuwhoo!
Tuwhit! tuwhoo! A merry note!
While greasy Joan doth keel the pot.

W. SHAKESPEARE

Lord Luton introduced the Trevor Blythe fragments from his proposed poem sequence *Borealis* with this appropriate disclaimer: "We must remember that these are the introductory attempts of a young poet striving to find his way. He had already proved at Oxford that he

could write the traditional three-verse rhymed lyric, and his sonnets
won him prizes, but later he felt obligated, and properly so, to ex-
periment with forms, length of line, rhyme and blank verse. What he
would have kept and what discarded we cannot conjecture; but obviously some of his attempts succeed much better than others.

"He began under the influence of the standard elegy, sixteen lines
of fairly competent unrhymed iambic pentameter":

> *Hark! From the distant village tolls the bell*
> *Summoning to prayer all those who feel the need*
> *Of more than mortal sustenance. These rites*
> *Can be discharged by those who hear the cry*
> *Of brass on brass to speed the well-worn prayer,*
> *To bless the child newborn or ease the gray*
> *And palsied head to its eternal rest.*
> *I hear a sterner call: the road untrod,*
> *The heathen who has never seen the light,*
> *The passage through dark seas uncharted still,*
> *The desert that they claim no man can pass,*
> *The virgin mountain peaks ne'er stepped upon,*
> *The lure of gold still hiding in the ground,*
> *The call, the call from some untended Grail:*
> *"Find me! Rescue me before I tarnish!*
> *And yours shall be the shout of triumph . . . ."*

"The long middle portion of the poem," explained Luton, "had not
been attempted, and although Blythe must have contemplated how it
would develop, he left no notes. However, he did leave on two pages
unattached to the longer poem, but obviously intended to be a part,
a lyrical passage celebrating his adventures on the Mackenzie during
the days when all was proceeding on schedule."

> *Broad Mackenzie helped to speed us*
> *Caribou came down to feed us*
> *Arctic winds could not defeat us*
> *Ravens came to guide and greet us.*
> *Endless nights were not oppressive*
> *For our minds flared forth in wonder*
> *Never mean nor small-possessive*
> *As we talked our world asunder.*
> *Blizzards whistled in but spared us*

Challenge tempted us and dared us.
  Borealis explodes in the night
  Leaping and twisting in tortured forms
  Conflagrations of shimmering light
  Heavens ablaze in celestial storms.
    Arcs in the sky
    Tumble and tremble
    Teasing the eye
    With forms they resemble.
  There leaps a bridge to the moon
  Here drops a chasm to hell
  Soars high that silver balloon
  Borealis ablaze and all's well.
    Patterns tremendous
    Clashes stupendous
  Behold that vast fire as it rages
  Then fades to pastel as it ages
  And drifts from the sky all too soon
  Borealis asleep and all's well.
    Spring days bring cheer
    No cold to fear
    New sun to warm
    Nothing to harm
  Arctic gods sat on our shoulder
  Whisp'ring to us "Bolder, bolder!"
  We became the lords of winter
  Brushing off the icy splinter
  Dangling from our frozen portal
  Till the cry came "You are mortal."

"At this point," Luton wrote, "Trevor was prepared to deal with the death of his friend and companion, Philip, but only eight unsatisfactory lines in an unusual meter remain of what he certainly planned as an extended threnody":

Mighty Mackenzie, enraged at our boldness,
Drew from the lakes she hid high in her mountains
Torrents of water locked up in the coldness
Sent it cascading in perilous fountains.
Ice blocks as big as an emperor's palace
Gouged out whole forests and left the trees bending

Lurking to snatch at young men unattending
Eager to drown them in hideous malice.

"Obviously dissatisfied with the meter though pleased with the words, he crossed them out, pencilling the caution: 'Graver, much graver rhythm!' Then he turned to the closing, the lines that had won praise from Harry Carpenter":

> *. . . the fault was mine.*
> *I visualized the Grail a shining light,*
> *Perceptible from any vale in which*
> *I and my helpers struggled. It would be*
> *A constant beacon, milestone in the sky,*
> > *Signalling far*
> > *Calling to goal.*
> *I did not comprehend that it could function*
> *Only by flashing back light from me. Its gleam*
> *Existed, but in partnership with mine,*
> *And I had launched the search a blind man,*
> *Nothing within myself to guide the way,*
> *No silver in my soul to match the blaze*
> *Of what I sought, nor did I test the peaks*
> *That would forever bar me from my goal*
> *Till I broke through with force and fortitude*
> *To conquer them and in my victory*
> > *Conquer myself as well.*
> *I see my fellow seekers lost in darkness*
> *And know that I have failed to lead the way.*
> *Mountains engirt us, rivers swirl, we lose*
> *Our trail and cry: "Reluctant Paladins we,*
> *Who seek our Golden Grail by fleeing from it."*

> TREVOR BLYTHE
> *The Arctic Circle*
> *Belated spring 1898*

The major part of this small and valued publication reappeared later in Luton's highly regarded *An Englishman in the Far Corners,* published in 1928, by which time he had become ninth Marquess of Deal, aloof and white-haired but still slim and erect.

REFLECTIONS

THIS SHORT NOVEL CAME INTO BEING BECAUSE OF A PHOTOGRAPH I first saw years ago. It captivated me from the moment I came upon it, and it now appears inside the front cover of this book.

It was taken in the studio of a professional photographer working in the tiny Northwest frontier town of Edmonton during the frenzied gold rush of August 1897. I had been doing casual research on the Alaskan portion of that rush, and had, at that time, no interest whatever in the preposterous madness in Edmonton, whose historical importance was unknown to me. But this photograph was so evocative of the thousands of amateurs streaming north that it registered profoundly, becoming for me the symbol of that period.

It is a little masterpiece, still in first-class condition, and shows a young woman gold-seeker, perhaps thirty years old, dressed in heavy boots, a kind of hunting uniform with shoulders excessively puffed out, and the sauciest cap you ever saw. Her sensible-looking, no-nonsense head is tilted slightly, and she stares at us with a resolute, almost defiant set to her lower jaw, her mouth pulled in at the corners. Her hair has been bobbed, I believe, in preparation for the long trek north. And her image has haunted my memory during all the years since I first saw her.

I was unable to learn her name or place of origin, for she might have been either a Canadian from some place like Ontario or an American from Michigan or one of her sister states. I could not even determine by what route she tried to reach Dawson, but I have always supposed she tried the overland one, and if she did, I fancy she may have died during the first terrible autumn when, miles from Edmonton, she awakened to the terrifying fact that she was never going to make it to Dawson and that she was too far from Edmonton to scurry back. She may have starved to death on the bank of some turbulent mountain stream she was powerless to ford.

On the other hand, her portrait is that of a determined young woman, a realist, and there is a chance, I think, that when the realities of this great delusion became clear she turned her back on the folly and returned to Edmonton, from where she quickly departed for her former home in Michigan or Ontario. Or, being the resolute woman she seems, she could well have gone down the Mackenzie, over the mountain divide, and on to her destination.

In the original version of *Journey,* I had no place for a heroine, but she went every step of the way with me nonetheless. She was my guide, my muse, my touchstone, and was so indelible that she kept fighting her way back onto my pages.

Journey is a narrative which depicts the courage that men and women can exhibit when dealing with adversity, even that which they have brought upon themselves. The realization of this tale has been a unique, revelatory experience for me, for I, too, learned about dreams and determination.

Although it now stands as a fully conceived novel in its own right, with which I am well pleased, *Journey* had its genesis as part of another work. Therefore, how the story of five men's tragic journey across Canada to the Klondike gold fields came to be written and then published deserves explanation.

It starts with my lifelong interest in Canada which began with a summer spent on Lake Muskoka in 1929. Canoeing into the wilderness north of there, I caught a glimpse of the essential Canada: open, majestic, wild, challenging, and filled with fine people and a commanding life. It was an unequaled introduction to a land of manifold beauties.

I followed it up through the years whenever an opportunity presented itself, with visits to various parts of the country: Halifax, the coast of Newfoundland, Montreal, Toronto, Vancouver, never in an orderly way, and perhaps more enjoyable because of the arbitrary nature of my travel. However, my main interest stemmed from my belief that every incident in Quebec's struggle for recognition of its distinct language and culture would one day be repeated in the southern United States, with Spanish in our country replacing the role of French in Canada. Canada thus became of vital interest, and I followed with a microscope the twists and turns of how this nation of two languages sought to apply intelligent answers to the problem.

I remember two incidents which epitomized the situation for the visiting observer. At a sports meeting in Montreal, where everyone on the panel had already demonstrated his command of English, an agitated member of the audience rose, pointed out that the meeting was being held in Quebec and was therefore obliged to obey Quebec's new language law, and warned that if the words of the speakers were not also translated into French, he would summon the police. Cowed by his threat, we sat through an afternoon of speech-translation-speech-translation when everyone present knew that this was both unnecessary and an irritation.

Later, on the same trip, I was in Toronto talking with businessmen of that city, one of the finest in North America, about how they had opted to close down their Montreal headquarters and seek refuge in Toronto, even though they had been happy in Quebec and did not want to leave. This seemed so preposterous that I asked for an explanation, and they informed me that under Quebec's language law all businesses in that province now had to keep their records in French, and the extra work this required had made conducting business there impossible.

After these two introductions to the friction between the two language groups, and with my conviction that sooner or later a similar movement for language rights would germinate in our Hispanic communities, I followed with the closest attention the implementation of official bilingualism in Canada and became, as a result, moderately informed on life north of the border.

Yet, like many Americans, who are poorly informed about Canada, I tended to perceive Canada for the most part through its expatriates: those Canadians who have met with outstanding success in the United States—Saul Bellow, John Kenneth Galbraith, Peter Jennings, Senator Sam Hayakawa—and whose achievements have led to a great respect in America for Canadians as a whole. I have admired, too, the successes of those who chose to remain and work in Canada, not least my fellow writers Pierre Berton, Margaret Atwood, Mordecai Richler and Morley Callaghan.

I did have one other contact with Canada, but it was personal. Once at a countryside picnic in Pennsylvania, where the Micheners of the world convened to celebrate the glories of their supposedly distinguished past, I met by accident my cousin the Right Honourable Roland Michener, the governor general of Canada, and we locals felt a bit puffed up.

My interest in things Canadian never diminished, and whenever I came upon someone in my travels who was familiar with the country, I engaged in long conversations about political changes, life in the western provinces and especially adventures in the arctic. So it was inevitable that when I began seriously to contemplate a novel on Alaska, I would spend considerable time pondering how to fit in a Canadian contribution. And, of course, there was always the vivid memory of that woman gold-seeker in Edmonton.

When I began constructing the intellectual outline of my novel *Alaska,* I had three special desires beyond the obvious ones that would have to be treated in any fictional work on that region. I wanted to help the American public to think intelligently about the arctic, where large portions of future international history might well focus; I wanted to remind my readers that Russia had held Alaska for a longer period, 127 years (1741 through 1867 inclusive), than the United States had held it, 122 years (1867 through 1988); and I particularly desired to acquaint Americans with the role that neighboring Canada had played and still does play in Alaskan history.

The reasons for these desires are easy to explain. I had found my first good luck in writing by dealing in a fresh way with the South Pacific and had always wanted to complete the cycle with work on the North Pacific. In the years after 1946, when I finished *Tales of the South Pacific,* scores of correspondents had urged me to write about either the North Pacific or Alaska or both, but I refrained because I was afraid I did not know enough. However, the urge to tackle such an enticing subject was ever-present, and I visited the area repeatedly to check my understandings in case I should later wish to try.

My interest in Russian Alaska is duplicated by many American historians and geographers who have knowledge of either the history of Russian, or of British and American, attempts to explore that part of the world. As a young man I had studied the eastward expansion of the Russian Empire to the Pacific with the same avidity that I studied American and Canadian expansion westward to the same ocean. I was moderately well informed about the steps Russia had taken to extend her empire eastward and I had been allowed to travel to many of her Asian frontiers, but not, alas, into Siberia itself. But if books can provide the portrait of a land, and as a writer I had to think so, I had acquired a powerful understanding of and admiration for the great, halting, confused and finally triumphant Russian push to the east. What I did not know very well, and I was dismayed to realize this, were the Alaska-Yukon border region and the events that had occurred there, particularly during the years of the gold rush. In fact, I knew of only three incidents that might be usable in a novel, and that was pretty thin gruel for the kind of book I hoped to write.

I was aware, as were most Americans with knowledge of our history, that the great gold rush of 1897–1899 occurred mainly on Canadian soil and that the Canadian police had saved the day when the American presence in the region had not yet been fully established. Many Americans, like me, regretted the fact that the boundary between the two nations had not been just a few miles farther to the east, which would have placed Dawson City and the Klondike on American soil, but we accepted its position as an unfortunate mistake that could not be corrected.

On the subject of boundaries, I had also read many years ago about the hilarious contretemps that occurred in connection with the important Hudson's Bay post at Fort Yukon, that strategic settlement just off the Arctic Circle where the great Yukon River stops flowing north and takes a ninety-degree turn to the west for its long run into the Bering Sea. When American surveyors got around to checking boundaries in 1869, they learned that this big Canadian post was not in Canada but in Alaska! An amiable agreement was worked out, with never a harsh word, whereby the Hudson's Bay people would move their trading store the proper number of miles to the east, which would put it safely on Canadian soil. In fact, the agreement was so amicably reached that American military personnel helped the Canadians not only to make the move but also to build a new trading post at a site called Rampart.

Unfortunately, the Canadian-American team moved the site the proper number of miles not as the crow flies but along the bank of the Porcupine River, which wandered this way and that, so that when the Canadians had finished making the move and were installed in their new trading post, the next team of surveyors found that they were *still* on American soil. In some disgust the Canadians abandoned their new home, which would be remembered as Old Rampart, and moved a substantial distance into Canada, where they named their post Rampart House. It had been a trivial affair with amusing interest, but hardly the kind of material on which to base the entire episode I wanted to write.

Of much greater significance was an incident I could use, one which glows in history because of the restraint with which both Canada and the United States behaved. In the years 1877 and 1878 conditions in America's new territory of Alaska were in dismal shape, primarily because no responsible form of government had been established for the vast territory. Matters deteriorated so precipitously that the few American settlers in Sitka, once the Russian capital and now the American, feared that rebellious Tlingit Indians were about to invade and slaughter all white people.

Justification for their fear has never been established, but in 1879 distraught citizens, unable to obtain protection from their own government, made a dangerous canoe trip south to the Canadian military outpost at Prince Rupert, imploring the naval command there to dispatch a warship to save Alaska on behalf of an American government that seemed about to lose it.

A daring Canadian officer made a snap decision to aid his American cousins, and on 1 March 1879 the Canadian warship *Osprey* steamed into Sitka Sound. This show of force dampened the Tlingit uprising, if indeed it had ever existed, and for nearly two months this Canadian vessel represented organized government in Alaska. When an American ship arrived belatedly, the *Osprey* courteously saluted and retired, taking with her the gratitude of the American colonists, who would forever after insist that "when the Americans would do nothing to protect us, Canadians saved the day."

That was the totality of what I had to work with regarding Canada's role on the Alaskan frontier, and it wasn't much, but when I started my serious research I came upon an American source which said cryptically that a Canadian writer named Pierre Breton, who from the entry I judged to have long been dead, had written a book about the gold rush, published in the United States as *The Klondike Fever,* and I asked a research librarian upon whom I often depended to see if she could track it down. In less than five minutes she called back: "The author is very much alive. He is one of Canada's most respected writers. Six libraries in our district have copies of his book, which was published in 1958. And incidentally, his name is *Berton*."

Since I could walk to the library nearest my home, I soon had a copy of this excellent work, one written with a powerful sense of organization and emphasis and in a congenial style, but as I read it in great gulps I realized that Berton was telling me what I already knew about the joint American-Canadian experience in the gold fields. I was not wasting my time reading the book, because Berton was continually throwing up bits of compelling information I had not previously known, but I was not getting much material about the strictly Canadian role in the gold rush. Then, in chapter six, I came upon a section dealing with the comic-tragic stampede out of the Canadian frontier town of Edmonton.

It was enchanting material, just the kind of story I had been seeking upon which to construct a Canadian narrative, which would keep my novel about Alaska from being narrowly parochial. It had reverberating overtones, provided correctives to standard accounts, and opened my eyes to the complex role western Canada had played in the gold rush. It was tantalizingly brief, only thirteen pages, but I shall ever be thankful to Berton for including that short glimpse in his book, for had he not alerted me to the Edmonton mania, I might have missed it completely. No other book I used had mentioned it.

However, his material, good as it was, did not provide enough data for my purpose, so, utilizing all the research knowledge of some very fine librarians in Alaskan centers, particularly those of the state historical library in Juneau, I came finally upon a very brief note in a learned journal. It said that the Edmonton story had been told in fascinating detail in J. G. MacGregor's *Klondike Rush Through Edmonton 1897–1898,* and it was obvious that it must hold the very material I sought. Telex calls were spread afar, and when after some days I had received no response, I concluded that the MacGregor book must have been privately printed and that no copies were going to be available. But some time later, the postman arrived with a parcel from a library in a distant city, and when I opened it, there in my hands lay the one book I needed to complete my Canadian research.

This is, I think, an almost perfect example of two aspects of writing: the necessity for a serious writer to keep following even the most tenuous thread, the slightest hint that somewhere in a distant library a book will be hiding that provides all the information he seeks; more important is the other side of this coin, that anyone who writes anything pertaining to human knowledge must, to complete the task, lodge that material in some library or archival center.

In my writing life I have worked on some of the most arcane subjects, topics on which one would gamble that no one had previously written anything, but with enough searching I have invariably come up with something, and most often with a full-length, well-written work like the MacGregor on Edmonton. I have found that many nineteenth-century English clergymen stuck away in far corners of the world with nothing much to do wrote some of the most valuable books in an amateur style, reporting on their hobbies such as travel or archaeology or the history of strange nations and tribes. German professional scholars, too, have been remarkably far-ranging.

From repeated experience I can confidently state that I doubt if anyone can devise a subject of even the slightest significance but that someone previously has written a substantial book upon it. The accumulation of usable knowledge in this world is staggering, and with the new computerized indexes, even the most fugitive document can be tracked down.

The value of my two books on Edmonton was demonstrated when two professional readers of the *Alaska* manuscript protested my having characters die of scurvy:

> Ridiculous. A full century earlier James Cook had demonstrated an absolute cure for scurvy. Surely, seasoned explorers like Lord Luton and Harry Carpenter would know how to prevent it?

Browbeaten and afraid that I had misconstrued something I might have read too hastily, I went back to Berton and found this passage:

> Wind City lay on Wind River, and here were camped fifty or sixty men, three quarters of whom suffered terribly from scurvy. When gangrene set in, their toes were cut off with hacksaws; and when they died, their corpses were stuffed down the empty mine shafts. . . . The death toll reflected the internationalism of the camp. On November 30 a man from Chicago died of scurvy; on December 13 a Frenchman died of scurvy; in early January two Dutchmen died of scurvy.

Rarely does one settle an argument so conclusively. Of course my English travelers would have known how to prevent scurvy, and during their first long winter in the arctic, with adequate food, they handled the problem easily. But this was the second winter, and a terrible one it was, with most adventurers penned up in tiny cabins without adequate food or medicine, and scurvy wiped them out.

The MacGregor book was a treasure house of historical information on Edmonton's role in the gold rush, and when I finished my first delighted reading, I saw that the actual men and women who trekked through Edmonton in those days provided such a wealth of character and incident that I was free to construct my group of men heading for Dawson as arbitrarily as I wished. Nothing I could invent would seem preposterous after one read what real people were doing in those wild days.

And here I reminded myself of a curious rule governing writers. We are advised by our lawyers not to read any books of fiction dealing with the subject at hand, because a work of fiction is the exclusive property of the author who invented it and to borrow from it is plagiarism, but the writer is free to refer to scholarly nonfiction research if he acknowledges the source, for it is considered an addition to the general reservoir of human knowledge. I had an amusing experience with this concept some years ago. Readers began writing to me, pointing out that an extremely popular novel had used whole pages from one of my novels, and when a major magazine printed excerpts side by side, the similarity was clear and something had to be done.

But now a curious impasse developed, because Publisher A is very loath to cause trouble for Publisher B about unauthorized borrowing from a work of fiction, because next week A might want to borrow legitimately from B, so lawsuits are avoided. In this case my publisher did complain quietly to the publisher of the offending book, and after some time received a letter of explanation, which deserves to go into the history of publishing as the best possible response to such charges:

> My client denies that she has ever heard of Mr. Michener as a
> writer, or ever read one of his books, or knew in any way that
> he had written on this subject. But since the similarity between the two excerpts is undeniable, we can only conclude

that both writers borrowed from the same original source, which we have been unable to identify.

Hoping that I might be able to devise a group of five interesting male characters to make the run from Edmonton to Dawson, I hit upon the idea of a group of four interrelated men of London's aristocracy and an Irish servant, and the more I worked with them, the better I liked them. From time to time I regretted that they were not all Canadians, but my knowledge of Canadian family life was too limited to permit that; I had done graduate work at a British university and had personally known moderately well the kinds of men I wished to depict. Besides, the geographical settings would be Canadian, some of the most striking in the world, and my Britons would encounter Canadians on their journey.

Very early in my planning I decided for two reasons that my five men would approach the gold fields by the Mackenzie River route. The overland route from Edmonton to Dawson was so terrible and so impenetrable that my characters would simply be bogged down in tragedy from start to finish, a grinding, grueling, step-by-step descent into oblivion, and I did not wish to write that kind of story. Equally important was the fact that I had conceived a deep interest in the Mackenzie River system, and although I had not traveled upon it myself, I had flown over great stretches of it and had read many accounts of its discovery and exploration. It is a majestic river and one admirably suited to what I wanted to say. Once I focused my thinking, I discarded all other options. My tale would be an evocation of this great, formless, wandering river as it heads for the arctic.

The three components of my Canadian narrative were now firmed: a river I respected, a historical incident of some magnitude, and five characters I understood and liked. With such material a writer is in luck. Holed up in a log cabin in Sitka, Alaska, I wrote diligently for several months, trying to knock my story on the gold rush into proper form, and as I toiled through one version after another, the segment that constantly pleased me was the one on the journey of this group of Britons down the Mackenzie River. I liked my five men increasingly and shared their trials with them. Tears came to my eyes as certain incidents devastated them and me, and I had an amazingly clear picture of the survivors: the Irish ghillie who would become a major character in the remaining portions of *Alaska,* and the nobleman who would become an aide to Lloyd George during the 1914–1918 war.

A manuscript is a subtle affair, and long ones such as those I most often write need to be carefully constructed; components that appear in an early episode are established there to be put to effective use in the latter part of the book, and incidents which seem almost irrelevant may have considerable meaning because they create values which become important later.

I do not mean by this the use of contrived clues, as in a detective story. I mean the inherent components of storytelling, whose proper use is so essential in establishing style and winning reader confidence and participation. And I mean particularly the phenomenon of resonance.

The classic example of resonance used with maximum effectiveness is prepared in one of the early scenes in *Anna Karenina* when in a railway station Anna notices the workman tapping the wheel of the engine with his hammer to ensure the train's safety, a presage of the climactic scene in which she will commit suicide under these wheels.

Almost any component of a narrative, adroitly used, can produce resonance. A novel is an interwoven series of freighted words and images, of characters who behave in certain ways, of a physical setting which carries its own unique identification, and of important incidents in the latter part of the narrative which can be strengthened, or foreshadowed, by comparable incidents that have occurred earlier. I try constantly to introduce words, phrases, incidents and meanings in one part of the narrative so that when they reappear later they will do so with intensified significance. One of the joys of reading is the friendly recognition of these resonances.

Resonance occurs, to the great advantage of any narrative, when the reader comes upon a phrase, a complete thought, a character or an incident with which he or she is already familiar. The reader then enjoys the pleasure of recognition or the thrill of renewed acquaintance or can admire the aptness of the passage. Classical composers of longer musical works relied on this device, Richard Wagner and César Franck with heavy obviousness, Ludwig van Beethoven and Giuseppe Verdi more subtly. Certain novelists use the tactic with marvelous skill—Honoré de Balzac to name one—and few readers seem to be aware of the extraordinary flood of coincidence in Boris Pasternak's exquisitely crafted *Dr. Zhivago.* Any young writers who are afraid of utilizing coincidence lest they be hit with the famous criticism "He jerks the long arm of coincidence right out of its socket" should read Pasternak and take comfort.

I have thought of my novels as seamless webs which could start anywhere, end anywhere, and that, I suppose, is why some have felt that my concluding chapters are unsatisfying. The criticism is justified. I do not tie loose strings together; I do not want to imitate certain composers of symphonies who start to end their music some four or five minutes early and proceed with a noisy series of crescendoes until they finish with a titanic bang. I prefer to have my novels wind down at exactly the same pace I used in starting them, as if to let the reader know that the basic situation goes on and on, and since it can't all be of maximum intensity, I am forced to stop my orchestra somewhere.

When I had finished writing the gold-rush episode in *Alaska,* having edited and cut certain portions that ran too long, I was happy with the result and judged that I had at least brought Canada into the narrative as I had hoped to do. As well, I had introduced certain events in this section of the novel that had been carefully foreshadowed by earlier events or that would be paralleled later in the narrative. But when my New York editor and I began discussing the finished manuscript, he urged me to consider cutting the Canadian segment. For the reader to appreciate why, several important facts about professional writing and publishing must be told because they pertain to the nature of creative work and the editorial process.

First, any publisher who has been in business a long time has acquired a wealth of knowledge about the pitfalls of writing. His editors may not themselves be able to write successful novels, but they can spot with uncanny skill defects in their authors' work. Sensible writers listen to cautions voiced by their publishers, as expressed through their editors; the writers may not accept everything said, but they do weigh it carefully. So when I was warned that the Canadian material was not in the best interests of my Alaskan story, I had to pay heed.

Second, there are writers, and some of the best, who, when they submit a manuscript, tell the publisher: "This is it. Print it," and permit no editorial work. There are others of equal merit who not only listen to critical opinion but seek it, even altering their novels substantially if that seems desirable. I fall within the second group. Regardless of the debate as to which attitude is correct and produces the best results, I avidly seek criticism before the book is published. After it's in print I do not, because then it's too late, and I would not have released the book for publication if I hadn't liked it pretty much as it was.

Third, I had from the very start of my Alaska project a self-set determination to keep this novel noticeably shorter than some of my previous works, even though my readers have insisted through the years that my books end too soon. I felt obliged this time to keep the total pages to less than a thousand and, if possible, under nine hundred. I was therefore attentive when one reader warned:

> There is a vast difference between a book of 1209 pages and one of 918. Both the critic and the general reader will comment negatively about the former and allow the latter to pass. The critic will cry: "Another thousand-page effort," and in the bookstore the potential reader will heft the book and look at the last page and moan: "I can't read a thousand pages of anything." In other words, the length of the book runs the risk of becoming the most important thing about it, and for a writer to allow that to happen, or even invite it to happen, is self-destructive.

So I was myself looking to identify segments that could be eliminated, knowing that at the same time my editor would be similarly engaged. Consequently, his suggestion for a cut did not come as a surprise, but the fact that the Canadian story was chosen did.

Fourth, there was another major objection to the Canadian section, fearfully obvious and damaging, once voiced. I was spending a lot of time on a river that played no further role in Alaskan history, on a town not in Alaska that never reappeared in the novel, and on five characters of whom only one, the Irishman, appeared in the purely Alaskan material, and his role could be salvaged by creating another Irishman for my Nome and Juneau segments. So far as characters necessary for the narrative were concerned, cutting the Mackenzie River segment completely, as my editor advised, would lose us little. Even as I was writing the Mackenzie River passages I had sometimes the feeling: Boy, we're getting pretty far away from Alaska.

These men are headed to the Arctic Ocean, not the gold fields. But I muffled that sneaking suspicion by pointing out to myself: But that's what the story is all about. Heading for a gold field but constantly moving farther and farther away. However, I never fully disposed of this unease, and when New York advised exactly what I'd been tentatively thinking, it struck fire.

All these reasons for eliminating my Canadian story were sound. They added up to one unavoidable conclusion: this segment, while a good and interesting story in itself, did not belong in *Alaska*. So the advice was accepted. A sequence on which I had labored arduously, and which I cherished for the great scenes it contained, would not be in this book. The general narrative was speeded up, and the focus was kept more sharply on Alaska and not disturbed by a diversion into Canada.

The cut had not been forced upon me: I had made the decision, and in retrospect it had many virtues to defend it; specifically, it served as an interesting example of how publishing decisions are reached.

Of course, when the cut was made many valuable cross references productive of resonance were lost, both earlier incidents which foreshadowed present ones, and present which foreshadowed future. Two of the first type were serious losses. I wanted the ease with which Captain Cook saved lives by his handling of scurvy to be contrasted with how Lord Luton lost lives by his mishandling. And I had planned for the comic scene in which the Russian tyrant Tsar Peter the Great, who hated beards, used a dull razor to shave his cossack to presage the later scene in which the English dictator Lord Luton shaved Fogarty with an equally dull blade.

In the present-to-future relationship I wanted Luton's exhibitionist fifty-mile trek down the middle of the frozen Mackenzie to pave the way for the ridiculous scene, founded on fact, in which Fogarty's replacement in *Alaska,* Murphy, rides a bicycle down the middle of the frozen Yukon during blizzards, an incredible eight hundred and fifty miles from the played-out gold fields of Dawson to the rich new field at Nome: I wanted this to be the Irishman's subtle comeuppance to His Lordship.

But eliminating the Canadian segment was not the end of this adventure, nor could it be. I had spent so much energy researching the Canadian episode that it had become almost a living part of me, and I was disconsolate to think that it would never see the light of day. Here an important characteristic of the writer surfaces: I had worked hard to tell the Canadian part of the gold rush because I had a strong conviction that this interlocking between North America's two nations which share the arctic region ought to be known, just as it ought to be appreciated that the Soviet Union also shares in that frozen terrain and in the responsibility for it. I had said something important, in parable form it is true and therefore limited in certain significant ways, but also with the potential of achieving the readership that sometimes accrues to parables, and I had a strong desire to see it published and in circulation, especially among Canadians for whom I had intended it in the first place.

On the day I agreed to cut the section, I placed the banished pages neatly in a folder and vowed: Someday I'll get you into print; and then I surrendered the matter in the rush of seeing the rest of the manuscript through the editing process.

But good ideas take a long time dying and the same is doubly true for characters into whom one has breathed life. Often in my nightly walks I would recall incidents on the Mackenzie River and I became increasingly forlorn over my failure to get their story published. One night it was as if my five characters rose in revolt, demanding my assistance, and a happy thought struck: Why not try to place this Canadian story with a Canadian publisher? Once that acorn was planted, it grew into a very strong tree.

Here, I must make an observation. The Mackenzie River story that lay unquietly in my files was far shorter than the one I would try to place with a Canadian publisher, since I had cut portions of the original manuscript and had refrained from writing parts I had planned because it was already running far too long. In preparing the manuscript for my Canadian publisher, I was able to set down the full story I had originally wanted to write. Parts cut were restored and parts originally intended but not written were added. Now that I was working on a short novel, not a segment of a novel, I was able to re-search my story further and to develop incidents and passages that I had not previously imagined. In short, I was able to give flesh to what had been bare bones, but in not one word was the story modified to make it more palatable to the Canadian reader. This was and is a story conceived for two purposes: to acquaint American readers with facts about Canadian existence, and to demonstrate to Canadian readers my respect for the history and achievements of their country.

To friends in the modern metropolis of Edmonton, I apologize for having dwelt so heavily upon the misbehavior of their ancestors in 1897–1899, but the propaganda about routes from Edmonton to the Klondike in those years was reprehensible and as a result many died. In later years, of course, the frontier town transformed itself into a major center and a force for good in Canada's westward expansion and in the development of the prairies.

Only another novelist or a trained researcher will appreciate the quiet joy I experienced in the final days of editing this book. My editor in Toronto, now aware of my infatuation with the Edmonton photograph of the intrepid woman gold-seeker, had urged the custodians of the Provincial Archives of Alberta to ransack their files to see if the name of the young woman could be determined, and one morning Toronto called to say: "Great news! They've identified her name. Mrs. Garner."

I gasped, for my high school Spanish teacher, a graduate from Swarthmore College who had arranged for the scholarship that sent me to Swarthmore, thus paving my way into the academic career I had enjoyed so much, had been a Miss Garner, so that to me the name was revered.

"Where was she from?"

The archivists did not know.

"What route did she take north?"

No one knew.

"Canadian or American?"

They did not even know that, but she was a real woman; she had been in the studio of Ernest Brown, photographer, in Edmonton in August of 1897, and as far as anyone knew, she had left that town for the Klondike. Even with that meager information I was content, for it dramatically changed her from a ghostly shadow to a living person.

Then, as we were about to go to press, Toronto called again: "Even better news. We've found out more about Mrs. Garner. She came from Fresno, California, with a party of eighteen men. They bought eighty horses in Edmonton and headed out on the overland trail with a great determination to find the gold fields."

That's all we know, but the phrases haunt me, for the questions are limitless. Was her husband, or brother, among the eighteen men? How did he allow her to go to Edmonton? And why in the world should she have gone there when Seattle was so much closer and was the start of a much simpler route? What happened to those horses? What happened to her? If she raised children somewhere and they had grandchildren, I hope that someone informs them that their great-grandmother was the guiding light of this book.

It is strange what sometimes transpires when we go prowling about through old photographs.

JAMES A. MICHENER, one of the world's most popular writers, was the author of the Pulitzer Prize–winning *Tales of the South Pacific,* the best-selling novels *Hawaii, Texas, Chesapeake, The Covenant,* and *Alaska,* and the memoir *The World Is My Home.* Michener served on the advisory council to NASA and the International Broadcast Board, which oversees the Voice of America. Among dozens of awards and honors, he received America's highest civilian award, the Presidential Medal of Freedom, in 1977, and an award from the President's Committee on the Arts and Humanities in 1983 for his commitment to art in America. Michener died in 1997 at the age of ninety.